Radiant Darkness

SETH LEON

Thank you to my sister who
supported me in writing this book.
Having someone give a small shove behind
can help a person move forward

PROLOGUE

Have you ever wondered why some people are afraid of the dark? Some may think it's an innocent fear that will eventually go away, a trick of the mind, although in reality it's a natural instinct imbedded into us. It heightens the fear within us making our instincts more alert, keeping the predators from getting the upper hand. The darkness is something that shouldn't be taken lightly, especially for a human. Unlike an animal, we are smarter and more vigilant, but we give up our heightened senses. We can't see as far like some animals, we can't smell or hear as good, all we have are our creativity moments.

Far from the morning sky where the sun can shine even through the gray clouds, there's only the illumination of the night moon. Visibility, low, the air gets colder, unseen shadows surrounds us. That's the perfect time for "them" to come out; natural predators that are never seen or heard of. Shielded from the human population they are known as imaginary beasts, demons created from self illusions.

We don't hear them, since they are silent hunters; they only make a noise when there's no other in sight. We don't see them since they hide in the shadows, camouflage; quick to show, quick to leave. Occasionally, a few of us might see them, but those that do are never believed, they are disregarded from society as mentally disturbed, and once again, our hunters don't exist.

They are damnations that shouldn't exist; they are the cause of the missed, and the missing. Feeding on the more preferably human flesh, they are the beings that cause fear to come at our doors and trouble the young.

Have you ever seen the child and the milk carton labeled missing? Or the boards full of missing people, never to be seen again leaving the loved ones to come back from time and time again hoping for a bit of news only to leave solemn in tears? Most are found again, but for the thousands of others who aren't, they are taken, devoured, and left among the many missing.

For me, the beginning was only a glimpse, then after, nothing but continued fear and cowardice.

CHAPTER

1

Here at night, I laid in my bed in my small room with nothing too visibly noticeable. My room is a plain room painted white, no posters or any real decorations. In the corner was a table with my very old desktop computer, just decent enough to run websites for research and projects, nowhere near fast enough to stream videos at full speed like so many my age were now doing. Next to my bed was a small lamp on a table, giving just enough light to keep me at ease from the surrounding darkness of my room. The wind blew fiercely outside as the wind gave its hollow yell, making me turn my head towards it. If it was one thing that stood out in my room, it would've been my curtains that covered the one small window. They were thick black curtains which blocked the visibility from either side.

Standing out was a decorated small white tree that was threaded in the center of the curtain, an odd addition to my ever so plain room.

"It's only the wind, it's only the wind," whispering the words to myself for bits of comfort.

Starting tomorrow, I would be moving away from here and with it a new life as a senior in high school, living in new place. As I looked back at the window, it gave me an uneasy feeling as the glass sounded with clatter. The longer I looked at it, the more I started to remember why I was so afraid. Not wanting to remember, I opened the drawer next to my bed, quickly shoving the earpieces in while still keeping the lamp on. Turning on the music, it drowned out the sound of the crying wind while I kept my eyes closed. Though the music played a soft melody, calming my fears a bit, yet didn't keep me from remembering. Remembering of my life years ago that has led to haunt me till this very day. I tried not to recall those painful times, fighting off my weary eyes from closing, but as I doze off, the bright sunny days of my childhood was brought back to life.

Walking down the street, I held onto my mother's hand, those were the highlight of my days. Looking straight ahead as the wind gave a gentle breeze blowing the autumn rustling leaves. The sun filled brightly all around us through the clouds and leaves as they fell to the floor while we enjoyed the blissful stroll. A fairly early morning, 6:30am, the two of us were out the door and already it was fairly bright outside. The two of us looked like a happy mother and child going on a normal morning stroll. It was our usual routine, every Saturday morning we would walk down to a quaint little pastry shop that sold a variety of small portion treats. Difficult as it was for me to pull off the sheets every Saturday morning, the reward afterwards was a welcoming pleasure. Originally, it started so that I could watch the morning cartoons every morning, but my mother saw this as me being lazy, that I was rotting my youthful brain away. Instead, she had encouraged me to start taking morning walks with her to get some outside air and exercise. Soon enough, it became a weekly routine that I looked forward to; to spend time with my dear mother. As for my morning entertainment, they soon became forgotten as I started to enjoy the morning outings. Still, when we did arrive back home, a part of me wished I hadn't missed them, wanting to know what happened to the superheroes and how they thwarted the master evil villains.

"Evan sweetie, what do you want to get today?" asked my mother.

She was a beautiful tall figured woman with blond straight hair and light blue eyes with ever so white porcelain skin. Standing at six foot in her white high heels, she wore a casual flowing white dress that went down to just a few inches above her ankles. With her long open tan coat wrapped around her, the cloths suited her perfectly with her slender body, classy hat and large shoulder bag that were strapped across her shoulder. She looked classy and a bit outdated, but at the same time, indifferent and uniquely refreshing.

"I don't know," shrugging awkwardly, clinging to my

8

mother's skirt. Being too short to reach her hand still, she made me cling to her clothing as to not get lost.

Being a cute little boy that I was in my tennis shoes and shorts, my features were a bit different from my mother. Like my mother, I inherited her unique white porcelain colored skin, though it made me look a bit too pale I thought, anymore and I would look sickly. I too had blue eyes but it wasn't like her wonderful light blue, mine were still darker, deeper blue. Instead of being a blond, I had a rustic brown colored hair that I inherited from my father, all which suited me.

My mother gave a slight smile, "okay, we you can choose one when we get there."

"I want a choux," I said with a big grin.

"Do you know what that is?" my mother chuckled.

I shook my head, 'no'. There were time when I do reminisce about what I said, giving me a delightful smile whenever I see the French treat now.

My mother gave a small laugh, "okay, you can see what it is when we get there, and if you still want it, we can get it."

After the trek through the park, it was only a short twenty minute stroll down the street to our destination, even with my short legs. With my little hand grasping my mother's skirt, I was enjoying the quiet slow walk. The nicely paved street, the stores standing tall to me, each one were lined right down the street, the buildings looked stuck together while occasionally leaving an alley in between. The streets were empty with the exception of a few others, which were understandable considering the time of day. Perhaps a car might drive on by after a short while. As most people would've been spending their day off sleeping in, it quieted the streets, where it might have been bustling with others on the normal weekdays.

As we both continued to walk, something caught my eye. Across and a little ways down the street, there was an alley way. For a second, I noticed a dark looming shadow, and without a moment's notice, it disappeared. Still clinging, I tugged with both hands on my mother's skirt, the sudden action making her wobble a bit in her high heels.

"Mommy, mommy, I saw something over there."

"Hmm, what did you see?"

"It was a monster," I had cried out then but could tell that my mother was skeptical, that I had seen anything at all. Instead she looked down at me and gave a smile filled with disbelief.

"Okay, well lets' take a look." Her words surprised me then as I wouldn't have thought to go over to the location to take a look. I should have protested, but I suppose due to my innocent age to follow my parent's instructions, it seemed to me at the moment; reassuring. That if we were to look and find nothing there, it would only prove that I was imagining things.

We kept walking until we stood across the street where we could see right down the alley. We both stopped and peered into the darkness. It was a bright beautiful morning and there was plenty sunlight, rays from the sun escaped the narrow space. The surrounding sunlight still made everything perfectly visible, yet it made me uncomfortable, for me to look down the dark desolated alley. We simply stood there for a few seconds, gazing at nothing in particular; the empty alley space was silent. Nothing moved, as if everything in that narrow space was frozen in time. There wasn't much there but some trash bins, a few trash bags, there were also a stack of card board boxes with scattered newspapers near the corner, once led by the wind to pile up. From the looks of it, a few bottles of empty glass liquor laid nearby. It looked like the home of some poor drunk homeless sap who was nowhere in sight.

"There's nothing there sweetie, you were probably imagining it."

"But I really saw it," doing my best to persuade her as we started to walk away.

"Well you know," my mother responded, "back in the countryside where I grew up as a child in a small rural town of Scandinavia, my mother told me and my sister a few stories. It's only a story, but she told us a few times about shadow men and monsters. She said that as a little kid, once in a while she would see the shadow of man moving from within the darkness."

"Is that what I saw?"

"Maybe. Your grandma did tell me something interesting once. She told me that there were other kinds from the regular shadow men who often left people alone." Now in a more serious voice, her fingers were up to her lips as she looked slightly down at me mischievously. "My mother, your grandma, also said that there were very bad ones too." I didn't say anything but I felt an uneasy chill. She continued, "'they', also moved through the darkness, unnoticed by most people, almost all live in their own world, wherever that is no one knows. But my mother had told me that a few of their kind lives here, in our world among us."

Her words made me quickly turn my head to glance back down at the alley. In a low voice, I turn my head towards my mother and asked in a whisper. "Why do they want to live here?"

"Oh, you want to know?" There was a slight pause as she thought of the answer, "I'm not going to tell you since you're too little, it's not something to tell pampered children like you," she said as she bent over and gave a big pinch on my cheek.

A bit insulted and now pouting, her cheek pinches hurt. "I won't get scared," tugging onto my mother's skirt with my tiny hands, "tell me, tell me, I want to know," pleading, hoping my annoyance would make her cave in.

We continued walking for awhile, me still pulling onto my mother's skirt, still trying to get the information out of her.

"Okay, okay."

Finally she was going to fill me in on the details after my insistent calling. We both stopped, my mother turned slightly towards as she looked down. She seemed like a giant as I looked up at her. Standing with one arm folded across, and a hand under her chin, she asked in questionable voice. "If you really want to know I'll tell you, but no climbing into bed with us at night if you get too scared."

There was a moment's pause between us and I gave my reply, nodding my head in agreement. It was a hesitant reply but I wanted to know. Curiosity clawed at me as I craved the information from her.

"My mother said it was the smell here," she begun again as we both started to walk once more. "It's the smell of people, which means that there are some out there that stays in our world so that they can, well, feed on us." Seeing the confusion on my face, she lifted both her hands in front of her, and made chomping noises as if she was tearing into a giant roasted chicken leg. Her silly facial expression made me laugh, and I understood what she meant. "They don't just go after anyone, they choose carefully on who they go after." Her voice grew lower and more menacing. They usually go after adult women and men, single and lonely if possible. Once in a while though, they go for beautiful succulent children like you." Saying this, she gave a smile towards me.

"My mother also told me that they preferred little boy and girls like you, since your meat and bones are soft and tender, and little kids also smell tastier to them."

Noticing me clenching her skirt tighter, she knew I was getting a bit afraid and with good reason. After all, I thought I had just seen one of them in back there. 'Was it going to eat me?' I thought.

She softened up a bit towards me, not wanting to frighten me too much. "They don't do it too often since people tend to search a lot harder for children than for grown-ups, especially if they have a family. They rather to be kept a secret from everyone, so if they did attack people with families, their loved ones would look really hard to find them. So you don't have to worry. You have your dad and I, we will always be there to protect you. I'll make sure to give whoever that tries to take you a little bit of hell." Her last few words seem to have eased my fears a bit as I continued to listen.

We suddenly stopped as I stood puzzled, wondering why. After a second, I realized we had already arrived at our destination, standing in front of the pastry shop. It wasn't much of a pastry shop but looked more like a place for an individual to casually relax, like a café but not quiet since they didn't sell any drinks. One would have to go to the coffee shop across the street, pick a drink up, then come over and buy some pastries. It made me wonder as to why the place just wouldn't sell the coffee as well.

The inside was decorated very nicely with wood furnishing with their goods under the glass. Lighting was slightly dimmed which gave the place a nice luxury feel. On the outside there were about six small tables, half filled with either couples or friends talking while enjoying one of the shop's tasty treats. The shop didn't have a big name across the top or on the window like all the others that surrounded it; instead, it had a small board stand next to the door with the French name, *Désir et d'appel.* I stood there not understanding what the name meant. All I knew was that it was a nifty name and I liked how it sounded as the name rolled off my tongue, unsure if I was even saying it correctly.

It may have looked small and quaint on the outside, it was actually a fairly large pastry shop and quite popular too, especially with the women. There were already a few people walking inside to see which kind of pastry they wanted, even at this early in the morning. Apparently the pastry here wasn't like any of the others in the area. My mother had explained to me once before that the store was owned by a young French gentleman and a Japanese woman, both whom studied various styled pastries. Most of the time they were in the back while the hired staff were out in the front taking care of customers. Unlike other places, most of the pastries here weren't as sweet, they were delicious because of this; one bite gave a fine earthly taste, some a slight tinge of sweet coffee. They were a bit expensive for such small portions, but they were delicious, and offered as a nice treat for those who could afford it. Another winning aspect about the shop was that unlike many others, they had a large variety from all around the world; each one had its own fancy yet delicate uniqueness to them. They didn't just have a wide range of to choose from; they were seasonal, so that each season there would be new selections of deliciousness to choose from. Smart of them to do since it always left the person wanting to come back for more, trying their new items, to never to tire from eating the same sweets over and over.

While the store attendants were busying taking care of the paying customer before us, the two of us took our time to browse through the options.

"Evan sweetie, so which one do you want?" my mother asked with a lovely smile. "This one over here is the choux."

Looking through the glass, I was undecided; the store really did have a large selection and made me dizzy from wanting them all. There were rows of choices, on top there were more, even more on the shelves, and even more inside pantry displays on the counter in the center of the room. It might've been too big of a store with too much of a variety, even to this day I would've like to peek into the back to see how the two couples could make so much every morning.

I turned to my right, "I want that one," I replied foregoing the choux, now choosing whichever was decorated most creatively.

"Looks like you've both decided." A nice brunette asked, smiling behind the counter.

"Yes, I would like the Cro-cro-cream."

"Looks like you're staring at the *Croquembouche*," said the attendant with ease, interrupting my mother, "and your looks like your son wants the *Tres Leches*?"

"Yes please," now a bit embarrassed as my mother gave a slight blush, as the woman behind the counter said it so fluently; I could tell she was a bit envious. "Can I also have this dark one on top?"

She was a nice sweet looking girl and very intuitive. Noticing the mother's discomfort, "sure thing, and you don't ever have to be embarrassed, I know some of the names here are a bit hard to pronounce. Most people come in here and try to pronounce them but they're usually off, even me sometimes."

"Yes, I know, but I usually come here with my son, and well, it's still a bit embarrassing still since we come every week." Feeling more at ease, "I'm a bit envious of how you remember these complicated names so well."

The attendant gave a reassuring smile as my mother handed casually handed her a credit card before being asked. "Well, actually, every season when the new pastry selections come out, the husband and wife here pronounces the names for everyone ahead of time. When I first started, it took about a week to get most of it right, but hey; I eventually got the hang of it. By the way, there's still a few of them that I just can't get right."

My mother gave a small laugh, one that said, 'it's fine, you're just like me.'

"Here you go madam, thank you and have a nice day," said the attendant. My mother took the box, thanked the woman kindly, and we both left the shop.

Not being able to wipe the smile off my face from being so delighted and impatient. I wanted to get home quickly now, being only able to imagine the taste of the desert filling my mouth. Slowly, greedily, I would devour and savored every bite. My mouth watered a bit as we both continued to walk. I soon snapped to reality from my moment of day dreaming when a ringing sound came from my mother's purse.

"Hey Clarissa, how's it going," my mother asked enthusiastically.

My mother stopped as I was again left standing puzzled from my daydream, wondering what was going on now. She then looked back; and I followed as we both saw a slender woman giving us a small wave as she walked towards us. She was a pretty woman with straight brown hair tied back that reached her elbows. With brown eyes, she stood about five foot ten in high heels.

Walking up to me and my mother, "hey Alina, you're monstrously tall as ever."

"Men prefer a tall slender woman," my mother responded in

a confident yet corny stance.

It was my mother's good friend; she was also our neighbor that lived right across the street from us. Clarissa was thirty-nine, a year older than my mother, and while being single and lonely, she and my mother would spend a great deal of time together, that or grieving to my mother after a more than often breakup. Though she had her problems with her relationships, she was always a kind woman to me, sometimes she came and brought cookies she just baked, other times after coming home from work, she would stop by and play with me or have girl talk with my mother, sometimes my sister would be there talking with the two as well, but rarely. Perhaps she came over so often was because she was lonely, maybe she really liked us that much, it might also be because we were neighbors and we lived right across from each other. Either way, everyone in our household had taken a liking to her, enjoying her company whenever she came by.

Clarissa and my mother started talking away, me not really caring to listen. Instead I began looking around at miscellaneous things. As I stood there, still clinging to my mother's skirt, I noticed a nice black cat with a red leather collar walking right by me. I stood looking while the cat slowly walked by into a big alley way, only a few feet away from where we all were. I was intuitive, I wanted to get closer to the cat, see where it went, and possibly even touch it. Letting go of my mother I followed it up to the alley and peered down.

It was bright, yet even though the sun was high in the sky, it was getting a bit cloudy now, blocking out some of the light, creating a dimmer darkness. Still, there were plenty enough that it filled the alley making everything visible. Being a big long alley, it extended to the street on the other side, with tall brick walls on both sides. It wasn't that wide of a space but still being pretty spacious.

I spotted the cat a little ways down, lying on top of some boxes with blankets. Was it the home to another homeless person? I didn't see anyone so I started to move towards it.

"Evan!" my mother yelled, which gave me a startle. She quickly walked the short distance towards me. Bending down she caressed my hair back gently. "You shouldn't wander from mommy's side sweetie. Letting go is one thing, but if you have to wander, it has to be somewhere safe and where I can see you at all times," she said in her soft yet motherly voice.

"But I want to pet," pointing down the street, pointing to the cat now napping on top a heap of cardboard boxes as I looked up to my mother for her response.

"Let him play," Clarissa said arms folded as she stood behind my mother. "It's just a cat, and your husband won't allow him to have pets of any kind, why not let him play with it a bit?"

Slowly, standing straight up, my mother gave her argument in an unsure tone. "Because, you don't know if it has flees or some kind of disease, what if it scratches him?" she replied with a worried expression. "We don't know if it's tamed or not, better safe than sorry."

That was my mother of course, she always worried about everything me and my sister did. I didn't mind it since even then I knew that she was only caring for our wellbeing, maybe that's how some mothers just are, overprotective and overbearing.

As I looked up at Clarissa, I gave a look saying that I really wanted to pet the cat.

"It looks okay, the cat looks like it's been well groomed and it has a collar," she tried to argue, not being able to resist my adorable eyes. "Alina, you're too much of a worry wart," teasing her.

"I'm not a worry wart; I'm just being how a good protective mother should be." Standing there for a moment, looking at Clarissa and then at me, she gave a sigh, which was practically announcing that she was giving in. "Okay, go ahead, I concede, go play with the cat."

Clarissa gave a smile and thumbs up to me. Nodding my head, I happily hurried over to the sleeping curled up cat, leaving Clarissa and my mother to chat.

Reaching the feline, I stood in front of it. Glancing over at the two, my mother stood on the sidewalk intently watching me. She made me pretty nervous as she watched me; I gave a small waved to her anyway. She stood there waving back while giving me one of her motherly smiles, letting me know that she was right there if I needed her.

I redirected my attention back to the cat. At first I just stood happily staring at it, examining it. After a few seconds, I gathered the courage inside of me and extended my hand out slowly. Starting from the feline's furry head and slowly sliding my hand down its back. It was a nice soft warm feeling. The fur was well groomed and the cat looked well fed. While breathing, you could see its small body grow a bit bigger, then slightly becoming smaller. Eventually its ears twitched, waking up, staring at me with its sleepy eyes, sticking its tongue out as it slowly licked my hand before resting its head back on its paws. Docile and used to humans, it didn't mind my company or touch. I gave a joyful look back at my mother which she once again gave me a smile, waving back.

My mother finally assured of my safety, knowing that I wasn't going to get clawed by the feline, she then turned back to Clarissa, refocusing her attention to their earlier discussion. I could hear what they were talking about a bit, it seemed like Clarissa had once more been asked out, being about a month now by a some guy named John, which I had actually met before. He came over once, had gone on a double date with my parents last week. The two of them stood talking as Clarissa was inquiring with her whether it would be okay to bring him as a date for that night's party.

Uninterested in their conversation, my focus turned back towards the napping cat as I started moving my hand in a petting fashion once more. Deciding it would be alright, I tried picking it up, to hold it in my arms, feel its weight. As I made the movement, it suddenly jolted its head up in alert, almost as if alarmed. Black ears twitching a bit as it quickly stood up, turning around to stare at the wall behind it. Retracting my hand, I stared intently at the cat, wondering what it was going to do next. Making no sudden movements; instead it just stood there staring down at the wall. The boxes was a bit high as I couldn't see what it was staring down at, so I decided to climbed on top the boxes. The cat scooted over for me as I climbed on top on all fours. Now thinking back at the moment, I'm astonished that that the boxes were sturdy enough to house my weight.

As we both looked down, I noticed a decent sized gap between the boxes and the wall, in the wall was a hole. The cat gave a sudden *meow* as it stood there looking down into the hole. Being a small hole just big enough where I could squeeze my way into it if I really tried. Peering down at the hole, it made me wonder if something was inside. There had to be if it was enough to capture the feline's attention so suddenly. We both stared together not moving. The cat's body tensed as it became more focused; its eyes gave a slight glint. With a hiss it stood there and continued in a threatening stance. As the cat calmed down a bit, it got off the boxes, jumping into the space between the wall and the boxes. With a slow and careful approach, the cat inched its way toward the hole, curiously.

I stared watching with my full attention, waiting for

something, not knowing what, inside of me, my stomach I felt as if it was in a knot. It was the feeling of fear and anticipation of knowing that something was coming. The sky grew darker as a large grey cloud covered the sun as I had continued my concentrated wide eyes, not even blinking. Fear grew in me, besides the chatter from my mother and Clarissa, it was dead quiet. The wind blew down the alley making me feel cold, yet I continued my watch. Not knowing why, I couldn't rip my eyes away.

Standing directly in front of the opening, the feline just stood there as it peered inside, into darkness. A quick hand extended over the cats face. Still bent over, I saw it clearly. A large black hand with elongated fingers extended out. It had untrimmed claw like nails, grasping its poor struggling victim. So quick was it that the cat didn't have time to make a noise or even a movement for escape. The grip was tight, strong as the fingers creased into the finely groomed fur. As quickly as the hand extended towards the cat, it quickly dragged the furry creature back into the dark black hole. Following quickly was a small but audible crack, like the snapping of a bone.

Petrified, I didn't move from the boxes, I couldn't move being too surprised as the surge of fear moved throughout me. I started to hear a noise. A voice came out to me, calling me. I didn't know what it was not being able to make the voice out. As if it was calling my name, a hand landed on my left shoulder. Startled, I immediately turned around.

"Evan sweetie, I've been calling for you, what's wrong?"

The sound I was hearing was my mother's voice. Relief flooded through me as I started to get off the boxes, still shaken from what I saw. My hands grasped onto my mother for some comfort.

"Alina, is something wrong?" Clarissa asked as she walked over. She gave a quick look around, "where's the cat?" Clarissa said bending down towards me.

I faced Clarissa, not even noticing her until now. "O-over there," I said in a panic voice. "Mommy, it was taken by a monster," saying with one hand still holding onto my mother's skirt as I pointed towards the wall behind the boxes. "It was a monster, I saw it, it came at the kitty and ate it," I continued. I was still afraid, refusing to let go of mother, not wanting to even go near the boxes now.

My mother squat down, "Evan, there's no such things as monsters."

"But you told me there were monsters earlier, you said grandma told you stories of monsters," I retorted.

"They're just that, stories are only stories, they're not real, so you don't have to worry about monsters or demons, it's just make-believe, which means that they don't really exist."

I was still unconvinced as I knew what I saw was real. I was frightened, tears started to well up because no one believed me.

She tried comforting me again, this time caressing my cheek

softly, "it's okay, there's no monster. Evan, it was just your imagination."

The sky was starting to get covered with gray clouds, bringing a slight cold breeze. "It's going to rain today, we should hurry back," Clarissa interrupting the two of us.

"But the kitty," again I was insistent. "I really saw it, the monster grabbed it into the hole," I remarked again, pointing toward the pile of boxes.

"I knew I should have never told you that story. Sweetheart, you don't have to worry," my mother repeating herself, not making me feel any better.

Clarissa went up to me and scuffled up my hair. "Okay, let me check."

"You don't have to do that, he was only imagining things."

"Don't worry about it; it'll make him feel better if someone checks it out, to prove that there wasn't anything," Clarissa said as she approached the boxes. "Parenting 101, right?" Bending forward, tiptoed to get a glance behind the boxes. "It's kind of hard to see." Making her way over next to the pile of boxes, she bent down to grab one of the corners, and with a little effort, she pulled them over, openly revealing the hole completely.

My mother and I stood there silently watching Clarissa, doing whatever she was going to do. The hole was visible so all three of us could see now. To me, it looked ominous like an opening into another world, where devils existed.

Clarissa bent down, peering into the hole. "I don't see anything, it's too dark, but the good thing is that I don't see any monsters," she said as she turned around with a reassuring look.

Making me feel a little better, I was reassured as I began to doubt myself. Perhaps what I saw really was just my imagination; maybe it was my mother's story that made me imagine that there was a monster. Confused, at the time being so young I didn't know what was really going on then. So sure of what I saw, yet Clarissa was telling me that she wasn't seeing anything inside.

"See, no monsters, the kitty probably went into the hole and wandered off somewhere," said my mother while Clarissa went back over to me again as she scuffled up my hair once more. "What do you say to Clarissa Evan?"

"Thank you Miss. Jones."

Clarissa stood there frowning, "didn't I tell you to call me 'Clarissa,' I always feel so old when kids call me, 'Miss. Jones.'"

"Thank you Clarissa," I said with a grin.

After standing there staring, as if my mother was feeling a bit left out, "okay you two, it looks like the sky is starting to get worse. We should head on back, you coming Clarissa?"

"Yeah, it's a bit early, but I've got to get ready for tonight's event, I still don't know what to wear."

The three of us started back. As soon as we turned, I felt someone glaring at me from behind. So, I decided to glance back to see if anyone was there. Nothing was there, but I looked at the hole one more time. Though I was a bit away while looking at an angle, I saw something. In a slight moment, two white glints, it looked like a pair of eyes focusing in on me. Continuing my look before the sight of them disappeared as we exited the alley.

I decided not to mention it to my mother or Clarissa of what I just saw. I forgot why. Perhaps I didn't want to sound annoying. Maybe I figured they would've said that it was the cat looking back at me, though that was doubtful. Inside, I knew that tiny docile creature was no more. Not as frightened as how I was then after leaving the enclosed space, I simply decided to keep that part to myself.

During the short walk back home while my mother and Clarissa continued their conversation. I Drowned out their chatter as my mind was occupied, thinking about what just happened, of that ghastly looking hand that I just saw.

CHAPTER

2

Perhaps it was later that night when it all started. If it wasn't for that night, perhaps I would've lived a normal life just like everybody else, inconspicuous of the things that shouldn't be known.

"Lisa, remember the rules?" My mother yelled as she hurried down stairs that eventful night. I still remembered her beauty that night as she had prepared for the outing. Wearing a nice violet dress, hair tied up leaving just a few bangs in front with her diamond earrings she got from my father for her birthday, she looked quite dazzling then.

The house itself was fairly decent. There were three bedrooms in the house, all which were located upstairs being within sight standing below. Along with it came a closet in the hallway and three bathrooms. One for me and Lisa that we shared on the second floor, one below, and another located in the master bedroom. Downstairs was fairly roomy, consisting of a few multiple rooms which included an average sized living room, small dining room, a spacious kitchen, and a den. We wouldn't have lived as good if it wasn't for both my parents working. My father being a successful tax consultant and my mother was a well like university college professor, so we could afford to live in such a house.

"Yeah, I got it mom," my sister yelled back with annoyance as she tried to shout over the TV and the pouring sound of rain from outside.

Lisa sat lazily on the couch next to me, both of us in our pajamas watching some cartoons which I could no longer remember. I do remember it being one of those big bulky old TV sets though, the ones that still needed an antenna which would still sometimes lose connections from time to time. Lisa was my fifteen year old teen sister, wearing jeans that had holes on the knees and a plain black t-shirt. Like our mother, she had straight blond hair and light blue eyes with clear white pale skin. With the exception of being five foot six, she looked very much like our mother, but a shorter version. Possibly she might have grown as tall as our mother given a few more years. What she really lacked from both of our parents was their kindness and consideration for others, though I still cared for her regardless. There were multitudes of times where we never got along, which is how siblings are. Even when she was angry at me I would still cling to her out of boredom or for comfort as she would look out for me, sometimes unwilling of her own will, but she was there for me when needed.

"Well, what are they? Tell me them, I just want to make sure." Putting on her violet heels while looking across the living room, my mother stood in front of the door waiting for my sister's response.

Lisa looking awfully annoyed, in the same tone, "absolutely no boys, no partying, no drinking, nothing illegal, look after the house, I got it already."

"Chris, what's taking so long, Clarissa and John is going to be here soon," my mother yelled up the stairs, rushing my father to finish up.

"Hold-up, I can't get this tie right," saying now, running down the stairs while trying to fix his tie along the way.

Chris, my father stood fairly tall, six foot one, dark brown eyes, his brown hair nicely trimmed, having had a slight beard growing which gave him a rugged look while wearing his black sleek suit. It made him look fairly younger than he should have looked. Though unlike the rest of the pale white family, he had more color to his face, darker, making him stand out a bit sometimes when all of us were together.

"Okay, how do I look?" just finished with his tie as he waited for his wife's approval.

"It's still kind of crooked," reaching over to fix it. "And Lisa, you forgot the most important rule."

"Look after the little brat, I know."

"Okay, looks great," my mother said, looking at my father with satisfaction.

"Great enough for a kiss?" my father asked.

"Hmm, no, not quite there," she said before quickly kissed him afterwards. "That one was just because."

She then walked over to me and bent forward slightly. "Okay Evan, me and your dad are going to an event hosted by mommy's school, so remember to listen to your sister while we're both gone, okay?" She changed the tone of her voice to a lower, softer voice, more childish as if she was talk to an infant, which I didn't mind at the time.

I gave a nod in response. A moment later, the doorbell rang. My father opened the door as the sound of the pouring rain came rushing through the house, nearly overpowering the sound of the television. It was Clarissa, standing next to her holding the umbrella was her date whom I had no recollection anymore. All I did remember of him was his name and his burly beard, and that he had dark brown neat hair. Being so long ago, I still remembered him standing a bit taller than Clarissa, but still shorter than my mother in high heels.

My father welcoming them both in, "Clarissa, John," he said joyfully, "come on in, me and Alina are just about ready."

As the two came in with their black coats, Chris shook their umbrella before entering. "Man, what a weather we have out there," he said giving the umbrella one last shake.

"Hey Evan, come give me a hug," Clarissa yelled as she moved towards me.

So I left my cozy warm spot on the couch to quickly give her the requesting hug. The bottom of her coat was a bit wet, but it was okay since I was careful to avoid touching the cold damp parts.

After a second, I let go, but before I was able about to retreat back to my warm spot on the couch, Clarissa reached out to hold my face in both her hands, "oh you're such a cute little man." This had annoyed me.

Clarissa stood up straight and turned toward Lisa, setting me finally free. Noticing this, she straightened up, "hi Clarissa," followed with a polite smile. Clarissa gave a smile back, "so Lisa, do you have a boyfriend yet?"

John gave a jab to my dad, "not until she's twenty-one, right?"

Giving an unusual uneasy grunt, he responded. "Better make

that never, she's going to stay single for her whole life."

"Dad, I'm old enough to date you know," sounding more annoyed than ever.

Again, my father gave an unsatisfactory grunt, "yeah, no you're not." He turned his attention to the two women standing in the room. "Now ladies, we should leave the kids alone, if we keep talking we're going to be late."

"Already, but I haven't even got to play with little Evan, and I was hoping to have some girl talk with Lisa," Clarissa whined.

"Well you can have a girl talk with me." My mother then pulled Clarissa away with her arm in arm. Everyone said their goodbyes to us, and before my mother went out the door, she turned back to us, "oh Lisa, Evan and I went to the pastry shop today and brought something back for you, it's in the fridge."

"Okay, thanks mom," looking evermore delighted.

Hurriedly leaving once more, a second later, the door opened again. Once again it was our mother as she popped her head through the doorway and shouted. "And remember, even though your father and I won't be back till late, even though it's Saturday, I don't want Evan staying up too late." About to exit the door, she stopped short. "I want you to make sure your brother brushes his teeth," yelling across the room toward Lisa.

"Okay mom," Lisa yelled, but without an annoyed irritated

tone I might have thought she would have. Perhaps it was because my mother had brought her a dessert. "We'll be alright, hurry up and go."

The noise of the honking car was heard muffled by the sound of the rain. "Okay, okay," my mother shouted, quickly retreating back behind the door, followed by the lock.

"Finally," Lisa said giving a sigh. Looking at the clock, it was just past eight. Getting off the couch, she headed up the stairs.

"Where're you going?"

"Nowhere, I'm just getting something from my room, I'll be back."

Leaving me to sit and watch television by myself. A few minutes later, Lisa came down with some red nail polish and placed herself back in the same spot on the couch as before. Opening the bottle, she began painting her left hand.

"Lisa, play with me." So began the annoyance of how the younger sibling in almost all family would give to their elder sibling or siblings.

"No, I'm busy, and don't move, you'll make me mess up."

"But I'm bored," again I tried to convince her.

"Well you have the TV, find something to watch."

"There's nothing to watch right now, and I want you to play with me."

"I said no," this time Lisa raised her voice, showing a bit more authority, that she was the eldest and I needed to obey her.

I didn't let up though, I suppose I was much more stubborn as a child, maybe you could even call it, 'defiance.' "Play with me," again I said, this time I reached out towards her, grabbing onto her sleeve, yanking. The action caused Lisa to mess up giving a red smear on her middle finger.

"Damn it, I told you not to move," turning towards me, looking angry.

Knowing that look, I retreated back towards the side of the couch, cowering like an animal waiting for some sort of punishment to come. "I'm sorry it was an accident, really."

"Whatever," Lisa stood up calmly taking no action; this was a surprise to me. Unlike our mother, I always thought Lisa had anger issues and I was sure she would've done something.

"I want you to stay here and watch TV, you got it?" She faced me, waiting to hear a respond from me which never came. "I said, YOU GOT IT?"

This time I gave a few quick fearful nods. Grabbing her nail polish, she ran back up the stairs not coming back down. Left alone, I sat still watching boringly at the picture box in front of me. It was nine past five and some sort of movie was playing then. Again, what movie it was eluded me, but it must've been dull enough to forget. When Lisa finally came back down, she flopped back down on the couch; both her hands and toes were neatly painted in dark red which in my opinion wasn't a good color.

I crawled over toward Lisa, spreading myself over her lap, "that was long."

"Yeah, well I was busy, and get off, you're heavy."

Obeying since I knew it would only anger her again if I didn't. Still, being the little brother that I was, this time I got off and leaned against her while facing the T.V. As Lisa rolled her eyes in response to my action, still, she wrapped her arm around me as I started to remember what happened earlier during the morning stroll with our mother.

"Lisa, are there monsters?"

"Huh, what's up now, where did 'monsters' suddenly come from?" Though she made no noticeable movements, this question seemed to have piqued her interest. I could tell by the tone in her voice. She turned down the TV a bit to listen more carefully.

"I think I saw them earlier, but mom and Clarissa said there wasn't any."

"Yeah, what did you see?"

"Mom and me were walking, and there were those spaces in the walls."

"Spaces in the walls, you mean the alleyways?"

I nodded my head in response. "When we were walking, I saw a shadow man, than he ran away." Trying to explain to her was difficult, being young and limited on vocabulary.

"Then I saw another one coming home. In the alleyway there was a big hand that came out from a hole. It took the cat and ate it." Being more alert now, perhaps the memory gave me a bit of adrenaline. Sitting up, I looked straight at Lisa, welcoming any form of comforting response.

Anticipating some remarks of, 'monsters not being real,' there was a moment of silence before she responded. "Yeah, you were probably imagining it."

Still facing towards Lisa, "but I saw them, it was there," even though I knew she wouldn't believe me, still kept hope that she would in the end.

"Oh, I almost forgot my dessert mom got me." Getting off the couch, she headed toward the kitchen.

I felt my face grow whiter as if the blood was being drained from me. Hurrying off the couch, I made my way up the stair. By the time I reached the top I could hear Lisa fiercely closing the kitchen door. She was coming after me.

"Evan, come here you little brat," she screamed as she ran.

Making my way into my room, I quickly closed my door behind me. Hiding underneath my bed, I stayed, waiting. I was so afraid of what she might do; I began to produce beads of sweat. My breath grew heavy; I was a bit tired from the running.

Hearing my door creak open slowly, I softened by breathing so she wouldn't hear me. It was dark, but the light from the hall outside gave me visibility as I looked beneath the sheets. Being perfectly still, I watched her dark red toenails move around the room.

"Evan, I know you're here you little twerp." She had one of those low creepy voices, the kind of voice you would hear only from the killers in movies. "You ate my share of the dessert that mom brought, didn't you?"

A hand reached under my dark bed, firmly grabbing my left leg as she forcibly dragged me out. "No!" I yelled trying to dig my nails into the carpet with no success as my small body was pulled out from under my bed. In a mere two seconds, I laid out from underneath my bed, faced up towards the overwhelming might of my sister.

Now she dragged me by both legs as we made it out into the brightly lit hall. Letting me go, I stood up with my back against the wall, fear encumbered me. Lisa stood there leaning against the railing; she looked down at my pitiful site.

"So Evan, did you eat it?"

From my past experience with Lisa, I knew lying had never helped in any situation. She knew I had eaten the dessert, and if she didn't hear me say it, she would've force it out of me by torment of tickles. It was oddly effective and terrifying at that age so long ago.

"Yes," I gave my answer while nodding my head.

She moved forward, coming closer to me. Bending over until she was eye level. In a wicked voice, "don't worry little Evan, I won't do," she stopped. She gave a silent pause which only made me even more uneasy as it meant she was thinking of something evil. She then stood straight, "I'm not going to do; much," saying as she towered over me.

Grabbing me by the shirt, we both made our way downstairs as she threw me on the couch. "Stay there," she said as she left me. Turning off the television and lights, she went into the kitchen, soon emerging with a stool. Turning on a small lamp on the table, she sat directly in front of me only a foot or two away.

"Well Evan, you didn't think you could eat my cake and get away with it did you?" I sat there silent. "Well, six or not, you need some discipline, and mom and dad aren't home, they left me in charge, which means I get to decided what to do with you myself."

There was a flash of light, then a roar. It was a thunderstorm; its timing was impeccable as it set the mood for Lisa.

"Perfect timing," Lisa said, the light from the storm intensifying her evil smile. I stared at her with a bit more fear. I gripped the pillow nearby, clenching it in with my arms. I didn't know what she was going to do, but I knew it wasn't going to be good.

"You know Evan; there really are monsters out there. After our little talk earlier, I remembered something. Before you were born, our grandmother in Russia was still alive and well. At the time, mom was seven months pregnant with you, so we all went to Russia to celebrate your upcoming arrival with grandma. After about a day, I asked her about her husband or our grandfather. Since I didn't see him around and after noticing a loving picture of them both, I wondered whatever became of him."

"Do you know what she told me?" I shook my head as Lisa continued in a lower voice. "She sat there by the fire place that night, and she told me with her old shaking hands and lips, 'he was murdered, by the demons living in the backwaters of Scandinavia, her home country where she once lived. She continued as I sat there listening to her, very much like how you're doing right now."

"It was ten years ago in the late night, before she, our grandma, mom and our aunt had moved to Russia. While the couple strolled down the street in the snowy weather, she wrapped around her husband's arm, the two madly in love, discussing of the various things that they would need for their new home. She felt like she had everything back then. Our grandfather was successfully employed, making a decent hardworking living. After just purchasing a new house in hopes to raise a larger family, they received news that grandma was now pregnant with mom. While walking home, the two had decided to take a short cut through the park. The park was cut down the middle by a river where the bridge was broken, soon to be reconstructed. A few days earlier a cart had rode through, carrying too heavy of a heavy load. Riding over the bridge, the wood below had rotted over the years, collapsing from the added weight. It was closed off of course, so they both needed to walk down to the next bridge, yet grandfather insisted that they go on. Already being so close, all they had to do were lean on the side and slowly walk across. Plus the next bridge was much too far away to be walking in such a freezing weather. Freezing cold that night with their young daughter waiting for them at home, they wanted to get back as soon as possible. In the end, they foolishly agreed as they both started there walk over."

"In the past, grandfather was a joyful energetic husband, dong a little dance before holding his hand out to grandma. Taking his hand, she was the first to cross over. Halfway across, grandfather deciding then to take a look down at the slow moving icy water, steadily flowing down, saying, 'some idiots really can't ride,' making her smirk. She too bent down and peered into the water with him. The water was high, so high that the water touched the wood below their feet; it was so close you could touch it simply by crouching forward a bit. Due to the weather warming up, the snow was melting, even though that night she felt as if she could have frozen solid if she stood in one place for too long. After a bit, she turned around to make her way across, hoping he would take notice and follow her. He didn't, instead she heard his cry for help. Turning around, he was reaching out for her, yelling, calling her name, calling out to her. He was clinging to the edge yelling for her to help pull him up. In a panic, she rushed over, trying to pull him up, but she couldn't. Instead, he was sinking deeper into the dark icy water below, as if something was pulling him down."

"'Something caught hold of me, something is pulling me in!'" she remembered grandfather saying to her.

"As grandma pulled with all her strength, she glanced over to the side to see if anything was grabbing hold of him. As she did, she noticed both his legs were in the water, and his pants were as if being gripped, tugged upon by some unknown force, dragging him down. It was then that she also noticed the four white glowing lights, like two pair of eyes staring at her from below the dark watery surface. She stood staring deep into the water while her husband slipped further into the abyss, out of her arms. Catching hold of his hand, she held onto him with everything she had, but she couldn't hold on, she wasn't strong enough to win against whatever *they* were. Little by little, her husband, our grandpa slipped between her fingers, holding on for as long as he could, the water now reached up to his neck. Still pulling, she then cried out for help, for anyone nearby to come to their aid, but it was a silent cold night, everybody was inside their homes near their hearth, warming up their own bodies. She was shouting pointlessly into the cold air. She could remember his head going down below the surface, the air rising out of his lungs creating large bubbled above the cold water, yet still, he fought for his life. She knew because his grip was holding her hand tightly still. Then, he was finally gone. Their pointless struggle came to an end as he disappeared below; the glowing eyes that once stared up at her had left with him. She still remembered stumbling as she tried to stand up, running into town, frantically calling for help. When she told her story to others, no one believed her. As they searched for him, his body was never found, not a single trace of him."

As I sat there silently, not knowing what to make of Lisa's story, were there really otherworldly beings or weren't there? That was how I thought, at least back then before the definitive confirmation later that night. Being such a young boy, I didn't comprehend the whole story, but I did get most of it. Her story at that moment did confirm a feeling in me that there was the possibility that at least some monsters existing. After all, I had knew or at least thought I knew what I had seen earlier that day. I didn't have much time to contemplate as Lisa sat in front of me with her evil mischievous look.

"Well Evan, what did you think, do you believe that monsters exist, because I do?"

I sat there silently, giving a nod, unsure of my own emotions at that point.

"Good," uncrossing her legs, she bent forward a bit, "because you'll be sleeping outside with them tonight."

Flashing a smile, showing her pearly teeth, she grabbed hold of my collar, dragging me out to the backyard door. Opening it, she gave me a strong shove from behind, almost making me trip and fall. Hastily, she closed the door as I ran to the clear glass door, yelling for her to let me in. As I shouted and screamed for her to allow me back inside, instead she simply stood inside, pulling the curtains, blocking the view of me. Calling her name, apologizing, I was disoriented with the sudden turn of events. This was the first time Lisa had done something as extreme as this.

I kept myself dry underneath our small patio. When Lisa pulled the curtains closed, I was a bit taken aback by her simple hateful action, which I simply stood frozen, shocked for a moment. Looking around, I walked over to a white chair and slouched down in it, sitting there in the cold, arms folded, shaking. Seconds later, the light inside the house came back on, along with it the sound of the TV being muffled by the pouring rain. Our backyard was a normal one; it was a fairly decent size. We had a lawn with the typical old fashion boarded wooden fence, separating our part of the house from our surrounding neighbors. My mother had a small garden to the left where she grew a variety of herbs and vegetables, sometimes using them in her cooking. Plain as it were, the grass freshly cut, there wasn't anything else outside, no grill, no playground set, just my mother's small garden, a table, and a set of chairs.

I was neither angry with Lisa nor sad at the current outcome. I did something wrong, and perhaps her actions might have been a bit extreme, I felt apologetic for doing her wrong. You could say, I was repenting, simply hoping that she would cease her anger, softening up after a few minutes and let me inside again.

With not much to do, I contemplated over the story Lisa had told me. Sitting there, thinking about what our now deceased grandmother had possible seen. I began to review the details and facts to come up with a more solid conclusion of whether monsters really existed, at least what could come up with at that age. Soon paranoia took over, quickly darting my eyes, looking around to see if I could notice any glowing pair of eyes were looking at me. Thoughts of them clouded my mind of them hiding in the dark night, watching me, a possible victim for them, just as they had done with my grandfather.

There was a noise nearby, a car driving through the rain. I could hear it, even with loud and occasional boom from the thunder. The tires moving through the water as it made a loud splashing noise as it tried to reach its destination. Thankful that it had come by, it had snapped me out of my delusions, distracting me from what was not there.

Curiosity foolishly took a hold of me. Deciding to get a look out in the front side of our house, I walked to the side, getting drenched by the rain as I reached the end of our fence. It was a tall fence, much taller than I was so I couldn't see anything over it.

Trying to peak through the holes, I still couldn't see anything. Our fence was never locked, so I decided to open it up, poking my head out.

When I did, I noticed a small figure running across the street on all fours. I stuck my head back in, my thoughts raced as to what it was. At first, I had figured that it was a monster, than a more logical answer came to mind, 'it must've been a dog of some sort,' but it wasn't. Though it moved fairly fast, I knew that shape, even with the poor visibility, I had a decent enough glimpse to know that it wasn't some animal. Whatever it was took a very *'human'* like figure.

Gathering my courage, I opened the gate to leave the sanctity of my home. My curiosity was too great, wanting a better look at what it was, my heart raced as walked out. Moving quietly as I could, barefoot, shaking from the cold rain, I reached the bushes at the end of our driveway. Cautiously peeking, there was a car with its headlights on about three houses down; most likely it was the car that drove by earlier. The owner still hadn't left their car yet.

Looking around, trying to locate the 'thing' I saw earlier. Scanning the area as the car lights went out. A figure came out of the car. It was hard to see, visibility was bad with them being too far away. An umbrella covered their face. All I saw was them wearing a long black coat, carrying something in their left hand, a bag, perhaps a suitcase or a purse. Disappearing as they went inside their home, I then noticed not one, but what seemed like three pairs of faint glowing eyes. Even from that distance, I was certain there were three of them. The glows were bright, mesmerizing as the image bore its way into my memory. Quickly, they crossed the street, moving toward the house the individual entered earlier, disappearing once more.

I should've stayed away. Normally the fear in a person would've kept them from going, from exploring the possibly dangerous unknown, to take caution under safety; it didn't for me. I wanted to see what *they* were, to confirm the truth, my bravery as a child was truly rash.

Making my way to the house three doors down, an audible banging noise was heard coming from that direction. Getting closer, it was the gate to the wooden fence of the house being blown by the wind, creating a slight not too loud noise as it opened and close itself. Approaching the gate, I looked into the backyard through the occasional opening the gate would make. There was nothing. This time, I trespassed into the backyard, my bare foot inside as I held the door. That's when the lights inside went out, a loud crash followed, coming from inside. Standing still, a scream of a woman, followed by another crash of what seemed to be glass breaking, this time from the backyard. This one was much louder than the previous. Still it was muffled by the rain, not loudly enough for our neighbors to take notice. Taking a deep breath, despite my fears I took a step forward, letting go of the wooden gate as it resumed its banging, frightening me. Swiftly, quietly I moved along the wall before peering around the corner.

A woman was lying on the lawn faced down; her long brown hair spread sprawled around her as she faced away from me. Shards of broken glass covered the floor from the broken back door. She was a plump woman wearing nothing but a dark blue robe which covered her, a single house slipper on her right foot while the other one was left missing. She didn't move. There, next to her were three ghastly black figures, their color helping them perfectly camouflage under the night. I could see them well, being so close. Two of them had their backs towards me, while the other one had its side to me, analyzing down at the unmoving woman.

There was no light outside, but the lighting flashed as I captured the images of them. They were hideous little beings, perhaps just a bit bigger than I was at that time. The flashes from the lightning made them all the more visible. Naked, yet muscularly build. The one that I could see from its side had some hair growing on its head, slimmer than the other two, still fairly muscular. From what I saw, their arms were long, perhaps as long as their own body, longer even. Watching, wondering what they were going to do, I stayed and watched. I should have ran but I was simply too amazed at what I was seeing, confirming their existence with my own two eyes. My tiny legs just didn't budge, mesmerized by the ghastly black figures. The three of them had their face down against the woman, possibly sniffing her, even though I didn't see a nose, at least not on the one I could see. One of them poked her a few times with its elongated finger. One of them with its back towards me stopped moving before tilting its head up, taking a moment to gaze up at nothing. In a response the others came to a halt. For some reason I knew what it was doing. It noticed my presence somehow and was sniffing the air, through some part of its body I did not know. Even through such heavy rainfall, they were trying to locate me by my scent. It was the same reaction as our neighbor's hound sometimes made.

The one that face my direction jolted its head straight at me, looking at me as I spied on them, seeing it's eyes piercing my entire being. From the distance it looked at me expressionless with its mouth opening wide. It had sharp pointy teeth, disfigured and crooked. Even they too were colored black, looking disgusting as the water streamed down its face into its mouth, between the gapes of its teeth. Seeing me, it gave a wide creepy smile stretching from one end to the other, one filled with joy and murderous intent.

My body moved back on its own, stumbling, falling to the ground. Getting up, I ran. Reaching the end, I pulled open the gate, as I did, I looked back to see the three pairs of eyes gazed upon me from the other end. My stomached turned as my heart raced in sync with my fright. Their faces were no longer visible, but their eyes were gleaming. Two pairs of yellows, the other one white. Leaving, rushing around the corner, falling hard as I made the turn. A faint call came to me as I got back up.

"Evan! Evan! You scared the hell out of me," Lisa said kneeling down, looking to see if I was alright.

"Lisa," I said rushing into her arms. Pushing away from her, I tried to utter an explanation for what I saw, pointing towards the woman's backyard. No words escaped my lips.

She held me, giving me a comforting hug which both startled and calmed me. It was the first time she had ever held me so gently, soothingly caressing my hair. It was quite nice as it eased my fears a bit, reminding me of our mother. She pushed me away and started looking at my face. Unusually, her expression was too, something that I was first seeing, filled with a sort of kindness, sympathetic, sorrow, yet worried look. I wonder why but I felt relieved that she was there, perhaps because it was the first time she treated me in such a way, or maybe perhaps it was because she looked a lot liked our mother that moment. It could also be that I was no longer alone, a feeling of some sort of protection from being with her. She was my bodyguard, my hero in that moment. I looked up to her then; like an almighty being who could do away with the three creatures had they appeared.

My senses came back to me, "Lisa, monster, monster," again, struggling with my explanation.

Glancing over, she saw nothing but the wooden gate opening and closing. She looked back down at me, placing her hand on my head. A gentle voice, "there's nothing there Evan, monsters don't really exist, I'm sorry, I was just trying to scare you earlier."

"B-but I saw them, really, there eating the lady," again, trying

51

to argue.

"Lets' go home, we need wash up before mom and dad come home."

"I saw them." Pulling down on her arm, trying to convince her with everything I had.

"Okay, okay," this time in her normal annoyed tone, back to her usual self. "If it really makes you feel better, I'll take a quick look."

Hearing her words, I immediately regretted it, "no don't, they'll eat us," I clambered, this time I pulled her arms in the direction home, "I want to go home," shouting as I was afraid of what might come if she did go over.

"Hey, don't pull!"

After that, she held my hand, making the short trek home. Looking back as we walked, their eyes visibly bobbed out, one pair after another, glowing poorly into the visible rain. Holding my sister's hand tighter as we walked, not taking my eyes off them, them not taking their eyes off of us, till eventually we were out of sight of one another.

After we had gotten back home, I took a bath as Lisa shower in our parent's room. I sat there with the foaming bubbles, warming up, brooding over what I had seen. The wind blew harder outside, it howled as if it was welcoming evil. Looking through the window, it was dark out; you couldn't see anything but the splash of water against the window panes. As I sat there for a long while, I grew tired.

There came a knocking on the door. "Evan, you done? Hurry up and get out."

I was so tired. I finished up, exiting the bathroom in my new dry pajamas, and made my way back downstairs. Lisa was below; she wore plain light blue pajamas, lying on the couch watching TV.

I reached the couch.

"Go to sleep, it's late," she said before I got up.

A bit disappointed, she simply had no sympathy. I was a somewhat scared little boy who just had a traumatic ordeal earlier, yet that was all she had to say? Displeased, originally wanting to lie next to her. Not having much of a choice as it was already 10:46pm. Pretty late I'd admit. Tired as I was, drowsily I headed back upstairs.

Reaching the top, the sound of the TV below stopped, as it was turned off. Glancing back, the lights turned off below with Lisa appearing as she hustled on up.

"Brush your teeth Evan."

"I'm tired," with my eyes half open.

"Too bad, mom told me to make sure you brush your teeth, so you're going to brush your teeth." Dragging me to bathroom,

Lisa started to brush her teeth as I reluctantly follow after. Afterwards, I was in my room as she tucked me in.

"Are you sure you're not hurt?"

I nodded my head; Lisa had asked me this earlier after we entered our home as well. Not saying anything, she exited my room, turning off the light on her way out. It was dark; I had a normal bed, a fairly normal room. Walls covered with construction paper, my toy bin on the side. Adjusting my position facing my window, watching the rain hit the glass as my eyes grew heavier. Dozing off, I blinked a few times. It appeared. The pair of glowing yellow watching me. There was only one of them this time. The body not being visible, all there was where its eyes. Wondering what it might have been thinking, nothing came to mind as exhaustion took its course, making me fall into a deep sleep.

CHAPTER

3

An incessant beeping, I couldn't sleep; my alarm kept on beeping as my consciousness crept upon me. Reaching over to my left, turning off my alarm clock, peace and tranquil quietness filled my room as I started opening my eyes. The time stood at 9:30am, exactly the time that I had set it to. Sluggishly, I got up, sitting on the edge of my bed. For a moment not doing anything, staring at the wall in my dark room as my body and mind started to function again. I could see a little sunshine creeping through my black curtains as I got up, reaching for my window. Turning away, I pulled the curtains open, the light blindingly brightened up my room. A good thing I had looked away. Squinting a bit at the magnitude of the new morning sun that impaired my vision, the sun hurt my eyes, but I quickly adjusted. The neighborhood kids below were already up biking down the street, a few of the other neighbors were seen below talking to each other under the shade of their tree, away from the brilliant sun.

Changing my cloths into a nice plain red shirt and plain jeans, I exited my room. It had been a few years since my family and I had moved, we still lived in a three bedroom two story house, but the structure itself was different. It wasn't the same house that I grew up as a child, having been forced to relocate years ago due to a fire. Unfortunately the location of the new place was still in Boston. Originally, I had wanted to move out of Boston since the incidents back then, to forget the awful times, the tragic moments of my early youth. Well, it was okay now since I would be living with my Aunt Emelia starting today, finally out of Massachusetts.

Reaching the bathroom, quickly washing up, I did my hair and looked at myself in the mirror for a moment, wondering how different my new life would be. I wasn't the same pale young boy I was back when I was a child under my mother's care; instead there was a flow of color throughout my face. I had darkened a bit to now resemble a bit more like my father. My brown hair had become a nice darker brown if I had to judge myself, I was also evenly built. There were some muscle but not much, I wasn't overweight or skinny, about average, wherever that would lie, and I had grown to six foot.

"Evan honey, hurry up, we don't want to be late," the call

from below reaching loudly up to the bathroom.

Hurrying downstairs, there stood Clarissa, much older now. She had changed a lot, the years taking its natural toll on people, aging everyone including her. Now with short hair, she was thinner having lost a few pounds from her daily exercise she now did every day. It did make her look a bit healthier. Her face had laugh lines, eyes holding some dark bags underneath them, though not very noticeable with her makeup, yet you could still see them. It was most likely due to my father and her not getting along lately, I knew she stayed up late, sometimes drinking her Burgundy red wine. There were times when the argument would get a bit too heated as I would hear them arguing while I lie in my bed at night. It didn't bother me too much anymore, though I would still pull out my earphones to drown their arguments out.

"Come here," she called out to me opening her arms for a hug. Reluctantly, I reacted as she instructed. Her embrace was warm and loving like how a mother's hug should be, although I hated every bit of it, but never once did I show it.

"Morning mom," I forced myself to say. The words, "mom," was something that I had never become accustomed to even after so many years. She wasn't after all my real mother, but I knew how much she tried, time and time again to be my dear real mother's replacement. Showering me with love and compassion, I knew with absolute certainty that she was treating me as if I was her own flesh and blood, as if I was her real son, never knowing of my actual dislike towards her.

She held my face in her arms as tears began welling up. Holding them back, not wanting to ruin her makeup, "oh my handsome little man is going to leave."

"Don't worry, I can come back during the holidays, we'll talk from time to time over the phone too." I forced myself a fake smile. It seemed to have appeased her a bit.

My father then barged into the house through the front door. He too had noticeably aged from the years. His hair had a touch of gray, he now looked worn out with heavy bags below his eyes, and he had obviously been working through the night. His hair no longer in a neat fashion as it was always in the past. No longer did he shave everyday as now a slight beard grew. The past few years were harsh on him. I knew he taken on more responsibility at work, forcing his own self to the limit even when not requested. A few times I had even caught him asleep right at his desk, sitting up as he worked. It started after my real mother Alina had passed away. He changed; work to him at first was a way to escape the reality of losing his wife and precious daughter. It kept his mind occupied, at the same time it was worrisome for his health. Its' been years since their passing, but perhaps he was now use to the work load, or maybe he really had gotten over the loss, I didn't know.

"Your things are in the car, we should get going," my father said in an emotionless tone.

I was excited yet at the same time nervous. After my mother and Lisa passed away, my father and I had never quite gotten along after that, Clarissa marrying him only made things worse for me, at least in my opinion. I would say she had helped supported my father with our loss. If not for her, perhaps he would've collapsed all together.

Every year my father would call Emelia to ask if she would like for me to stay with her for a little while during breaks. It was a way for me to get away, to relax while he and Clarissa could reconnect. After some time, I would return back home before break ends so that the three of us would have a short vacation out somewhere. A sort of win-win situation for all of us, for me, it was that I could get away from the two as I did enjoy my visits to Emelia's. It wasn't until a few weeks ago as I was visiting her during summer vacation, when she asked how Clarissa and my father were doing. Telling her the truth, that they would occasionally argue which was typical, it was nothing new that she didn't already know. That it was sometimes difficult living with the two of them, but we were all doing well in general. It was then that she had surprised me when she asked if I wanted to move-in with her. If I did, I could attend the high school nearby to finish out my last year of high school. I remembered asking her why. Her response was that it might be a good idea to give some space between Clarissa, my father, and I. At the same time, since we enjoyed each other's company, it would be nice if I could enjoy a setting where I could be more comfortable, unlike how it was now with me living with my father and Clarissa.

Agreeing immediately, Emelia eventually talked it over with my father and Clarissa to get their consent. I could have only imagined the conversation they had. Most likely Clarissa would of course have been reluctant, throwing a fit and accusations at Emelia and my father, fighting to have me stay. I would imagine my father agreeing, but he was sometimes too difficult to read, and would do the opposite of what I would sometimes think. If he did though, it would be that he trusted Emelia. He had always trusted her. Not only was Emelia the sister of his deceased wife, she was educated, responsible, and he knew that the two of us got along well. A part of me told me that it was because of something else. There were certain times I would see the two of them talk, hints from my father's feelings of guilt sometimes showed, perhaps the guilt made it difficult to say no to Emelia. Guilt perhaps?

The image of Emelia that day she had flown over after hearing what had happened to my mother and sister would forever be ingrained in my mind. She blamed my father for not being there to protect her sister, even becoming somewhat violent towards him. Shortly after, she came to own senses and stopped blaming my father for her sister's death, but I'm not sure my father ever did.

During the drive to the airport, no one said a word. Odd as it maybe, it was fairly nice. Often times, moments like this was when Clarissa would continue talking non-stop. Now she silently sat in the front seat, simply not saying a word, pouting for my leaving her care.

As we drove, I watch the passing view of the place I would no longer be living in. Out the window, the other cars moving to reach their own destination, I didn't have any feelings of remorse.

Arriving at the airport, my luggage was already checked in, consisting of a large suitcase and duffle bag, along with my backpack strapped around me behind me. I didn't have much else as my other stuff would be packaged and shipped over. All that was left was to say goodbye, finally being released from the state of Massachusetts.

Clarissa stood resisting her tears once more.

"Bye mom," again I called her my mother with reluctance, forcing myself to give her another hug. "Dad," I said extending out my hand to him, awaiting the usual firm handshake.

"Evan, take care, don't cause any trouble for your aunt," replying as he then shook my hand, once more looking at me with his emotionless expression. Even at this moment, he didn't force a smile on his face or seemed sadden by my leave.

"Remember to call us when you land," Clarissa said.

"Okay, I will, take care," starting to leave, giving wave back as I walked away.

"And be sure to eat properly, remember to stay out of trouble," her voice called out to me once again.

Turning around while walking backwards, this time I nodded

and gave two thumbs up. My father then said something to her, word of comfort, possible to say that I would be fine; there were nothing to worry about. I turned back around, knowing she wouldn't yell anything else as I made my leave. Once boarded, the feeling that it was finally happening. I really was going to start my new life in Middleton, Idaho. There weren't any feelings of anxiety or nervousness. Joy, calm, anticipation, these were the feelings that welled inside of me at the thought of finally starting over. A new slate in my life, away from all the misfortune and memory that once happened in Massachusetts.

When I landed, Emelia had already arrived, waiting for me. "Evan, over here," She yelled for me, waving her arm in the air as if I wouldn't be able to spot her. She stood out like a sore thumb in her black pants, tennis shoes, and bright green t-shirt. With a slight Russian accent unlike my mother, she too had the same blue eyes and beautiful skin, with some aging wrinkles, blond straight hair cut short to her shoulders. She wasn't as tall as my mother, but she was fit and beautiful for her age without really trying to be.

"Aunt Emelia," I called out, making my way to her.

"You ready to live with me?" She stood there in a confident stance, much how my mother used to. She would do lots of things like my mother, cooking, gestures, the way the spoke. Growing up with one another gave them similar habits.

"Yeah, I am."

Giving me a warm welcoming hug, "we're going to have lots of fun together, well maybe not that much since I do work a lot, but we'll still have a good time." Letting go of me, "you don't have to worry about a thing, I've got lots of room at my place, oh sorry, our place, you're going to be living with me after all, it is going to be your new home."

She drove us to her place as I viewed the landscape of the new town that I was going to be living in. It wasn't my first time, yet I had never stayed long while only being to a select few locations in the surrounding areas. Now I wanted to take everything in that the place could offer. Middleton was a nice small town city with a decent population. The city itself was fairly modern while retained some oldness in many parts. It wasn't the typical bustling sky scraper business oriented city. Instead, it was filled with small district shopping malls; the people seemed like decent homely folks. There were nice homes as they were built in a place to live in if you wanted a quiet urban lifestyle.

Emelia pulled up to the drive way. Looking at her large house as I hauled the luggage in, it wasn't my first time, but I was still pretty excited. It was a big luxury two story house with multiple bedrooms and bathrooms that were left unused. Greenery surrounded the outside of the house. Tall old aged trees that reached the sky as they did many of the other houses. Though old looking on the outside; inside was fully decorated and technologically modernized, upgraded with some of the best appliances. Even with her job as a surgeon for the city's hospital, I assumed it would have been difficult to buy the house by herself. Lucky, she didn't even have to put out much finance as most of the costs were paid for by her ex-husband.

A few years ago, Emelia had married a wealthy self-made business man. The two had a dream, an idea of being able to raise a large family. Right after their marriage, they searched for the perfect community as well as their dream home, fit for them and their future kids, which they eventually came across this large house. Being as wealthy as her ex-husband was, he paid off the house in full with a giant check. The dream was soon shattered after only a year and a half later when Emelia caught him cheating with a business associate of his. Their marriage slowly broke down after that. They went to marriage counseling for a while, trying to work things out, but a slew of problems arose and the trust between the two of them were too hard to salvage. Divorce was the only option left.

According to the details during the divorce settlement, instead of splitting everything, she originally chose not to take anything. She hadn't married him for his money or material possessions. Not needing his money with the current pay she was getting, nor were she particularly interested in his money. Still, he felt burden with regret, eventually leaving her with the car and house with everything inside. That was all she took from him, even though her lawyer insisted that she could have taken much more.

I remember once, she had told me of how lonely she was,

living in such a big house all alone by herself. Multiple unused rooms, some she had only entered a few times a year now only to clean the dust off. Coming home to an empty large house, it made her feel depressed and lonely. Dating once or twice after, but due to her busy job, it became too difficult and tiring to date. After a while, she simply gave up on dating all together. The hospital she worked at had too few surgeons, especially ones with knowledge and experience in certain fields that only she could perform. Not giving her much of a choice, lots of people were counting on her, so she was made to come in often, leaving her with not much of a personal life.

As I walked into my room, it was now different since the last time I came. The room was repainted from the yellow color it was before to the now light blue walls. New furniture was also brought, only the necessities though. A new bed and desk replaced the old ones that once were there. On top of the desk was a new desktop computer still in the box unopened.

"Do you like it?"

Startled as Emelia's voice came up from behind me, "I do, but you really didn't have to, the old stuff would've been good enough, I mean they still worked right? Plus I'll only be here a year."

"Yes, but the old furniture didn't appeal to my eyes, and the computer before was pretty old and slow. If you're going to be living here, you'll need a new one for doing research papers, and, well, other activities," giving me a small nudge with her elbow.

I smiled back a bit awkwardly thinking what purpose she was assuming I would use the computer for, something inappropriate maybe.

"Even though you know the house inside and out by now, I'll let you settle in, maybe you can start by setting up the computer. I'm part of the elderly generation, so I'm pretty bad at the technology side of things." Walking off she left me alone to unpack, settling myself in.

Finally, I was alone. Today would be a start of an almost new beginning. As I unpacked and setup the computer, I realized that she didn't spare any expenses. It was a top of the line computer with a 31.5 inch monitor. I felt happy with such a high performance machine, however, guilt crept upon me that she was doing so much for me. It made me wonder just how much money was she actually making? I then began to question for the first time whether it was the right choice for me to have moved in with her. Late as it was, I was now here. I would make the best of my situation, make life better if possible, even try to curing or at least lessen myself from the terrors of the past.

Wednesday came as with the start of my new school life, the second day that I've been living here and already I was attending school. A prudent choice, the new semester had started and I had already missed a week of school, it wouldn't have been good to miss anymore. Biking the way to school wasn't too bad either. Even though being seventeen and having a driver's license already, the school itself was pretty close, about a ten or so minute bike. Nothing to complain about and I didn't want to trouble Emelia with purchasing a used car for me. She did insist on doing so right after my father and Clarissa agreed on my moving, wanting to get me car or at the very least a used one to. Through my adamant denial, she conceded giving up after a certain point. I just didn't find it very necessary.

Emelia had taken care of all the documents ahead of time, even having my schedule ready to go before leaving the house. All I needed to do was find my classes. I had always liked that about her. When she was in charge of something, she would be very detailed about it, making sure there was nothing less but perfection. If she wasn't working in the medical field, I could have imagined her working in the business sector, running her own company.

Arriving at the school grounds, the front was packed with cars dropping off their kids, or those who had cars quickly drove in, filling the parking lots. Quickly locking up my bike, I still had a good amount of time left before first period began. Deciding the best course of action, it was to start off by finding the location of my locker and all of classes. It was normal school filled with other teens my age. I felt a bit nervous as if I was a freshman again. To explore another high school once more, wandering around aimlessly looking for my classes made me feel out of place. Everyone looked so carefree, laughing together without a care in the world as if it was a perfect city with no worries. It made me feel small, at the same time comfortable and curious with how my senior year would turn out.

Walking through the halls as the other students passed me by. A girl bumped my shoulder, giving a quick turn-around reply, "sorry," before making her way up the steps to the second floor. She ended up slipping on a piece of paper, causing her to fall backwards, catching herself using the hand rail. I stood behind her with my hand on her back, poised to catch her body weight. She didn't end up crashing down as I had anticipated.

"That was pretty dangerous, are you okay," I asked helping her regain her footing as she turned around.

She was a pretty girl, blond wavy hair, with blue eyes and a light touch of makeup. Her body looked petite, yet she was average height, about five foot seven. She looked her age but perhaps a bit more mature, at the same time with a hint of immaturity.

"Yeah, thanks, you really saved me there. That's pretty embarrassing having others see me slip like that." Her shoulders scrunched together as she gave an innocent smile, covering her embarrassment.

"I didn't exactly do anything, you pretty much caught yourself. By the way, my names Evan, I'm a senior, and this is kind of my first day," I said gesturing my hand out for a handshake.

"The name's Alice," she gave a more welcoming relaxed smile, reaching out to shake my hand. "I'm also a senior, not my first day. Hey you know what, since you're new around here, how about I show you around?"

Before I could respond, a big thuggish brute stepped beside her, interrupting. "You okay, I saw you almost falling over back there, didn't hurt yourself did you?" he asked.

Alice gave a glance at me, "I'm good, it's a good thing Evan over here assisted me."

It was pretty obvious that he was her boyfriend, since after she said that, he turned towards me, wrapped his arm around her waist, and forcefully pulled her towards him. It was as if he was monopolizing her, telling me to back off. Alice seemed pretty uncomfortable with this, but she didn't resist. Seeing this, I had wished she hadn't told him that I had, 'assisted' her when she was about to fall, when I hadn't done much of anything. His actions told me she was the possessive type, the kind of guy that would get both angry and jealous easily.

"Yeah, this little punk?" he said with an intimidating look.

"Well I was right behind her, so good timing I guess, besides, she was the one who caught herself," about to continue, but before I could, he let Alive loose and approached me up close, face-to-face, him being only two inches or so away from me. I knew I wasn't in a good position, dreading this school already on my first day.

"Well you know what pretty boy, something about your face

really ticks me off," he said in a threatening voice. "How about I rearrange it to make me less pissed off?"

"Jason, stop it, he didn't do anything, and I really don't like it when you act this way. The guy was just being helpful." I looked over his shoulder to see Alice pulling on her muscular boyfriend's arm, persuading him to back-off, but he didn't, it had only stirred his anger further.

Shoving me away from him with just one hand, I nearly fell back from the force. That was with just his one hand. It made me nervous with the thought of what he could do to me if he did decide to, "rearrange" my face.

"Don't look at her when I'm talking to you."

His intimidation on me was working. Even though I was slightly physically fit myself, I had never personally fought anyone before, and he was twice my size. I didn't know what to do, all that went through my head was that it was the first day and I was going to get beaten up by some bodybuilding jock.

Instead of panicking, I calmed myself, relaxing my shoulders, doing my best to stabilize my heart beat, just like how my therapist taught me. "Hey look, I'm new here; I'm just trying to get through my first day without any trouble." Composed and cool headed now, I continued, "I pretty sure we both don't want any trouble, but your girlfriend over there fell, and all I did was give her a hand," reluctantly admitted having helped her when I really didn't, "it's a reasonable thing to do, to help someone when they're about to fall, right?"

The thug didn't respond, merely looking at me and the surrounding, so I had assumed reason was getting through his thick skull. Everyone was looking at us as they all walked by, others standing nearby listened in while staring at us, most waiting for a conclusive violent outcome. It was how most kids were, they craved violence, for something eventful to happen, to gossip about for the day and after, entertainment is what some of my fellow classmates seek.

"Listen, I don't want to cause a scene on my first day here," making my way up the stairs around the two, doing my best to calmly walk by.

In the corner of my eye I could see his arm reaching out towards me, and I knew I had failed to escape. He would now clobber me into red bloody puddle. Unexpectedly, Alice took his outstretched arm and wrapped herself around it, giving way for my escape.

"Hey come on, it's over okay?" was all I could hear her say leaving the two.

The periods flew by quickly with no trouble as I made my way to each class having scouring for them ahead of time. It was a good thing none of the professors cared enough to introduce me, all they did was assigned me my seat, leaving me alone. As the end of the school day approached, I only had one more class before the school day was over. Taking my seat, I saw Alice in the corner of the room as she gave a smile towards me. I gave a smile and a wave back. Looking around, I didn't see her boyfriend anywhere, which was a good sign, not wanting another piece of his jealous rage. 'Was she in my other classes,' I wondered. I hadn't cared enough to look at my fellow classmates having been too busy seeing what materials I had missed and I needed to catch up on. I figured becoming chummy with them could wait a day or two.

When class ended, I exited the room to head for home. Alice shouted out towards me, "Evan, wait up," as she quickly made her way beside me. We continued walking, her keeping up with my pace with a cheerful smile. "I wanted to say sorry about what happened this morning, Jason can be a bit, overprotective."

"No, don't worry about, he has a reason to be," I said looking at her.

I knew I shouldn't have said that, seeing how she liked what I said. Making a slight gesture, moving her hair behind her ears, I could tell she gave a blush that she tried to innocently play off. Only trying to be nice, it seemed to have come out sounding as if I was hitting on her.

We exited outside the building.

"Listen, don't worry about earlier, in any case, I didn't get beaten up, so no harm no foul." Leaving, I felt her hand on my shoulder.

"Wait, since this is your first day and all, I'm guessing you just moved here?"

"Yes, I did just move here. I'm currently living with my Aunt, but I'm not entirely 'new,' to here, I've visited her on a few occasions, you know, for vacation. So yeah, I'm new, but not entirely unfamiliar to the area."

"Oh, so you've been to the surrounding areas, but I pretty sure you don't really 'know' the place. How about I show you around town, I've lived here since birth, so I really know the ins and outs? Think of it as an apology for my boyfriend earlier."

Seeing the eagerness in her eyes, she really wanted me to agree, however, I wasn't quite up to it. Attractive as she was, I didn't want to cause another run in with her brutish lover. She was one of those girls who tended to bring trouble and drama with her, I thought to myself, knowing that refusal was the best option.

"Are you sure it's a good idea, I mean I don't want your lover to get the wrong impression, he does seem like the overly jealous type." I faked a small laugh, hopeful that she would be reminded of the earlier incident that day and agree.

"Jason? It'll be okay, he's at football practice so he won't find out."

A bit baffled by her response that she was able to so casually disregard him. Worried about rumors, if word got out of us two together, my safety would be in jeopardy. I would definitely get pummel by that football jock. Before I could express another excuse and worm my way out, Alice wrapped her arm around mine's, pulling me along. This annoyed me; I hated women who forcibly dragged me along.

"Wait, what about my bike," I protested.

"I'll drive you back to school afterwards."

We went to a movies theater first, which wasn't what I had expected as, 'showing me around.' The movie itself had also made me a bit uncomfortable, since it was a horror movie, making Alice cling to my arm. Just the movie made me exhausted being with her, wanting to hurrying up and head back already. One more place I thought, then I'll ask her to take me back.

The next destination we ended up in was a coffee shop nearby. The place was fairly modern yet casual, specifically furnished and arranged for casual relaxation. For a person to come in, take a seat, and order a beverage, perhaps have some of the simple prepared food they already had.

As she sat at the table, I offered to get her something, hoping to get a few minutes away from her.

"One Caramel Latte Macchiato please," she responded, again, joyfully.

Not knowing what that was, I simply nodded in agreement. Moving towards the counter to order, cursing in my head that there wasn't a line to further drag my time away from her. Once I had gotten to the counter, a pretty girl with long black hair faced me. She had a confident stance with a confident uncaring look.

"What are you going to have," she said in a fairly straight forward rude manner, her voice said that she was in a bad mood and that she didn't really care if she showed it.

My right eyebrow rose a bit in astonishment. "That's quite a welcome," I responded with a grin, leaning forward on the counter. "One Caramel Latte Macchiato and a double shot regular Americano."

The coffee girl grinned at me as if mocking me. "I'm assuming you want it strong for that attractive blond over there," she said tilting her head to look over me.

Glancing back but not all the way, I gave an uneasy laugh. "Yeah, she's quite a handful," I responded back at her. Saying this seemed to have cheered her up a bit, her eyes where a bit wider, looking more awake now.

"I can definitely say I understand that," replying with an attractive smirk as she went off to work on the orders as she was the only one working. Besides her, one other male waiter was walking around the room cleaning up. A short while later she came back with the drinks in two large colorful glass mugs. "I made your coffee extra strong by the way," she responded with a smile. "A word of warning though, that attractive blond you're with, has an overly jealous boyfriend," she said as I paid her.

Sighing, "I know, I met him already, thanks for the warning though," I replied as I walked back to Alice, wondering if she went to our school. Had we met somewhere, perhaps she was in one of my classes.

Sitting down at the table, Alice went on to dominated the conversation with her ranting that I didn't much care for. After a while, I started to get a bit tired, simply smiling, nodding my head, made a few remarks once in a while instead of trying to actively contribute to the conversation. Looking at the time, it was five past seven, the sun outside was started to go down which made me worry.

After Alice wrapped up the latest segment of gossip she thought would intrigue me, I interrupted her before she could continue. "I hate to do this, but I really should head back."

"Oh, so soon, it's only seven."

"I just moved here to live with my aunt, so I'd rather not stay out too late and make her wonder where I am." It was a lie of course; Emelia wouldn't be home till much later I knew. I just wanted the evening out with Alice to end. There was one other reason why; I wanted to get back before nightfall.

Making our way out, I looked back to how the coffee girl was doing. She was busy with a small line of customers. Instead of the unfriendly demeanor she showed me earlier, she was giving smiles to the customers, giving them a pleasant service, acting completely opposite from how I was treated. Well, I supposed it was a good thing that she had some friendly customer service attitude in her.

We both arrived back at the school. As I got out and thanked Alice for the evening out, she offered to walk with me, which I found odd of her to do since my bicycle was a fairly short distance away.

"That's alright, it wouldn't be much of a walk since my bike is right there," refusing her offer with a chuckle.

Still, she got out of her car anyway. "I need to go watch Jason's game. It's a bit early, but oh well." Alice didn't seem too enthused about it, almost reluctant to even mention him. "Evan, about today, thanks for going out with me. Even though I dragged you around, it was nice that you were able to play along and keep me company." She said this while trying to avoid direct eye contact. Her body seemed to have shrunk a bit as she scrunch her shoulders together. Her childish face and petite body only made her look delicate and weak as she said those words.

"I had fun Alice, so you don't need to thank me. If anything, 'thank you,' for caring enough to show me around, it means a lot, being new and all." Seeing her relaxing, giving a glad expression from my words.

We both looked at each other in an awkwardly fashion.

Leaving, making my way to the bicycle racks, I looked back. I caught Alice looking my way, which she then tried to quickly deter her gaze, making as if she wasn't staring at me; a bit too late. Knowing that I had caught her watchful eye, she looked back at me, giving a wave before leaving towards her own destination. Grinning at the thought of how awkward she was. Sure she was controlling and she annoyed me a bit, but Alice also had a nice, innocent, caring side to her as well.

Looking up at the sky, it was now an orange red. As the sun started to set, the air felt   colder. A small weak gust blew, giving me the chills. Hurriedly, getting on my bike, I rode home. The sun started to set more rapidly than I had anticipated. As the sky grew darker, so did my thoughts that something would show itself. Knowing it was only my own thoughts rambling on out of fear, the delusions persisted. Riding harder, faster, as the light from the sun faded into the new night sky, as the street lamps began to brighten themselves to life one by one. Beads of sweat came pouring down my face, not from the exhaustion from pushing myself as I pedaled, but out of fear, out of fear that *they* would show themselves. Remembering what my therapist told me, the countless sessions I've had, that they simply didn't exist, and I told myself just that. Yet an image of them kept reappearing in my mind. My mind created flashes of them running across the street, watching me within the trees, from the shadows of the buildings, when I knew it was only me creating those images. There wasn't anything to fear, I told myself consistently in my head as I neared home. A few more corners were all I needed, but there was only what seemed like a few seconds of sunlight left.

Once the sun disappeared, the darkened sky enveloped me from above, my body shivered from the chilling wind that brushed against my face as I biked. I began to gasp for air. All of the sudden, breathing became much harder, as if the air was suddenly thinner, as if I was suffocating. No, it wasn't the air, it was me. I felt as if multiple eyes piercing me with their stares from all around, even though I profusely knew I was mentally playing a trick on my own self. They stared and stared while I wished they wouldn't.

Once reaching the house, I hurriedly approached the door, leaving the bike to the side as I shoved my shaking hand into my pockets, trying my best to take a hold of my keys. Forcing the correct key into the door proved more difficult than it was suppose to be. Due to my shaking hands that I couldn't properly control anymore, it took endless precious seconds to turn the locks. Making my way into the house, I closed the door quickly and locked it. Turning on the nearby lights, I slumped down towards the wall.

My breathing quickly stabilized as I calmed down, taking in deep breaths. The uncontrollable shaking of my hands settled. Looking down, I realized my shirt was drenched in my own sweat. Standing up, weakly I made my way into the living room towards to the couch. I hated my simple minded self. All this time, and I still was afraid of the night outside. Disgust and self-loathing was what went through my head. After so many years, after so long, to still be afraid to this extent was an embarrassment. True, I recover a good extent over the years, but my fear of the night outside continued going as strong as ever. I was never able to calm myself down, at least not when I'm alone, that was true even now. No training from therapy proved helpful, nor was I able to apply anything in practice properly. There wasn't much I could do at the moment. I'd been like this for a long time, even if I did brood over the situation, I needed to move on. Tomorrow was once again new day, and I had to prepare for it. Wishing that I would one day be able to overcome this hurdle, I hoped a new start here would help me slowly do so.

CHAPTER

4

The next day back at school, I dreaded the thought of seeing Alice once more. Sure, she was a nice girl, but I knew with obvious notions and hints that she portrayed last night that she liked me, or at least was heading in that direction. This was definitely something that I didn't want. Even though she was a beautiful female with a great personality, I knew it was a bad idea to match someone of my nature with hers. Not only was it a personal preference, my instincts were telling me that it wouldn't work out. What's more, there was the danger of perhaps rumors possibly spreading around school, eventually reaching the ears of her brute of a boyfriend, Jason. This would leave me in a bad situation where he would eventually beat me down into nothingness. Not being on his good side already, it was most likely a good idea to avoid them both. Figuring that was if I wanted to live a normal peaceful school year.

As I locked up my bike, making my way to the front of the building, I saw Jason and Alice together in a group, chattering away with a few others. The group consisted of other fellow sports players, most wearing jersey jackets of the school's team. They stood out like a sore thumb, laughing aloud, expressing what seemed to be a great game last night as you could hear them talking about their win. How they made that one amazing tackle, pushing their team to victory. Not giving a damn about anything or anyone around them it seemed, as they simply cared about having a good time.

Typically, I wouldn't mind. If people were having a good time, than great, it didn't bother me even the slightest, as long as it didn't invade my personal space. In my previous school days of the past, I simply ignored them as I would have done in this situation; after all, they never really bothered me so I didn't need to make myself bothered by them. Besides, no one else seemed to have cared either, nor did they invade other's space, they were simply a bit overly loud. Simply put, I would ignore them and they left me alone. This situation was bit different. The bad part was their location, which was right at the entrance of the door, meaning I would have to walk by them, which I really didn't want to do. The thought of having to encounter a possible problematic situation so early in the morning only exhausted me further, already after having to wake up and pedal myself to school. I could imagine the situation in my head. Walking myself to the front, the two would notice me, only giving a slight confirmation with a casual smile while I would try to continue to walk away, but without success. Jason would eventually stop me, ask where I was headed, which would have been obvious to most that I was going to class. That's where I stopped thinking. I just couldn't imagine how I would have acted afterwards in that situation, or how his responses would be once I did reply.

Instead of entering the front, I decided to fine another route into the building. The school itself had to have more than one entry point; it was a fairly large school, so perhaps a side or backdoor. The only problem was that I didn't know the school that well yet, and class would be starting soon. Should I really risk being late when it was only my second day here? No, I didn't, I was too much of a school boy to do so, "too diligent," I told myself as I gave an exhausting sigh, making my way to the front entrance. It wasn't just being late, it was the fact that I didn't want to feel intimidated. After all, *they* were more fearful then a bunch of kids my age could ever be. Already, I've lost the mental fight against *them*; I didn't want it to be the same towards my fellow students. My legs felt a bit heavy, but my I had relaxed a bit, forcing myself not to show any anxiety.

"Don't worry about it too much new guy," a familiar voice came from behind.

Turning around a bit to see who it was, it was the coffee girl from yesterday. Standing there with a one arm bag strapped over her shoulder, arms folded, she seemed more enthused towards me then the other day, but with no smile, the enthusiasm reflected from her eyes. Now at that moment, I took a good long look at her, registering her into my memory. Before, she was simply a person that served me coffee, someone who would come and go in my everyday human life, someone that I would hardly see besides when I would go again to that particular location just to get coffee, if or when I chose to do so that is. So at that moment, knowing now that she attended this very school, knowing where she worked, and for the fact that she came up to me was enough for me that I needed to remember her. Looking into her eyes I took all of her in, the more I looked, the more for some odd reason, I wanted to continue looking, not just wanting, but as if needing to remember her. This had never happened before. Often, if I had to remember a person, I would glance quickly and that was enough, but for her in particularly, something about her made me crave to memorize her, more so than anyone I had ever met in my life, and I didn't know why or what it was about this woman that made me desire to do so.

Her long straight hair that was no longer tied back as the night before, now visibly showed that they reached her elbows. Eyes of dark brown, almost to the point of near black like a void, dragging me into them, how gravity was pulling me down to earth. With a simple yet at the same time a small beautifully confident facial structure, with not even a smile on her face but an eyebrow raised up as I simply stared at her, questioning why I stood so silently watching her. Standing confidently as she had before, wearing casual clothes, a bright orange shirt underneath her jacket which I thought didn't suit her. It made her look like an adult lady, mature, but at the same time, young, even though her features obviously portrayed that she was only seventeen or eighteen, and the color of the t-shirt was too bright for her overly serious collective expression.

"Just walk by them without paying attention to them," she said to me, "or you could fine some other way to get inside, but you might be late for first period," this time she said with a mischievous smile. As if she knew that I had obviously thought of the fact, simply saying it just to mock me as she walked on by.

I smiled a bit, she was definitely mysterious. At that moment, I knew she wasn't like the other childish teenage girls that ran around spouting gossip, only to care about popular pop idols, cloths, what's trending. Instead she portrayed that she was sharp, confident, but not the happy merry type. Instead, she was the sophisticated kind of woman, a woman that could take charge and handle problems and situations as they occur with ease and with a stern calmness. A doer and a leader I thought, perhaps even what many others might have seen in her as well.

As I walked, following behind this mysterious girl, passing Alice, Jason, and their group, they didn't pay any attention to me, not even a glance. I didn't stare at them but I knew they didn't as I continued to walk on by, trying my best to look forward while seeing their expression through the corner of my line of sight. Once I did past them, a smirk of satisfaction came to my face; second morning at school with no trouble.

Losing sight of the girl from before, not knowing where she went, I was too focused on making my way past the group of jocks and their cheerleading squad. Shrugging it off, I continued to my first class. We just met, so it didn't really matter too much I thought. Making my way into my class just as the bell rang; the teacher had yet to arrive. Hurriedly, I took my seat to my empty newly registered spot. Right after, the coffee house girl came in, taking the seat in the desk right next to mine, without even a bother to take notice towards my direction. Taken aback a bit, I hadn't even noticed that she was there other day. Then again, I haven't yet cared to remember anyone's face since I had come to this school. Perhaps it was due to my first day, there was already too much to take in, especially since those that sat around me never bothered to approach me either.

"Thanks for the advice earlier," I said still looking straight ahead. "But how did you know I didn't want to go pass them in the first place," I inquired, though I had a good guess at the answer. Perhaps I might be wrong though, so as a test to my own perceptive judgment and for conversational purposes, I decided to inquire.

"Don't worry about it," was all she said as she saw the teacher come in, closing the conversation all together.

Not sure why, but I stole a glance at her. Her face was stern as usual, without a smile, solely focused on the class at hand. Her posture was straight and upright with legs folded, seeming a lot classier then any of the other girls. The way she acted exuded confidence, making a person feel as if it would be hard approaching her, including me.

As the class dragged on, I kept the girl next to me in my thoughts, doing my best not to look in her direction, as not to seem weird or creepy if she saw me looking her way. To peak a bit at her, taking in her image, analyze her reactions. As if for some strange reason, the air around her drew me towards her, wanting to know more about her.

Once the bell rang, the class began their usual transition to the next lesson, dispersing quickly.

"My name's Evan by the way," I said as the girl was getting up.

"Lilith, good meeting you," was all she said, rushing with the rest of the students to get to her next class.

I couldn't help but give a small defeated smirk as I was left alone. We had roughly ten minutes to get to the next class which was a decent amount of time to talk, even if it would only be for just a moment, only to be shoved aside as if my existence mattered little to her, even insignificant. It made me feel embarrassed. 'That's it,' telling myself, I tried approaching her, to get to know more about her. From her reaction, it seemed that it would be a bit too difficult to approach her, like she didn't want others approaching her. Intriguing as she was, the thought of approaching her once more made me a bit tired, my mind quickly telling me to give up on Lilith. I simply didn't want to put in the effort to know someone who didn't want to be known.

It than gave me question as to why she had spoken to me that morning. Could it that I was simply there, on a whim she had chosen to talk to me? Laughable, only just meeting Lilith and already she kept me thinking of nothing but her. It wasn't as if we could ever date, I still had my *fear,* if I had to put it correctly, to yet recover from. 'They,' were the one part of my life that I could never tell others about. A secret I had to keep hidden from everyone.

It was a depressing thought. Having a friend would've been nice, to share my fears and worries with, it was awfully lonely with only myself, with no one else whom I could share both my joy and worries.

Throughout the day, I was nothing more than a mechanical human, going in and out of class just like all the others. Seeing both Lilith and Alice occasionally passing by, I didn't approach them and they didn't approach me. I would have thought Alice might have come up to me, she didn't, which made me feel a bit relieved.

Lunch time came. Once again I was lost trying to find my way through the crowded cafeteria, this time more familiar than the day before. Crowds and groups of people made me feel uneasy as I never took to friends or socializing much. In my earlier school years, people did invite me out on occasions, helping me along, to be my, "friend," if I had to put it that way. I never accepted them, I wouldn't. Most often my fellow classmates and I would discuss things in classrooms, getting along perfectly fine, but that's where it ended, it stopped at school. At some point the individuals would take a liking to me, why, I didn't know, yet soon after they would start inviting me to group events, social gatherings, hang outs after school, all in which I either turned them down or away. To be by myself was the best choice for me, a decision I made after so many anguish memories of my childhood past, most which left me partially scarred from trusting others. It wasn't normal I told myself many times, to force myself away from mingling with others after school, or technically after school which might have led throughout into the night. I was too different from everyone else. I wasn't completely healthy in the head, at least not yet. They on the other hand lived a normal life how regular people should be doing. Someone as sickly as me wouldn't be able to befriend others, bringing only a burden to them if they knew about my condition and were kind enough to still decide on being my friend. And what if they really knew about me and they weren't as kind, they would mock me, question my judgment, my mental health like how the countless others have done. This was how I thought whenever I was in crowded places, seeing everybody act so normal. It wasn't as if I couldn't converse with another person, it was that I chose not to incase they decided to want to hangout. It left me to rejecting them time and again. It was also in order to protect myself, to live a peaceful life without other's bullying treatment.

Leaving the cafeteria after getting my food, I headed outside to the open, fill with other students. Wandering around, moving farther away to a more desolate area, it became more and more deserted. Knowing that I couldn't just keep walking, it would be unusual to eat so far away, and as I continued, I felt that I would've eventually walked right off the school grounds soon. I needed to sit down somewhere and enjoy my lunch. Eventually, I did find a place. A bench under a big large maple tree, beautifully fully grown, that gave plentiful shade below. No one was there oddly, even though it seemed like such a nice place to have lunch. I knew this spot was a place that I was going to make mine from now on.

Sitting there, right in the center of the bench, I sprawled my arms open under the tree, simply sitting for a moment, enjoying the relaxing school setting, not even caring to eat. Feeling at ease and tired at the same time, exhausted already of the new school year. I was still glad to have moved here, to start over from scratch. At least I had gotten away from Boston and my past.

"It's unusual to see someone sitting here besides me," the voice seemed to echo next to me. Peering through my open eyes to see who it might be, it was Lilith, standing there with a brown bag in her hand while the other shoved in her pocket. She looked a bit annoyed to see that I was there.

"Sorry, you're more than welcome to join me," replying as I moved to the side, giving her some space.

"This is a surprise, I didn't expect to find you here at this spot," she said as she began setting her items down. "This is where I usually sit to eat by the way, if you didn't catch that earlier. It's quiet here, no one but me sits here most of the time, everybody else are usually back there, eating with each other," directing me with her head towards the school's filled open quad. "So what brings you here to this school so late, I'm guessing you recently moved since you just started showing up?"

"Good guess. I recently moved from Massachusetts two days ago. I like it here. It's a quiet and nice are to live in. I enjoy the air, the stores, and the coffee shop around here is another one of the perks, especially their help," I said giving a joking smile.

She chuckled. "So, it's that great huh?"

Her laugh was charming and adorable, this was the first time that I saw and heard it, but what made it unforgettable was the smile she had. It made me mesmerized by it. Perhaps adorable would be the wrong word. It was a more confident laugh that suited her personality, combined with her smile that made her charmingly innocent. She noticed me staring at her, not saying word, her faced straightened quickly back to its usual unforgiving stern self, but with a questionable look.

"What is it," she asked.

"Nothing," I looked away embarrassed for what I just did, it wasn't like me to do something of the sorts. "It's just that you looked really beautiful when you smile, I guess you could say it's was a bit mesmerizing." Uneasy after what I said, I quickly thought of something to move away from the conversation. "By the way, is that your lunch," pointing to the vanilla pudding and banana she had laid out earlier. They were neatly placed on top of her brown paper bag. "That looks," pausing for a moment trying my best to gather the right word, "good," I finished with a mocking smile.

Catching her off guard, she seemed conscious of the fact that her lunch consisted only of the two items. This time, even though I wanted to continue looking at her, to see what kind of look she was making, I diverted my eyes.

"My mom and I aren't really people who enjoy cooking," she said. "Don't worry, lunch isn't always pudding and fruit, I do get real food from time to time."

"If you mean 'real food' as sometimes doughnut, maybe slice of cake, or even a bag of chips, then it doesn't count as real food, just junk food." Another voice came from behind, friendly and familiar. It was Alice to my surprise. She leaned forward against the bench, popping her head right in the middle of the both of us to look at Lilith's lunch. "Healthy as ever, but I'm surprised you brought something decently good for you this time," she said as she picked up the banana, peeling the skin and taking a bite.

Lilith was back to her normal calm self. She crossed her legs and arms confidently, looking at Alice, filled with annoyance. "Are you going to eat all of that or are you going to give me some," she said as she open her mouth, waiting to be fed, and indeed she was.

Alice complied with a satisfied smile as if she was enjoying Lilith's demanding tone, feeding her a bite of the fruit as if she was a queen.

"This is what's usually at my house," Lilith continued talking while trying to eat. "My mom and I usually get takeout or frozen dinners, so this is usually what's left that easy and effortless to bring to school. Occasionally, I will buy lunch in the cafeteria if I feel like shifting through the crowds, or if I'm desperately starved."

"So you two know each other?"

"We do," Alice said wrapping her arms around Lilith, giving her a gaily hug from behind, while at the same time feeding her another bite. "Even though you can probably tell right off the bat that our personalities are polar opposites, Lily here is actually by best friend. We've known each other since we were toddlers. B-T-W, she really does bring real food from home once in a while, not just things like this."

"You're right; you two are pretty different," directing myself towards Alice. "I would say you're dress pretty bright, and you seem to happy almost every much every time I see you, while on the other hand," slowly directing my gaze at Lilith who flashed a glare of evil intent at me, but it only made Alice break out in laughter, leaning against the tree for support.

"You over exaggerate Alice," Lilith said, her voice full of annoyance and perhaps slight anger.

"I'm sorry but that was my first time actually hearing someone say that directly to you, they usually say it when you're not around," Alice replied. "You see Evan; this really is my first time hearing someone saying that directly to her, so you've definitely gave me a surprise. Lily is one of those people who gives off an intimidating atmosphere, maybe because she likes to wear gloomy cloths and she hardly ever smiles, always so stern, so proper, lacking color, which is why I was a bit surprise to see her wearing bright pink yesterday. Even now she's straight and upright, sitting like a lady, but thank god you lost that shirt, it didn't suit you," again, Alice teased her.

True in every way I thought. Lilith in her own sense was very mature and hard to approach, as if she didn't want others to approach her, much like myself I thought.

"You should go Alice, you're lover is probably waiting for you," Lilith said, this time moving on to her pudding as I began to start on my own lunch.

Alice didn't say anything after that, she simply smiled happily and mouthed the word goodbye towards me, and I waved back. Once again I was left alone with Lilith.

For a few moments there was a slight pause as the both of us fell silent, listening to the chattering of the crowds on the school grounds. Others passed by, enjoying their time while the two of us sat there; eating what was left our lunch, not knowing what to say to each other. As my mind rushed to think up topics, trying my best to figure out what the next thing to say would be, I was left with my mind blank, feeling frustrated. A good minute had passed by like this. Lilith had finished her lunch as I was finishing the second half of mine.

"I'm surprised that the two of you are best friends, since you're over here with me I mean," finally managing to say something. "If you don't mind me asking, how come you're not with Alice right now, hanging out with her and her group?"

"Oh, you're giving me all sorts of questions and comments. You're really throwing me off today. I didn't assume you would ask me such a question right off the bat," she said, though her expression didn't show any such suggestion. "But it does make sense for me to be with her and her crowd, so you're right, it's definitely odd, but not really if you think hard about it."

"I'm assuming personality wise; you wouldn't get along with the others?" I inquired further.

"That's one of the reasons, but there are others."

"Such as," knowing I should have stopped asking. Something was telling me she didn't want to say, but I had asked anyway. Simply put, I wanted to know more about her, she had caught my attention. Intrigued by her expressions, over confident gestures, and the fact that she wasn't the usual immature high school girl you could find all over. The other was to avoid another awkward silence.

"Well, the other reason is that Alice can really bother me sometimes. There are times she likes to play around just a tad too much, so her actions can really annoy me; a lot. That's really the reason why I don't hang out with her during lunch. She enjoys socializing while having lots of fun. I'm the opposite. I prefer being by myself, reading, having an intellectual conversation. Though I enjoy having conversations with Alice too, but I feel that she can be too much for me to handle. You don't have to take my word though, after all, she's taken a liking to you so you'll be experiencing much more of her. Something tells me that you'll understand what I mean," saying this while giving me a rather wicked look.

Unsure if whether her smile was to say that she was joking, or if it was to say that she was feeling sorry for me. "You don't need to worry about me, Alice has a boyfriend, and I don't think she has any real interest in me, at least I hope she doesn't. We also don't have that many courses together so we won't be running into each other much."

"So I'm assuming you don't actually consider her your best friend, only Alice thinks you two are?" I asked bluntly.

"No, she's still my best friend," she said quickly, almost defensively. "Just because I find her a bit annoying from time to time, doesn't mean I wouldn't consider her my friend, if anything, I wouldn't rather have anyone else but her as my friend. You could say our friendship is a bit odd. Even though I say those things, I still care for her very much. It's not just that I've known her for so long, but we've been through thick and thin. She annoys me, yes, but she does it knowingly, after all, if it's anyone, Alice would be the person who knows my personality the best, and that's just how she likes interacting with me."

"Sure, we don't spend much time at school together, but we do hangout outside of school. If I had to say, seeing Alice during lunch too, would only exhaust me, time apart from one another is good for any healthy relationship. You might notice this too if you spend more time with her, but Alice is someone that I can trust no matter what, she's someone that would help me if I was in trouble, no matter what, a real true friend to the end." A look of satisfaction washed over her face, filled with content of how their youth and friendship had become what it is today.

Continuing to speak of Alice, she became more joyful, captivating me. There was something else about her though. It wasn't just her beautiful smile, the way she looked or acted that enticed me towards her, there was a particular feel about her that brought back other feelings, feelings that I had tried hiding so long ago. It was then that my hands began to sweat. I was getting nervous for no reason as I continued to listen to her, watching this angelic woman which was pulling me towards her. The more I tried to think of what it was about her, the more uncomfortable I became. An itch in the back of my mind wanted to reach back, to find out what it was about her. I couldn't reach it no matter how hard I tried. Intoxication was the word I had to describe it, I wanted to continue that moment longer, for some reason, I was immensely uneasy, the warped feeling was growing. Whether it was a good or bad thing, I wasn't sure at the moment. The moment didn't last long as the bell rang, signaling the end of our lunch break, both of us about to go our separate ways.

"Oh, you can call me Lily by the way. I prefer it rather than Lilith. It's what everyone calls me, so you should too."

Slowly as the days went by, the two of us grew closer as we shared our thoughts under the maple tree, becoming more sociable towards one another. Seating ourselves next to each other at lunch and during the classes we had together, learning what each of us liked or didn't. The tense feeling I felt towards her went away as well. When no one else was around, Lily became more open about herself, she wasn't the same antisocial person everyone thought she was, or I had once thought she was. With just the two of us, she became passionate in her speech, enjoyed smiling, laughing, expressing a particular charisma or charm about her that would have made anyone fond of her if they knew how she really was. Time flew every time we were together, as the more I talked to her, the more I learned about her, her and her childhood days with Alice. There were also her interest in politics, technology, music, and drama. She played the violin as a child, her mother made her pick up an instrument, listing various benefits a person gets from learning how to play one. Then in middle school, Alice grew interested in bands, deciding later to start one of her own, which she then recruited Lily as a member. So she ended up learning how to play the electric bass guitar as well. Unfortunately, the band itself only lasted a few months, but her mother had already purchased the instrument and she felt that it was a waste to suddenly stop learning, so she ended up becoming adept at playing it.

Listening to her, I had now known how close both she and Alice were to each other. They hardly spent time with each other at school, but afterwards they would spend nights and weekends seeing each other, whenever Alice wasn't spending time with Jason that is. It wasn't always just the two of us; there were times when Alice would stop on by to talk to Lily and me. If the topic of her and Lilith ever came up, she too would indulge in the past. Alice expressed the same joy and enthusiasm Lilith would when reminiscing of her best friend. They were closer than just mere friends, like a sisters to each other, as if the two were inseparably, tied by a strong unbreakable bond.

During times when the conversations did turn in my direction, naturally I express myself, sharing my interests, my past of what I could divulge into, which wasn't much different from the average person in my own opinion. I didn't care too much about topics that embarrassed me or made me seemed like an idiot, or even if it would make me seem overly cocky, angry, or just downright evil, which there weren't many. Everyone had moments such as those I imagined. Telling others once in a while wasn't much a big deal in my opinion, even more so, it sometimes added a bit of spice to conversations. But there was one thing that separated me from everybody else. It was something I had learned to keep to myself after learning firsthand the type of consequences that could come after telling people. That I have a fear of the darkness and of enclosed spaces with limited lighting, with the exception of my own bedroom. Even then, I still sometimes panic. Unlike most people, I shared what I thought was appropriate, instead of spouting out all I could about myself, I thought carefully of every particular word I would say before saying it, making sure not to include my questionable past.

In my life time up until now, I have only told about my fear to a few people, most whom I had once thought I could trust. The others would simply laugh or mocked me. I still remember the boy back in my elementary years whom I had once believed to be my best friend. A few days later during a birthday party when all the kids had gone to the house of another's student, he has spread the word to nearly everyone of what I had told him. When Clarissa and I arrived to the house, when the grownups weren't looking, when they were outside having martinis and cake, the other children pushed me into a corner. Never would I forget that day, how they, all of them, grouped together, joining and cheering in. Two of them, a boy and a girl pinned me down to the floor as the others riled them on. Not one said anything to stop them, as I said before, all of them, each and every one of those kids that day joined in like crazed tiny people, hypnotized, drunk on the flow of bullying. Once pinned faced down, someone, I didn't see who, dragged me along the floor and up the stairs where I had bit my tongue, starting to bleed, they didn't stop. Once reaching the top, another flipped me over. It was only then a that a few of them stopped with their spur of young adolescent evil when they saw the blood coming out of my mouth, me crying from the pain. A few of them knew then that they had taken it too far, standing near, frozen, yet still they didn't say a word to stop the others, they simply stood staring, watching the reactions of the others, and of me. The others were not deterred from the bloody crying sight of me before them. Pulling me up, they pushed me into a closet, locking me inside the tiny dark space.

It stung inside, when I knew the next day that it was he who had told the others. It was a betrayal of my trust that I had in him, and I was left alone, let down, only to be ridiculed by my fellow classmates. It didn't come as a surprise to me when the boy drifted further away me, no longer being my friend. That, I knew would happen, and after the birthday party, I didn't exactly want to be near him either. It was an utter shock though, during the party, when he collaborated with the others to lock me away in that dark pitched closet. I still remember calling his name as tears ran down my youthful face, telling him to make the others stop, but he continued to laugh outside the door. I knew it was his laugh, I recognized it having heard it so many times. Lesson learned, I never told anyone else until later when I was in eighth grade.

Once more during my last year in middle school, a girl had taken a liking to me. We both had dated for a few months. Almost immediately, she became questionable of my reactions and responses. She was a kind individual, shy, yet willful at times, never asking why I never wanted to go out with her at certain times, or why I always left so early so suddenly. I felt guilty for it, leaving her each and every time when I left with nothing more but a vague excuse. My lies ate at me like maggots devouring my heart as I watched the poor girl become more confused every time I left, rejecting to go out with her. It felt as if I was growing rotten on the inside every time. In the beginning, she didn't mind me leaving, nor did she show that she cared, soon after, she began to worry, as if it was her fault, like something was wrong with her, as if she had made a mistake somewhere down the line that turned me off. Never asking, never voicing her emotions, it was all too obvious in her reactions. My guilt gave in eventually, telling her of my fears, not everything of course, and she understood.

The consequence? Not as traumatic an episode as the previous story, but it left me feeling lonely. We did continue to date for a few more weeks before she politely broke it off. Telling me simply that it wasn't going to work out anymore, and so she left me. The girl never told anyone else that I knew of. I wasn't exactly depressed to be dumped as I had never actually liked the girl that strongly. I treated her as how a boyfriend would treat his lover, but my feelings never grew for her. In the end, I walked away still depressed and feeling miserable, not from the break up, but with my life in itself. I became more worried about my future and what others thought about me, about what was wrong with me. What happened after that? Slowly my thoughts took a hold of me and I became evermore distant towards others when I could. The two particular incidents left me too afraid and wary of others. Being able to still joke and socialize with others; during the daytime at least.

It was the same with Lily. I could feel my emotions growing for her as we spent more time together, getting to know more of each other. Realizing my feelings that I liked this girl, but it wasn't enough to trust her, at least not yet. She might be like everyone else I thought; if she knew, soon she would come to reject me just like the many others, which was the normal course of action for a person to do I thought, but I didn't want her to. Beginning to dig an emotional pit, it left me to drown in the hole that I created, telling myself that there were no way out. To not have any trust in others, don't get too close to them otherwise I could end up hurt, or even hurting them emotionally. I knew my feelings were increasing a little at a time for Lily, day by day I thought of her just a bit more.

CHAPTER

5

Saturday, I've been l living with Emelia for a while now, in my new found peaceful life. School itself was a bother, it wasn't difficult, or proved much of a challenge to do learn or do the assignments, the subjects that were taught didn't give me any trouble. The teachers themselves were mediocre, teaching straight out of the book without giving any real insight to the subjects' apart occasional opinionated comment. For some reason, I still found myself coming home, unusually exhausted as of late. Dreams filled my head as I slept, most of them unpleasant, fragments of the past which would shake me awake in the middle of the night. A good thing for the weekend, I would be able to sleep a much as I wanted.

Emelia was given the day off, which was rare, and we both

ended up sleeping in till noon. She herself had slept for a good fourteen hours after coming home, dead tired with bags below her eyes. I remembered how the day before, she came home utterly listless. Emelia had simply come into the kitchen, dazed after hearing my voice, offering her some of the dinner that I had prepared for the two of us. So tired was she, it was as if she didn't hear me. It was a simple dinner, spaghetti with garlic bread. I called out to her once more if she would like me to get her a plate. Not saying anything, she then came up to me with an exhausted expression and caressed my cheek with one hand, which was awfully odd. For a good ten seconds, we stood there like that, unsure of how to respond towards her action, I stood there letting her touch my face. Moments later, snapping out of daze, she told me that she wasn't hungry, that she was simply going to shower and head to bed. It made me worried seeing Emelia like that; to drive home in such a state was dangerous. The hospital she was working for was definitely overworking her, even if they were understaffed on specialists. Not like I could do much about it, the most I was able to do was to help out by making her some food. At least this way she wouldn't have to worry about coming home and wonder what she was going to prepare to eat.

My days off were the days I had always looked forward to, as with most people. There was nothing better than sleeping in, wrapped under a thick warm layer of comfortably warmth. It was especially enjoyable now that winter was rapidly approaching, so the feeling was an extra pleasure. The only displeasing fact was the knowing of having to eventually get up, to continue the existence of daily life. Lazily, I got out of bed with the sheets still wrapped around me as I haggardly woke up, beginning my daily morning rituals.

I made my way down the stairs into the large luxury kitchen. Like the rest of the house, it fitted right in. The walls painted white, and there were plenty of windows letting the sunlight flow through, brightening the room. The trees blocked a bit of the sun, added a relaxing atmosphere to the room. The shadows from the leaves danced around in accordance to the outside gentle breeze. The cabinets were a dark wood that gave the kitchen a luxury feel with modern expensive appliances, largely left untouched from never being used. Sure, I would occasionally cook, however, I was still a beginner, having only cooked the basic dishes before, never needing to make use of a blender or juicer. In the past, Clarissa and occasionally my father did most of the cooking. And even though I enjoyed coffee, I never bothered to use the cappuccino machine in the corner, neither did Emelia.

As I wrapped an apron around, I pulled up my sleeves as I began making a very late afternoon breakfast/lunch. Emelia made her way down the stairs in her violet silk pajamas. Hair still in disarray, eyes half opened, plopping herself in the empty seat of the table in the open room nearby. As she huddled her head in her arms on the table; closing her eyes as if she was going back to sleep, I gave a slight grin. I knew that her sitting there meant that she was waiting for me to finish making her breakfast. I happily complied by speeding things up. The poor woman was worked to the bone nearly every day, she needed as much rest as she could get. After all she does and had done for me, it made me glad that I could do something for her, even if it was something as small as a morning meal.

"Aunty," I called to her; no movement. "Aunt Emelia, it's ready," calling out to her again, placing our plates down.

Two glasses of orange juice, one for each of us sat on the table. A simple morning meal, pancakes with sunny side eggs, sausage, and bacon. Rarely cooking when living back with Clarissa and my father, yet I had never found it difficult to do the basic cooking, nor did I bother to try anything more advance. I supposed it was because I had never needed to. Granted, the first time I did cook wasn't so great, only to get the hang of things after a few attempts. I still remembered making pancakes for the first time. Not knowing that I had to mix it more thoroughly, large clumps of the pancake mix was left floating around, leaving some bites filled with powder. I remember blaming it on the mix, not on my talented cooking skills.

Emelia slowly brought her head up with a yawn, her eyes slowly becoming more awake, opening larger once seeing the hot meal in front of her. "You got any plans today?" she asked more alert now.

"Well, I was planning to stay in and relax, you know, doing pretty much nothing I guess."

"Oh?" Emelia replied. I knew what came after. In my

experience from visiting her over the years, that, 'oh,' meant that we would be going out together to do something, which I didn't mind.

"Hmm, I'm planning on heading out to the mall, I need to restock on my ladies stuff, and to get a few other things while I'm at it," she told me, pulling her hair back to fix it with one hand while biting into a sausage. Her movements were both sluggish and sloppy, making me laugh seeing her like that. She was so at ease and carefree, I figured it was an admirable trait of hers.

"I'm guessing you want me to go with you? No need to ask, it's a yes," answering ahead of time as I knew she was going to ask sooner or later.

"That figures, you know me well young one, as expected from my sister's son." She reached out as she softly pinched my cheek mockingly, giving herself a laugh as I looked at her feeling shamed, like I was being treated as a child, which only made her laugh a bit harder. Laughing along, not actually caring, I knew she was only having a good time, enjoying the moment with her. It was more natural and comfortable than I had ever been with my father and Clarissa. I was happy being here, able to eat, laugh, rest so casually. Living with Emelia provided me with an unusual sense of warmth that I thought I wouldn't be able to feel again, a feeling that was long forgotten. Perhaps it was because Emelia was my late mother's sister. A few her actions were similar to hers, providing me with a nostalgic feeling of the past. It must have been times like these with Emelia which was causing me to dream of the past so often now. Pushing the thought out, I tried not to think about it.

Finishing our meal, we got ready, heading out to the mall. The weather was brisk, what looked like a nice breeze from inside the house was actually a frigid cold wind. As we entered the mall, it was crowded, packed with people shopping; we both had predicted this. It wasn't my first time coming to this mall. It was this packed on the weekends every weekend, as people loved to get out, being one of the more popular destinations to kill time during the day.

As we made our way around, Emelia childishly roam from one store to another, now bursting with renewed energy after her long slumber. I would wait outside uninterested in any of the merchandise the stores had to offer. Occasionally, I didn't have much of an option when Emelia saw a nice sweater or beanie that she thought might look good on me, pulling me in and out of men's stores to have me try things on. She charged the items on her card as if not caring, not even looking at the price at certain items. It was nice to see her enjoying herself. Often times she stayed home, rarely did she go out to shop or buy things for herself, perhaps once every few months or so, or whenever she really needed something.

Roughly two and a half hours had passed. I was fairly exhausted as we I sat at a table, stuffing ourselves with an order of chili fries split between us, Emelia still peppy and enthused; and on her second frappuccino. Next to me were bags and bags that she brought from a variety of stores, most of which I carried. Emelia did carry a few, but they consisted more of the much smaller and lighter items.

"Sorry for making you accompany me, I know it's your day off and all," Emelia said looking down at the multiple bags next to my sides as she finished her coffee and the last of the fries.

"Don't worry about it. I'm just glad we could spend some time quality time together." Since I had moved in, she was so busy with work, we both rarely had the time to even converse with one another, so I really was glad to hang out with her like this. "Besides, I don't ever get to see you so peppy and childlike, running from store to store. If you're this happy, I wonder how you'd be if you went to Disney World. Should we buy you a Cinderella dress?"

She chuckled. "Awfully cheeky aren't you, but I'm glad you're like this, to see you happy outside with me. You know, you really remind me of your mother Alina. I remember there was a time when the two of us as kids had gone out to buy clothes. I was pretty hyper like I am today. After running around for a while, we sat down on the cold stone steps, and she jokingly offered to buy me Cinderella dress. There weren't any made or marketed obviously, but when we got home, your mother secretly made me a dress from our sheets, making it puffy and everything. When our mother realized this, boy was she sure angry. I actually still have it you know. I remember being so happy about it, I just couldn't throw it away, so now it's sitting in a box somewhere at home."

Looking at her, hearing those words, it made me feel awkward. I was also happy, I never heard much of my real mother's childhood, so it made me feel closer her, even if she was gone now.

Both still sitting, enjoying our time, relaxing still, discussing about our lives whether it was regarding school, work, the economy, even music; a topic I now found out that we had no commonality in. We talked about whatever popped into our head. It ended when a loud call shouted out to me from behind.

"Hey, Evan, what a surprise to see you here," the voice called to me from behind, a resounded familiar voice.

Turning around, I noticed Alice a few feet away behind me. "Alice? Seeing you here sure is a coincidence."

Quickly, I glanced around to see if anybody else were with her, especially looking through the crowd to see if Jason had come with her. Luckily he was nowhere in sight. A bit away, I noticed Lily a short distance from us, leaning against the hand rail, looking away to who knows what.

"And I see you're with Lily," pointing towards her.

Looking behind her shoulder, it was as if she was baffled as to why Lily was all the way over there instead of with all of us. Hurriedly, she places both her bags down, went over to Lily, and dragged her over. Lily on the other hand looked obviously tired and bothered, carrying two medium sized bags herself.

"Dr. Lawrence, it's good to see you again," Lily spoke up, but in a kinder nicer expression than before, looking politer as well.

"Yes, it's a pleasure to see you again Dr. Lawrence," said Alice.

"Well, well, good to see you two again. You both seem to be in good health," responded Emelia, no longer as hyper as before. She now sat straight, more composed. "It seems you both know my nephew, Evan. Forgive me, of course you two do, all of you go to the same school after all."

Sitting there out of loop, "how do you two know my aunt," I interrupted.

"It's not much of a story," Lily replied. "You don't know this, but my dad died when I was really young, a little bit before that, while he was still alive, Dr. Lawrence had done surgery on his heart. At that time, Alice and I had already known each other, she was worried so she stopped by and stayed with me in the waiting room, giving me support. When the surgery was done, Dr. Lawrence came out and greeted the two of us; that was the first time we had met. Our parents kept in touch with your aunt a few times after that, and occasionally we would bump into each other from time to time like now."

"I never knew about that," I responded a bit more depressed, thinking that I should have.

It also made me depressed that it only solidified my knowledge of how close Lily and Alice were. After hearing the details, my relationship with Lily was growing day by day. My relationship with Alice was growing reluctantly closer as well. Being on good terms with Lily was great. I knew that I was falling for her. She was what I wanted in the opposite sex; however, it meant that it unfortunately came with Alice. Alice had become more and more attached towards me as I started to become more and more bothered by her presence. As much as I had tried to avoid her, she somehow had taken a strong liking to me despite her current relationship with her boyfriend, Jason. It made it both awkward and unsettling when I talked to Lily as she hung around every so often. Making it unnerving whenever I walked past her boyfriend as he recently started giving me hard cold stares whenever I was within in his sights. Alice had also recently begun to cling to me more, wrapping herself on my arm, pulling me along, even though I would refuse. Going as far as inviting me to events where she would openly express a flirtatious feel towards me daringly while her boyfriend was in the vicinity close by, or Lily was next to us. Placed in a fairly uncomfortable position, I wanted to push Alice away, yet I knew I had to be nice since she was Lily's best friend. For now, there wasn't much to do but put up with her.

"The girl's mothers and I are actually still close acquaintances," Emelia interrupting my train of thought. "After I had performed the operation on Mr. Rothschild, or Lily's father, her parents including Alice's and I had a friendly discussion. Since then, from time to time, not often, we would get together for social gatherings and such, maybe even for just lunch." Her comments and sudden proper demeanor made the conversation stiff.

"In any case, we saw the both of you sitting here, and we were wondering if your nephew, Evan here, wouldn't mind accompanying us," saying this, Alice placed her hand around my shoulder.

Alice caught me off guard. There was anticipation for her to bother me, but not to be whisked away, becoming her toy for the day. Perhaps I showed on my face my unwillingness to go, since Emelia sat across the table grinning, looking at me a bit sadistically. Seeing her watching us, I knew Emelia would surely agree. My mind rushing itself, trying to come up with an excuse to weasel my way out, I couldn't come up with one. My head was in too much in disarray from the unexpected question.

"You bet you can; how can I say no to you two love birds," Emelia said so agreeing, it nearly made my eye twitch.

Too late I thought, my fate was sealed, there weren't any reasonably excuse that I could come up with. Being Saturday with nothing planned, which Emelia knew, she left the three of us alone. Carrying the multiple bags with her, she looked funny carrying so many as she walked off. Emelia drove, so I would be with Alice and Lily until they grew tired of the day.

The three of us didn't spend much time at the mall as both Lily and Alice had done most of their shopping beforehand. Finding something to do, we decided to kill some time at the movie theater which was conveniently close by. We saw a high budget apocalypse movie that the three of us found enjoyable. Filled with action scenes, drama, and a twist at the end, it had all the aspects which made the movie great. It was worth every dime the producers put into making it I thought.

After seeing the movie, we sat at one of the benches that were in the halls. Our time together wasn't too bad, thankfully Lily was there. So instead of endlessly pestering me, Alice's attention was split, occasionally drawn towards Lily, giving me an occasional relief. Thinking this made me randomly smirk, drawing their attention towards my direction.

"What's so funny," Lily inquired as she had her scarf adjusted by Alice.

"It's nothing; it's just that from Lily's personality, I wouldn't have thought that you two would get along so well. Yet here you are, the best of friends, like you both told me. If I had to say, the two of you kind of, even each other out."

Alice gave a laugh, "that's true, she maybe a looker, but she's a big stiff with no feminine personality, I wonder why I stay friends with her."

"Okay, I'm a bit rigid and not as happy-go-lucky as you are, but maybe I would smile more if you didn't pester me so often," Lily responded, taking Alice's white ski hat, then throwing it as far as she could, which didn't go too far.

"Hey, that was mean, I really like that hat and the floor here is dirty," responding as Alice walked after it, amusing Lily.

Expressing her dislike, you could tell Lily didn't have any real hint of anger being bothered by her friend's action.

"I'm going to the ladies room real quick," Alice said a few feet away as she picked up her hat.

We found ourselves alone in an uncomfortable atmosphere, at least I was uncomfortable. Fairly quiet, most people were inside still enjoying the big screens. The only noise in the hallway was the roar of the movie's speakers behind the closed doors. Another good time to get a bit closer to Lily, I thought.

"Sorry about dragging you everywhere, I know you probably didn't want to come," Lily voice was low, not the usually self-righteous tone it often was.

Sitting next to her, I glanced her way. She seemed confident still while straight ahead. Her legs crossed, posture upright leaning against the back wall, she wasn't smiling now, merely looking off into the distance, where, I couldn't tell. Oh how I wanted to see her smile again. She did flash a smile before with Emelia, however, I knew it was a forced polite smile, and there wasn't any feeling in it, reminding me very much of myself. I didn't want just a glad friendly expression from her either, inside I craved more. To be different from everyone, different from the times we spent at school where we were mere regular friends. No, what I wanted was to make her smile; at me, only for me, to give her a feeling of joy in a way where she could express herself only with my presence.

"Its fine, you helped occupy most of Alice's attention from me, besides, I had a pretty good laugh watching you two just now."

"Sorry for having such a rigid personality," mumbling as she gave me a light punch, opening my eyes wider in a bit of disbelief at her action.

It was something that seemed unnatural for her to do, to act, well, girly. Looking at me, she realized what she had done, quickly diverted her eyes from me to look at the wall ahead. Her hands now stuffed in her pockets, shoulders a bit scrunched together making her seem smaller, showing how uneasy and awkward she felt. I gave a laugh. I couldn't resist, her response was adorable and funny. She charmed me over even more so than before.

"Shut-it, is it that weird for me to act," she gave a slight pause, "natural?" Seemingly more bother by her use of the word 'natural.' "I don't really talk to others a lot. The only person I'm really close to is Alice. Sure, there's my job at the coffee house, but that's just customer service work, you have to force yourself to give the customers a pleasant experience."

"No, its fine, really, it's just that I didn't expect you to see this kind of side of you. I'm actually glad, you always seem so reserved and composed around me. Seeing you act this way is nice."

"That's enough, I know it was a bit odd for me to do," looking down at the floor, muddling over her actions, "at least I feel like an idiot."

Knowing how it felt, the feeling you get when you do or say something out of place or out of your norm. The more unnatural the action was, the more uncomfortable I always felt, and then I would think back, groaning over what an idiot I had been. This was especially true when I was a child after my mother and sister's passing. Seeing Lily this way, I felt the need to say something, to cheer her up, lighten the mood.

"Don't worry about it so much, there's nothing wrong in showing that side once in a while."

"Yeah, sure, you're just saying that because I gave you good laugh." Quickly recovering as if she never showed her innocent shy side, she was back to her normal self. Not all the way there, but more composed like she'd always been.

"Yes, I laughed, but I also liked it, not because it entertained me, but it was you just being yourself. Seeing you that way, I thought you looked pretty adorable."

After complimenting her, there was no immediate change from her. She did take out her hands from her pocket, pushing herself to sit up straighter. Now was the moment I thought. Deciding to take a step forward, for a change between the two of us, I gathered up my courage.

"And that's probably why I've fell for you."

With a small gesture, extending my hand towards hers, I grasped hold of her soft delicate hand. Never being put in such a situation where I confessed my feelings for someone, I felt extremely embarrass, I couldn't even look in her direction. Nervousness with a small sweat, I simply waited for a response from her, any response.

"Adorable? Huh," her response was flat as if she was questioning my confession to her. She didn't remove my hand which still lied upon hers.

Not daring to look towards her, afraid that if our eyes met, she would reject me. So I waited, waiting for her to saying something, even a mumble. Just a little bit more, show me just a bit more of a reaction so I could know whether she liked me in the same way or not. I felt her other hand on top of mine, lightly squeezing it. Her warm soft hands made me feel glad from her response. Feeling a bit more at ease, my body loosen from the simply gesture. Though my heart beat fiercely, my nerves were stronger.

I began to look at her, wishing I hadn't. What I had hoped to see was of acceptance, a joyful look that would've been just for me. One where she showed a feeling of happiness, relieved that I had just expressed my feelings towards her, embracing me with her own feelings. Any positive reaction, some sort acceptance of me, but there were none in sight.

What I saw gripped my heart. My once adrenaline beating heart slowed down drastically. Once hopeful thoughts of her sharing similar emotions towards me now vanished. She was saddened. All there was were defeat, as if her soul was beaten into submission. From simply being depressed, it was a merge of agony and anger. Not the anger one would have at another, but at herself, at her own being. For some reason, it pained me to see her this way.

Staring up at the ceiling calmly, the dim lights reflecting off those beautiful eyes of hers, collecting her thoughts for a response. Trying to compose herself back to normal, "I like you too Evan, I like you a lot, but I'm sorry," she said to me as she removed my hand from hers. "I can't give you the reason why, I can't tell you what it is exactly, but it's a personal problem that I have, I'm sorry. Alice should be back soon, I'll pretend like this never happened."

Watching me, she gave that forced smile, the sly beautiful smile I've seen her give to Emelia earlier that day. 'What was happening,' was all I could think of, how do I act now?

"Lily," I said. Before I could continue, Alice was back.

"Hey guys, you okay Evan, is something the matter," Alice stood there, concerned for me.

Why? I thought, why did she have to show up now, why did she have to ask if something was the matter with me? Knowing that it was best to keep quiet about our earlier conversation, I came up with a random lie. After all, what I took from Lily's last comment was that she wanted to pretend that our confession didn't happen. I assumed that she was implying to still want to be friends, to act like how we've always been towards each other. Deciding the best case was to comply, I gave a big smile, "nothing, I'm just a bit concern that's all. I was teasing Lily how much better she looks when she laughs. I think it's she's more attractive when she does. I was thinking just now, over how we could make her be a bit livelier."

"I know Lily, laugh a bit more," Alice said using her fingers to create bad attempt of a happy face on Lily.

Not resisting, "happy," Lily said back which made Alice burst in laughter, even giving me a chuckle.

"What the heck is up with that," Alice cried.

Lily saw me, pleased from my response. Perhaps she thought everything was okay now, I didn't know, she confused me to no ends. I wasn't okay with this outcome though. Even if I laughed, putted up a good front for her, I was depressed on the inside. It didn't ease the fact that Lily had rejected me. I didn't want to be here anymore. I needed time to be by myself, to properly think over my recent confession, and of what Lily had said, not being able to be in a relationship due to personal reasons.

After a bit more time together, we had some food before I received a text from Emelia asking me to come back home, to help her with some things. Emelia said that she would wait for me at the mall if I was nearby as she was still there. Emelia knew of course of my fear, my past traumatic history as a child. Grateful that she did, it gave me a plausible reason to leave as the sun would've been setting soon; making me tenser the longer I was with Alice and Lily.

Arriving at the mall, we went our separate ways. Watching the two of them leave, I knew things were going to be awkward from now on. I wouldn't be able to look into Lily's eyes anymore. The merry times at school would become still and stagnant. Other questions still lingered in my mind, especially of the reason she gave me.

That night, contemplating various things, the conversation that I had with Lily was one. "Adorable," I said aloud, "I guess I really do like you." Saying these words in my dark quiet room, it seemed louder than what it was supposed to be. I had never having actually liked anyone before. I liked women of course, but the girls back in the past had never seemed to attract me as Lily had. Even with the girl whom I once dated in middle school, there just weren't any real feelings towards her. She wasn't the same, not as with Lily. Remembering her shy expression at the movie theater, I could feel the smugness inside of me. The more I kept thinking of her, the more my heart ached.

I needed to ask her out once more. She would only say no if I simply asked her directly, especially with what just happened. I needed to consider other things as well. My fear was also largely problematic, since it wasn't as if I could tell her that I believed in demons, that I had a feared the night, of dark isolated areas excluding my bedroom. That my bedroom was the one dark place that allowed me to be comfortable by myself. Heck, even after moving into Emelia's home, I wasn't entirely at ease with my room until a few days later. I even remembered the days in which I would check below my bed and closet before I slept. I still do it on occasions, when I'm overly paranoid. I took a lot of courage to check myself, knowing from experience that I needed to, if I didn't, I wouldn't be able to sleep that night. My therapist also mentions it, that I should check myself, by myself, to gather the strength inside of me and realize that they were fictional hallucinations.

Man, I had real issues. I didn't even consider them when asking Lily to be with me. As the thoughts went through my mind, I became more and more weary, my eyes grew heavier, and I knew I should keep my distance from her, but I kept thinking of how I should go about courting her. I lost track of time, eventually dozing off into another one of my dreams of the past.

CHAPTER

6

The next day was more normal than I had anticipated. During class, I didn't speak to Lily, even though she sat right beside me, we didn't speak or have eye contact with one another, merely awkward air surrounded us. I wouldn't be able to win her over like this if the situation continued, I thought, so I decided to try and lighten the mood during lunch time, in our usual spot.

Contemplating the situation ahead of time, I made scenarios in my head of what to say to her when we would be together. As my fellow students walked past, time seemed to move quickly as I waited. My appetite lost, waiting anxiously for Lily. As I sat there by myself, I began to feel that things might just be hopeless for us, depressed as there were only minutes left until lunch would end. Was she now avoiding me? She had never missed a day since we first met, always showing up at this location on the bench, under the same tree day after day; we would talk and laugh like the rest of the normal students that we were always surrounded by. The bell rang for our lunch break to end. Getting up, I felt a bit lonely making my way back to class. It wasn't as if I'd never been by myself before, or even lost a friend, but this was more than those previous times. This was Lily. Despite my condition, I just didn't want to lose her.

For the rest of the day, I was left dazed. Classes seemed so frivolous that I didn't care to pay much attention. I did my best to look awake, maintaining my eyes, gearing them towards the teacher, but I was simply staring off into space not listening. The rest of the week followed in that similar pattern. As I waited day after day for Lily, she never showed up, we never talked during class or in the halls. Enough was enough, at the current rate of things, our relationship would never recover. So when I saw her after school, I called out to her a few times. Ignoring me, she pretended to be in a rush to get to her next class. That only made me sadder, to be ignored in such a way. It was as if she didn't want to have anything to do with me anymore.

Oddly enough, Alice seemed normal. Like nothing was wrong, she would sometimes show herself at lunch as I waited for Lily, not caring to ask where she was. Did she know that something was wrong with Lily and me, or did she just think that Lily was off, occupied with something else, not being able to eat with me? After a few more days, Alice began showing up more often. I had found myself talking with her during lunch more, the halls, classes, and even when Jason was around. It was as if she was strategically replacing Lily with her own presence. Starting off by coming around, teasing me a bit, then the next day we spent the whole lunch together. After that, she would proactively start conversations with me throughout the day.

I didn't like how things were going. My current situation reminded me of how my family was. Alice actions reminded me of Clarissa, my step mom. Thinking of her left me with a bitter feeling once more. In my mind, it was as if Alice was trying to step in and take Lily's place, like how Clarissa did when my real mother had passed away. I knew it wasn't a fair comparison, especially for Clarissa who tried her best to fill the role of my mother, treating me like her own son, but I just couldn't bring myself to accept her.

I knew Alice had some feelings for me, but she still was dating Jason, even more so, she didn't show any concern for how Lily was avoiding me. Then again, I wasn't her, I didn't know how Alice think, for all I knew, she could have simply noticed me being by myself, alone, wanting to simply keep me company. Alice was a kind hearted person I knew, having spent so much time getting to know her. Conflicted, wanting to think the best of Alice, her actions reminded me so much of Clarissa that it angered me a bit. It was exactly what Clarissa did to my father. First, casually appearing more and more, comforting my father a little at a time, then she started showing up every day. At first it was just during dinner time, to occasionally help out with a meal or two, going about with casual conversations. Then she was eating at our house nearly every day. After a while, she spoke more flirtatiously towards my father, and finally she began showing up at my school, picking me up. Gradually, Clarissa had progressed into my life more and more, making her moves, biding her time until she made a permanent mark in my life, becoming my step mother that I could never love. I didn't hate Alice for this, knowing she wasn't Clarissa, it was just that I found their actions to be so similar, that it bothered me.

As the week moved forward, it was Friday once more and the school week was ending. As I made my way out of the school building, Alice had caught my eyes. She was talking to Jason next to her locker. Noticing me, the two of us made eye contact, and then she started to move towards my direction. As Alice made her was towards me, setting aside her conversation with Jason, he acted a bit confused with her sudden brush off. Turning around, he caught sight of me. The look in his eyes wasn't good, it was the look of frustration and anger, and I knew it wasn't a good thing. I was already on is bad side since we first met, since then he had never taking a liking to me. He always simply glared at me with a look of disgust whenever he was alone and I came to his attention. His anger must have grown as of late as Alice and I had become chummier with one another. This look was different; he was glaring at me, looking down with pure loathsome hate.

He caught Alice by her arm and pulled her back towards him, a bit too roughly. Knowing better than to stay, I left, knowing full well that Jason wouldn't actually hurt her or make too much of a scene, especially since the hallway was crowded with others and they were at school. She remained relatively safe, I, not so much. It wasn't going well for the two of them I knew. Knowing that I was the cause, I knew for certainty to never cross paths with Jason, I now had to avoid him at all cost, if possible.

Walking to the bike rack, a cold breeze blew as it made me shiver. Even as the bright yellow sun fill the cloudless sky, the air was becoming colder as of late. Winter was approaching, shortening the time the sun would stay out, the thought made me want to quickly head home.

"Evan, Evan!" a voice called out, I knew it was Alice shouting out for me, but I didn't respond. It was just one of those days where all I just want to do was head home and simply rest. Not having to turn around to know that there was some distance between the two of us. Considering that it was Friday, all of the students were rushing out to either get back home or have some fun. They would be trying to leave the school grounds like me. This meant they were blocking Alice from reaching me. She would have to maneuver her way around them. Hurriedly, I rushed to reach my bike. Once I did, a hand tapped my shoulder. Startled, I looked back to see who it was, disappointed to see that it was Alice.

"Hey there," I said as I saw her.

"You know, you left so quickly I had to practically run to catch up with you, well, I speed walked, but still. You seemed like you're in a hurry, do you need to get home or something?"

"Not really, no, it's just a bit chilly right now. I was hoping to get back home, turn on the heater, and sleep the weekend away."

She smiled from my comment, "I get what you mean, it is starting to get cold lately," she said rubbing her hands, shoving them into her thin jacket.

"Is there something you want to talk to me about?"

"Well, I was wondering if you were free this Saturday. We rarely spend any time together besides at school, Lily and I was wondering that maybe the three of us could go bowling or something this weekend. You know, to build some memories and stuff. We are seniors, after we graduate, we might not see you anymore. You don't even need to bring anything, just yourself; the two of us will plan everything."

"You and Lily," questioning her.

"Yep, it's usually just the two of us, but I suggested in bringing you?" Her expression was a bit shy as she said it in such an uncomfortable way. She was really embarrassed admitting it. "Lily doesn't mind, in fact, she said, 'the more the merrier.' You know what she said after that? 'Besides, it would be nice if there was someone else there to listen to your ranting.'"

That gave me a good laugh. "That sounds like something she would say."

"Hey, no laughing," Alice said as she gave me a playful light punch in the chest. "Well, you coming or not," getting back to the subject on hand.

"Sure, just tell me where and when?" not exactly wanted to go anywhere with Alice, but it was a good chance to talk with Lily.

"Don't worry about where, I'll pick you up bike boy," again she lightly gave me a small weak punch, which now slightly annoyed me this time around. "As for when, well, we usually meet up at nine, so I'll be at you house roughly ten or so minutes ahead to pick you up. They close at eleven so we got a good two hours of bowling, which is a pretty decent amount of time."

"Did you say nine, as in nine pm? Why so late, and how do you know where I live?"

"What are you, afraid of the dark, or do you have some kind of early curfew or something," she said making fun of me. "As for how me knowing where you live, your aunt and my parents are acquaintances remember. You might not know this, but when your Aunt was still married, the two of them would occasionally host dinner parties together with my parents, so my parents have been to your house before. They gave me your address yesterday after I told them about inviting you to bowl with us tomorrow."

This unnerved me. My shoulders felt tense with the thought of having to go out so late. Giving an awkward laugh, "could we do it a bit earlier, like in the morning," asking weakly.

"Come on, you know we can't, Lily has a morning shift that day. You don't *have* to go if you can't make it, if have plans to do something else, then that's perfectly alright, I mean, I don't want to force you or anything."

I was hesitant. Thinking about going out after sundown made me light headed, nervous, but this was such a good chance to meet up with Lily. I wouldn't be able to discuss anything with her at school with how things were, and I most definitely couldn't impose on her during work. I did know her number but she screen the last call and message that I left her. I knew that it would've been better to talk with her in person. This was my chance to fix things. Having a good time out, Alice would be there too, she would actually lighten the mood. Hesitant, 'should I really risk it,' I thought. Would I be able to maintain my composure outside during the night?

"I'll see you then," quickly saying before I could think any further. I had too; this was an ideal chance to talk with Lily. Plus, I was supposed to be getting better, to fight against my fear of the dark. I had to consider that this was a good attempt in that direction.

"Be ready by the time I come."

Before I could say anything, she had slipped into the crowd with the rest of the students, making her way back into the school building.

I was terrified inside. As I rode my bike home, the shaky disturbing feeling within me wouldn't stop. Perhaps it was the cold wind against my skin, but I had goose bumps.

I couldn't sleep that night, tossing and turning. My body itself grew heavier as the hours passed, my mind wouldn't let me rest. Not being able to sleep after tossing and turning so long, I placed my hand on my chest, counting each time my heart beat as a way to calm myself, lessening my anxiety. As the seconds passed, each time the hands ticked, it felt as if my heart was beating harder, so hard that it was the only thing I could hear in my quiet room. Time was slowed down considerably, oh so ever slow it was. Feeling a bit better now, my mind was still wide awake. Eventually, I found myself walking through the other rooms of the house, not knowing what it was that I was searching for, what purpose in aimless wandering would have. Walking into what looked like a private office, which I knew of course that Emelia always had. She never used it, but she kept the door closed. I've had a few glances inside from my previous visits, just never entered since there wasn't much that I considered to be enjoyable interesting inside. It wasn't as if I wasn't permitted from entering, Emelia gave me complete freedom to enter and exit any room within the house as I pleased, with the exception of hers of course. Not having to tell me, I knew out of common courtesy not to enter her private bedroom.

Inside, I got a good look around office. It seemed like it was mainly used by her ex-husband. Emelia had kept everything the way it was I could tell, as there were a few documents and notes were still sprawled out on the desk. The room was tidy, but gathering dust. Closely examining the room was a beautiful Mahogany desk. Around the office were a large globe, and various art pieces. Overall, the room felt a bit overly classy, refine, but gaudy and out of place from the rest of the house. The shelves where filled with novels, the majority consisting of many novels that I wouldn't have figured Emelia ex-husband to be interested in reading. The genre varied from science fiction to romance, fantasy, and non-fiction, to painting techniques, law and neuroscience. It was an array of books all jumbled together along the shelves in no particular organized order, making me to conclude that Emelia was the cause for this disorder. Most likely she brought various books, then not knowing where to place them, she ended up cramming all of them here. I knew her husband, he wasn't the reading type, didn't have various interests, and only read engineering, business, and politics.

Since feeling that I wouldn't be able to sleep anytime soon, I pulled out a book at random, the cover drew me in. I took a seat in the leather chair behind the desk, it was more comfortable than I had imagined. *The Witching Hour* by Anne Rice, a novel about witches. This had to be one of Emelia's books for sure, it seemed like it would have suited her taste. Sitting there throughout the night, captivated, the novel was rather intriguing as the plot and characters slowly drew me in. As the sun rose, I continued to read, even as my eyes were half open. 10 a.m., two hours before noon and I was quite exhausted. Not even moving from the spot, I decided to sleep with my head rested on the desk, even though it was only short walk to my room.

Feeling something ruffling over me, I woke up. It was Emelia standing behind me, covering me with a blanket. Her hair was wet, her shirt a bit damp from the moisture. She smelled like lavender.

"Sorry, did I wake you," she asked in a caring gentle low voice while rubbing my back. Her soft voice was soothing in my weary state, making me wanting to fall back into a deep sleep. She looked worn out. Dark bags had accumulated below her eyes again; she lost a bit of weight from when I had first moved in, making her look somewhat sickly.

"Are you alright aunty, you don't look so good," I asked.

"I'm alright, there's nothing to worry about. I'm just exhausted from work. I had to put in some extra hours again, so I'm lacking sleep, a few hours of sleep will do me good. By the way, what are you doing sleeping in here?"

"I couldn't sleep so I came in here for a book to read. Sorry for intruding into this room."

"Evan, don't be so silly," she said caressing my hair. "You live here, you can go wherever you want in this house, and besides, we're not strangers," she paused, "we're family, and I'll always be here if you need anything, you hear me." Lightly she kissed my head.

Treating me so well, I felt like she was my real mother, in fact, it was exactly the actions my deceased mother would do. It brought back a memory when I fell asleep on the couch down stairs. My real mother, Alina, came home and pulled a blanket over me. Waking up, she too had asked what I was doing sleeping there, before kissing me on my forehead as I dozed off again. Becoming sentimental from the memory, knowing those joyful days with my mother could never come back. It was nice to be able to at least feel the comfort and care from Emelia whom gave off a similar aura.

"What time is it, when did you get home?"

"A little bit before six, I got home roughly half an hour ago. I noticed the light in here before, but wait until after I showered, had a bit of blood on me from the surgery earlier. "

"Did you eat, you should get some food." Getting up, ready to prepare something, Emelia gestured that there wasn't any rush.

"That's alright. I had a light snack while I was driving home. I'm actually more tired than hungry, so I'll be heading to bed now. What are you going to do, do want to get some more sleep, do you want to order some food? I'll give you some money if you want to, is pizza okay?"

"Thank you, I'm okay, I just woke up so I'm not feeling too hungry. Get some rest, you seem like you're about to pass out."

Taking off the blanket she gave me, I wrapped it around her, guiding her back to her room. Doing so made her feel like an old woman to me, no longer the vibrant youthful woman she usually was. "Also, do you mind if I go out for a bit, later tonight?" She didn't respond right away, which gave me a mixed feeling. I wasn't sure if I was nervous, afraid of her saying no, or the opposite, nervous and hopeful that she was going to say, '*no.*'

"Y-you can," she said a bit emotionally, her words a bit shaky. Her dark eyes wavering under the hallway light, the rings gave emphasis that the lighting was hurting her eyes as she tried to keep them open. "I'm sorry, I'm just a bit glad to see you going out," rubbing her eyes with the blanket. I was afraid that you weren't able to go out after sundown anymore, so it made me a bit worried. I'm really glad that you're finally starting to feel more comfortable after all those years. When I first suggested you staying with me, I was hoping that it would change you, even if it's just a bit."

Her words pained me to hear. I had no idea she was worried about me like this. I knew I was her nephew and that she was worried about my wellbeing to some extent. It touched me to know that she felt this way about me, at the same time, my heart clenched to know that I was causing her worry, emotionally burdening her like so. I would have to try harder to make myself better, going out with Lily and Alice tonight would be a step in the right direction.

Leaving my side, going into her room, I knew she consented. As she began to close her door, I called out to her, "aunty."

"Is there something else?"

I paused, "no, nothing, make sure you don't overwork yourself too much."

Giving me a slight smile and a nod, she shut the door. Standing there, placing my head against the door, "thank you."

Checking the clock, 6:05 pm it read, it was much too early before Alice would be arriving. Wondering what to do with the rest of my remaining time, I showered, came down, whipped up a quick meal for Emelia for when she woke up, in case she was feeling hungry, leaving a note for her to find. Going back up to the office, I grabbed the book from before. Slouching myself into the couch, I made myself comfortable.

My symptoms started to rise. My hands began to sweat, looking at the clock multiple times, about a half an hour left before Alice would show up. Trying not to think about it too much, focusing on the words in the book. As I continued to read, the information wasn't being processed, I wasn't remembering anything of what I just read. It was me glancing over at the words. Knowing that the book wasn't helping, I tossed it aside.

'I should cancel,' telling myself, but I knew I couldn't. I wanted to get rid of my fears. I had to if I wanted to move forward in life. They were only self delusions. Emelia was so proud of me earlier. To bail out now would only make her sad if she knew. It wasn't as if she could find out, I thought. I could lie and just make everything up, she wouldn't know. My conflicting rambling thoughts persisted.

"Since you were little you haven't seen them since, so it's only you playing tricks on yourself," I told myself out loud. It helped calmed my nerves bit. Before I knew it, I had my hand on my cell phone. Neither my eyes nor my hand moved away, sitting there like that for a long time.

Placing the phone on the table, I got up and began pacing back and forth. I needed to go through with this, I had to. I have to go through with it, going out after sunset was a good experience for me. It was to show myself that there wasn't anything to fear, repeating this to myself in my head. I would be with both Alice and Lily in a crowded room so it wasn't as if I would be alone or anything.

My phone gave a loud vibrating noise, startling me. Fumbling as I went to picked it up. "Hello, Alice?"

"Hey, I'm here, I'm parked right outside, are your ready or do you need a minute?"

"Y-yeah, I'll be right out," I responded and hung up.

This was the moment of truth, telling myself. "I'll be right out," repeating the words out loud.

Opening the door, Alice was in her car, engine running as she waved to me, giving me one of her big charming smiles. Giving a good look outside, I took in the darkness. Truthfully, I hadn't been outside past sundown for a long time, not once. Already, I felt the creeping darkness of the outside sending chills down my spine. It wasn't so bad I tried telling myself. There were street lamps outside which gave plenty of light. Briskly, I made my way towards Alice's car, seating myself inside, only then realizing how sweaty I was. Almost instantaneously once closing the door, my body relaxed a great deal, knowing I was safe while having Alice besides me, in the confines of the vehicle. Still, I couldn't shrug off the disturbing feeling in my gut.

It didn't get better either. Both Alice and I made random small talk along the way, the conversation we had didn't ease my nerves. As we got out of the car, I stayed close to Alice. Taking advantage of the proximity between us, she pulled my arm around her shoulder. Out of natural instinct, I pulled her close to me. She didn't say anything, I knew I shouldn't have, but I couldn't let her go as I held her tightly for security. Stealing a glance at her to see her response, she seemed happy, blushing even.

Not until we were safe inside the building that my nerves started to disappear. I gave a deep sigh of relief. Inside was warm, filled with white, bright, florescent lighting. Surprisingly, there weren't many other people there. There was only one group in the corner and a couple in one of the middle lanes. In the center lane, Lily was sitting there waiting patiently for us while reading a book, how very like her I thought.

"Sorry about that," I said, letting go of Alice. Hoping Lily was too distracted reading to notice my arm around Alice.

"What are you apologizing for, you didn't do anything," Alice grinned. "Well sure, I got a boyfriend, but so what. We're just two friends walking, that's it."

"I know," I paused, "why don't we head over to Lily?"

As we approached Lily, Alice called out, "look who I brought with me?"

Ripping her eyes away from her book, she looked up at the two of us. "Good to see that you two made it. You know how to bowl," directing the question at me.

She looked and sounding a bit irritated, making me wonder if she saw both me and Alice coming in, or was it that she just didn't want me to be here. I smiled, "I'm an average bowler." This was true, having tried my hand at bowling from time to time during my school breaks. Even I couldn't stay home all the time, though I probably wouldn't have started if it wasn't recommended by my therapist to explore recreational activities.

"That's perfect, were both only okay bowler ourselves," Alice replied. "But we do try to make bowling a bit more interesting."

"A bit more interesting? How so?"

"A small wager," Lily said with a sly smirk.

"Okay, I'm listening. What kind of wager do you ladies have in mind," I asked as I seated myself.

"It's nothing too serious," Alice spoke up, "it's basically a truth game, the winner asks the loser a question no matter what it is, even if it's personal, and the loser answers truthfully. You don't really have anything to be afraid of, it's usually something small, like, 'who do you hate the most at school and what made you hate them so much?' Something like that, not so bad right?"

She was right; it wasn't so bad. "That's fine," I readily agreed.

"By the way," Lily spoke. "Only the winner asks the loser the question, so think up of one before the game ends," this time she gave a weak mocking smile as she made her way towards the bowling balls.

As the game progressed, it was a pretty even match, we were all equally decent, or so I thought. During the last few rounds, both Alice and Lily made either perfect or near perfect strikes one after another, that was when I knew I was hustled. They were much better than they had led up. By the end, they both scored in the 190's while I was left with a score of 164. Lily was in first place, so she had the honor of asking me. It didn't bother me too much, what could she possible ask me that I really needed to hide, as long as it wasn't something dealing with my trauma.

"So, what do you want to know about me?"

Lily sat pondering for a bit, "I've been thinking about it but still haven't come up with one yet, how about getting us winners some soda, I'll have one by the time you come back. Two diet cokes by the way."

Laughing at her demand, "okay, sure, I hope you go easy on me though." As I made my way back, I saw the two of them chatting away, Lily, still in her cool composure, while Alice seemed to be enthused as usual.

Coming back, "here are your two diets. So, ask away."

Lily gave a smirk, "what's your biggest fear and what caused it?"

Her question gave me a bit of a surprise. A direct question at my weakness, it was really the only question that I had hoped she wouldn't have asked me. Even making me wonder why she asked it, considering that there were so many other things. Being one question I'd rather no one would ask, I pondered at what I should do. 'I should lie,' I told myself. They didn't need to know. I sat there in silence as they both stared at me, probably wondering what was taking me so long to respond. I could feel a bit of anxiety coming up.

"Are you going to answer?" Lily asked. "And remember, we prefer the truth."

"Why this question in particular," I asked.

"I'm just curious about something that I heard," Lily spoke up. "Our parents know a few people, and they told us that they heard something about you through the grapevine that came from your aunt. This was a while back long before you moved here. Supposedly from what others told our parents, you were traumatized as a kid, so you now have night fears."

"I told her that I couldn't be true. I wanted to ask you something a bit more interesting. But well, she did win, so it's her question, whatever she wants I guess." Alice sat back with her legs crossed. "Is it true though," sounding a bit concerned.

I gave a sigh, uneasily adjusting myself to sit straight. "If you really want to know, yes, I am afraid of the night, so I can't exactly go out anywhere after sunset, especially by myself. To be precise, I'm afraid of the dark night outside." I looked up at the two and for a moment, there was no reaction, then Lily started to chuckle.

"What are you, some eight year old kid," Lily responded. "Sorry, I just never thought I'd meet someone you're age that's still afraid of the dark."

Alice on the other hand appeared a bit dumbstruck. Alice gave an awkward smile towards me, "well, everyone has their fears, who are we to judge." Giving a nudge to Lily as if tell her to stop laughing.

I knew it was a bad idea to tell them the truth, now feeling self-conscious. I should've told a lie, I thought, something like being afraid of spiders, lots of people had fear of spiders, and rightly so.

"Well, you have to tell us how you got the fear," Lily spoke again, still grinning. "It's kind of cheating, but it's a two part question."

"I know, I know." I wasn't sure how I would explain it to them as I started to form the story inside my head. Having them know already that I was afraid of the night, I decided that I mind as well tell them instead of covering everything up. If Lily did ever decided to date me, she would have needed to know at some point. At least this way, she could make a clear judgment now instead of down along the lines.

"It was at night when it happened years ago, I was a kid, in a really loving family. My parents were out, and while me and my sister stayed home, our house was broken into." I gave a small silence before I continued. "Before I knew it, I found myself running outside during the stormy night, running into the street barefoot, I was afraid, all alone, trying to escape from whomever it was that was chasing me. I blindly ran into an alleyway finding myself cornered."

Staring at the two of them, they were silent, waiting for me to continue. I had to choose my words very carefully, so I took my time as I knew they weren't going to rush me. "While I was cowering in fear, my mother appeared, she ran to me, to my safety. However, she was killed that night in front of me. Before she reached me, someone came from behind her, and that was it, she was killed, right in front of me. It was moments later that the police arrived, just in time before I was killed too. That night, both my sister and mother were killed, and my house was burned to the ground. As for the one who did it, they got away, they never found them, nor do they have an idea of who did it. In any case, that's how I got my fear. I'm still traumatized from the past."

The both of them sat there seeming a bit more sympathetic now. I felt a bit better though still embarrassed. I left out a lot of the story, omitting a lot of details on purpose, but they didn't need to hear what happened exactly. I also knew that after hearing the edited version, they wouldn't ask for me to explain too much if any. That was how most people were, they don't like to pry too much into people's personal past, especially if it was a particularly touchy matter.

"Sorry for asking something like that," said Lily, avoiding eye contact, seemingly gloomy. "Can I ask just one more question?"

"Sure, what is it?"

"How did they get away?"

"The sewers," I replied.

The fun happy atmosphere before took a nose dive. All three of us remained silent, not sure what to say next. Forcing an uncomfortable weak laugh, "you don't have to worry about it, it happened a really long time ago, and besides, it's dark outside and I'm here with the both of you now, aren't I? So yes, it's true that I'm still afraid to go out at night, but being here right now means that I've gotten a bit better since then. Before it was a lot harder to do, but I'm getting better." Waiting for a response from them, they didn't answer. "How about another game?" I asked.

They both happily nodded in agreement.

For the remainder of the night, it was seemingly normal, the place gave an announcement saying they would be closing in ten minutes, so the three of us made our way out. Having lost again for the final game, neither of them brought up any questions they wanted to ask of me. I suppose my one personal story was enough for them that night. Alice was as talkative as usual, while at the same time avoiding eye contact with me, occasionally taking a few glances in my direction. Lily was her usual self, calm demeanor, composed as usual. We walked into the near empty parking lot, parting our ways as Alice gave me a lift home. Even though I was still fearful, this time I kept my hands to myself as did she.

"Evan," Alice suddenly calling my name during the drive.

"Yes?"

"Just letting you know, Lily and I, we're not going to tell anyone else. We're not the kind of people who would, especially when it comes to something so sensitive. For personal matters, Lily and I share things only with each other. Also, we don't think any less of you because of what you're afraid of."

"Alice, thanks, I feel a little bit better." The rest of the way, the two of us remained silent.

It wasn't so bad, comforting myself. I was curious how the two of them saw me now, did they think of me as strange? Perhaps feeling pity for me? It was a good idea not telling them the full story, who knew what their reactions might have been, keeping it as normal and as believable as possible was the best idea. Alice, I had a feeling that I could trust in her words, that the two of them would keep my secret at least. As for Lily, unfortunately, that night there weren't any moments where I could have been alone with Lily. Unsure of whether things between us had gotten better or worse, the only think I could do was wait until the next time I saw her again.

CHAPTER

7

Dreams. Lonely self-desolated horrors that I occasionally recall on my own, reminiscent of the past whenever I sleep. That is what I come to think of whenever I hear of the word, 'dreams.' Not of goals, of the possible exciting future that could be waiting, but of my past coming back to take hold of me, reminding me of what is or could be out there. They've haunted me since I was a boy, haunting me still to this very day as I try and struggle in vain to escape them. It wasn't as if I never have a good dream, but when I do; they usually fade away from my memory when I wake. During the day, I simply go about my waking hours like any other, as I sleep, in my temporary state of a coma, which is when my self-delusions rapidly creep upon me. It is the nightmares that tend to leave a mark throughout my day, perhaps even longer if it was terrifying enough. The worse they are, the more I tend to agonize myself over the troubling thoughts of what once was, or possibly never were.

After spending the day with both Lily and Alice, that night as I slept, brought back both the good and the bad memories.

I was a young boy again, remembering the sunlight shining through the window as it blinded me as I opened my eyes. Bathing me with its wonderful warm rays as my sister Lisa pulled them open.

"Hey, get up, mom's making breakfast, you want some or not," my sister Lisa said, pulling the blanket off of me. I knew it was coming of course, trying to hold onto the blanket, but she was much stronger than my weak meager self.

No longer able to sleep in such conditions, I drowsily got up. I remember walking out into the hall, my father exiting his room, greeting me with his warmth.

"Hey buddy, you're up early," picking me up in his arms, "well, that's good, your mom is making breakfast, and all that's left is your sister." My father walked down the hall, knocking on my sister's bedroom door, "Lisa honey, time to wake up!"

The bathroom door then opened, "I'm already up dad. God, it's a Sunday, do we really need to wake up early just to eat breakfast together on a no school day?" Lisa yelled out, exaggerating the words, 'on a no school day.'

"Yes, it's important to your mother and me that we do more things as a family," my dad yelled back turning around, realizing that she was in the bathroom not her bedroom.

This caused Lisa to moan aggravatingly from his response before closing the door.

"And let your brother in to wash up too," my dad yelled, releasing me from his arms.

We both finished up as I headed down, while Lisa went back to her room. Moments later, she came hurryingly down the stairs as my mother began to pass out the plates. My stomach grumbled as the pancakes started to soak up the sweet syrup, the eggs and bacon slowly started to drown in the liquid syrup goo as my mother began to poor it over each plate. Tall glass of orange juice included.

"By the way, I want to give you a heads up Lisa. Me and your father will be out Saturday of next week, so don't go off making plans," my sister grumbled as a response while me mother gave a slight smile as I looked at her. She placed both hands on my cheek and rubbed them gently in a playful way.

I loved those mornings. Oh how I could live those wonderful days again. When my day is going bad, these types of memories were where I often tended to go to. There were times even when they had helped me from breaking down, it was something that I had to slowly learn, to help calm myself down. Later, I learned that doing so was a double edge sword. They were making me run away from reality too often. Finding myself thinking of these sunny happy mornings one too many times, it was me being reluctant to seeing reality. Secluding myself from others or simply spending time all day in a corner, daydreaming. Realizing this when one day the topic was brought up by my school teacher. She became troubled when she saw me doing nothing but daydream throughout class all of the time. Once my parents knew of this, they brought this issue to my therapist, and concluded that it wasn't helping me. Instead it was having an adverse effect, keeping me from recovering. Since then, I began moderating myself, only using this method whenever I was in a panic. Sadly, as I grew older, the effects wore off, they no longer helped me. Now, they simply bring sadness to me, realizing that these moments were no more.

That morning my parents and I left the house, leaving Lisa whom wanted to stay behind to get some extra shut eye. As we left the house, the sky was now partially clouded, the grass and trees stood still, still soaked from the down pour from last night. My body gave a shiver thinking of those *things* from the night before. My mother saw my reaction as I shivered, simply thinking that I was just cold, she zipped up my little gray jacket all the way up. Sitting in the minivan, I looked down the street. I could see the house of the woman from the previous night. As I focused my stare on that house, a dog ran out onto the street, giving me a scare as I thought it was one of *them*. Not wanting to think anymore, I slid back down into my seat, readying myself for the outing with my parents.

It wasn't until a few days later in the early morning that a police officer came to our house. We were all sitting at the table, eating breakfast, right before my father had to go work and my sister and I had to get to school. My mother had answered the door only to come back looking concerned.

"Who was that," my father asked biting into a sausage.

"That was a police officer, apparently Jenny from down the street has gone missing," my mother sat down, getting back to her breakfast.

I sat there and took a big gulp of orange juice as I listened intently on what my mother had to say. Reminded of the woman laying in her yard, with whatever those creatures where crouching beside her.

"It seemed that her work called," my mother continued, "they were worried about her since she didn't show up for work these past few days. Being gone so long, her friend and coworker called the police. So last night, the officer went to her house and found her car and keys still there, Jenny even left her purse with her ID and credit cards too."

My father slowed his eating pace, listening with a bit more focus, "what else did the officer say?"

My mother shook her head, "he wouldn't tell me anything else. He then asked me if I might have seen anyone strange around the parts or if I knew anything about her, and where she might possible be." She hesitated; "you don't think she was kidnapped do you?" No one replied. "Lisa, I'm driving you to school with your brother today."

Rolling her eyes, "its okay mom, you don't need to, you're just worrying too much, tell her dad," everyone's eyes were on him now. My eyes would shift back and forth from my frowning mother and my annoyed sister, while my father sat becoming uneasy from being put on the spot.

"She's right Alina," my father responded. "Like she said, you're just worrying too much, I'm sure Jenny will pop up real soon," he gave her a warm smile, patting hand. "Besides, if it was a kidnapper, he would have some balls to take Lisa right in broad daylight, but just in case, your mom will drive you to school." My father gave a smirk, while my mother gave a victorious smile at Lisa. It was childish of them to do, having so much joy over my sister's now dissatisfactory look. Remember that scene filled me with happiness.

"That settles it, let's go you two." My mother got up, gesturing toward my sister and me to follow.

"Wait, at least eat something," my father called out to my mother.

"If I don't take them now, Evan will be late, I'll finish up when I get back," my mother yelling back as all three of us exited the house in a hurry.

As I made my way towards the car, I could see the officer car parked in front of the woman's house. He himself was a few houses down across the street, knocking on someone else's door, making his rounds to the nearby houses hoping to get some sort of lead. Knowing that no one really would be able to give him anything useful, wasting his efforts. I wondered then, wondered if those creatures left any traces. Surely, if someone investigated hard enough, thoroughly enough, they would find some evidence, traces of those evil things, wouldn't they? No one else had come by after that, to question or gave any information regarding Jenny's disappearance.

Saturday quickly approached, it was seven o'clock. The weather was just as bad as the weather man on TV had predicted. Raining fiercely, the noise of the water splashing against the windows as the wind maneuvered the rain drops against our house was very loud. There was no thunder thankfully, but the wind howled and roared outside, making it ever more unsettling than if it was just the boom of thunder.

My mother was still getting ready up stairs. I was sitting with Lisa on the couch as our father joined us, watching whatever was on TV as he waited for her. He sat right in the middle of the two of us as he wrapped his large arms around us. Those were the days when he was still truly happy, when he still cared.

"Did you pull out the trash," my mother shouted from upstairs.

My father gave a sigh as he got up, heading towards the kitchen. Shortly after, returning to the room with a full trash bag, he headed out the front door, being left alone with Lisa again. A second later, the sound of the rain got louder. I assumed it was perhaps because my dad didn't close the door all the way and the wind blew it open. Too preoccupied with the cartoon, I didn't bother closing it. Then something caught the corner of my eye, darting across the far corners of the room, like a swift shadow of some sort. Frightened, I tugged on Lisa's pants, but she ignored me, continuing her sights on the television. Deciding to take a peek, I got off the couch. Cautiously, I went to the door. My father was standing there shaking the water off of his umbrella.

"Hey buddy, what are you doing all the way over here?" Lifting me up, he carried me back to the couch.

Moments later our mother came back down dressed up from head to toe. They said their goodbyes as my sister recited the babysitting instructions before the two of them hurried out the door, once more leaving me alone with Lisa. Time moved forward quickly, now half past nine as the rain outside was still coming down hard. Through the window, I took a peek outside. Visibility was poor. It reminded me of that night when Lisa had locked me out. The weather today was much worse as now the harsh strong wind came with the heavy rain. Lisa sat on the couch studiously finishing whatever assignment for school she had left. Slumped next to her, I decided take a short nap. It was short lived indeed. Moments later, the sound of her text book closing woke me back up.

"Finally finished," a voice shouted next to me. Getting up groggily, I stared at Lisa, now looking at me satisfied. She was enthused with herself, glad to be done with the burden of school assignments, to now enjoy the rest of the weekend comfortably lazily. "Let's go sleepyhead, it's time for you to go to bed," she said to me.

Looking up at the time, it was almost ten. I was asleep for about half an hour. Though Lisa had thin skinny arms, she was able to pick me up just like our parents would; carrying me up the stairs. She was a good sister when she wanted to be I thought. She was warm and made me want to sleep in her arms just like so. By the time I brushed my teeth and was snuggly in bed, I was wide awake. The preparations before bed had woke me up, and though short, the nap earlier now gave me a burst of energy. As I lay in my bed, I stared at the ceiling, trying to fall asleep again. Closing my eyes, concentrating on my breathing, a loud audible screech came from behind me. Immediately I turn to face the window, but there was nothing. There was only the sound of the wind and rain, pounding against the glass. What was that sound? I wondered.

Crawling out of bed, I approached my window, looking out to see nothing. Well, it wasn't like I would've been able to see anything, all I saw was the blurred darkness; all I could hear was downpour of wind and rain. Facing away from the window, I scurried my way back below my sheets. Not knowing why then, but I ended up looking back. Perhaps it was what some people called, 'instinct.' Sensing the cold stare from above peering down upon me, undoubtedly it was there, a pair of blurred white glowing eyes staring down upon me on the other side of the window. I moved away, collapsing backward, falling to the floor; not once parting my eyes from it. Steadily, the pair of eyes descended down the window, knowing it saw me and I it. Focused on nothing but me, the pair of eyes made its way downward. Two swaying glows moving side to side were disappearing down and out of sight.

Jumping onto my feet, I flicked on the lights, threw the door wide open, and hurriedly ran down the hall to Lisa's room. Pounding vigorously, "Lisa, Lisa," I called out to her over and over again, shouting her name out in a panic. All I could think about was the woman down the street, us ending up like her. Her limp body in the backyard, drenched from the rain, being surrounded by those ghastly creatures. Lights quickly appeared from under the door, half a second later, it flung open.

"Evan," she yelled, "what's wrong with you."

"Monster, there's a monster," I yelled as I moved away towards my room a bit, pointing in that direction. She didn't move, so I ran to her, pulling her along in the direction of my room. She hardly budged. "Come on," I said again, still struggling to pull her over.

"Evan, calm down. I'll take a look, but you need to calm down." She held me with both her hands, forcing me to look at her.

I looked back, up at her face and froze. Gazing up a bit more, I saw one of them. Right there, it was right above the door way behind Lisa, outside of her view. The hideously black naked figure, about as big as I was, laying flat up against the wall as close to the ceiling as it could be. With its large yellow eyes, it stared down into mines, giving a joyful wicked grin. Its grin grew bigger, stretching larger and wider than any human could. So far did it stretched, that it reached from one ear to the other as it showed its ugly distorted pointed teeth. When did it get there I thought, how did it even get in? I didn't need to think 'how,' as I knew the answer. It was the shadow earlier, the one that I had thought I saw when our dad was taking out the trash, slipping in then.

"Okay," Lisa said with her hand to her head, looking exhausted and annoyed.

Standing up again, she stepped out and around me. Before she could utter another word the thing sprung down with such force, it made her topple forward as the two of them sprung right over me, pushing me to the ground. The *thing* gave a loud scream as it hung on her back, full of excitement and glee. With two fists full, it gave a ferocious pull of Lisa's hair, sending her screaming in pain as she wailed in agony, her head forced back. The pull was so strong that her whole body threw itself almost. Somehow, before her tumbling towards the floor once more, she managed to grab the railing, standing herself up. Her hands frantically tried to reach for the creature behind her. She clawed out of fear and panic. This time, the monster pushed her head forwards, and then forced a strong pull back once more, driving the two of them backwards into Lisa's room. Through the struggle, Lisa screamed, fighting frantically, kicking her door shut in the commotion. The two of them were out of sight.

Standing there, my jaw was dropped. My hands and legs wouldn't stop shaking. A second later, the lights began to flicker before turning off completely. I had wet my pants out of fright. Not knowing what to do, I clumsily got up, fumbling in the opposite direction from the two. Another loud scream was heard. It was Lisa's voice but I didn't look back. I kept moving forward, both my legs struggling against their shaking will. Running into the nearby closet, I maneuvered to the back, as far as I could behind the thick coats.

Grasping one of the coats, I felt something in one of the pockets. Rummaging through as another scream echoed down the hall. I pulled out what felt like a pen; I couldn't see it, but I knew by the feel of tip that it was one of my father's fountain pens. Holding it tightly with both my tiny hands, wrapping my fists around it, I prepared myself to trust it at the creature if it dared to open the door.

The screaming stopped as I felt the tears flowing down from my eyes. She was gone, Lisa was gone, that thing outside took her. I knew it and I also knew that I would be its next victim. Not knowing what to do, I stood there for a while, trying to listen. Not hearing anything for some time, I decided to go through the other pockets in the closet while still holding onto the pen in my right hand, ready at any moment. While my left hand quickly moved itself, making its way around, a lighter and a pack of cigarettes was the only thing I could find, once again they were my father's. Shaking, I tried to get the lighter to start; there was a few sparks and then on the fourth attempt, a small fire lit itself in the tiny enclosed space. As I looked at the flame, it waivered back and forth from my quivering hand.

I was able to see it from below, a shadow from the other side of the door. *It,* was on the other side now. My body stopped shaking. Altogether, my entire being was still, I even stopped breathing. Moving my body against the wall, I waited bit in that lightly lit room. After a few seconds, nothing happened, so I moved my head to the door, listening, my right hand a bit higher in the air, ready to come down. The light in the closet grew now, unusually brighter as I looked up to my left. One of the coats had caught on fire. While I was occupied, staring at the flaming clothing, the door swung open. I lashed my gaze at the opening, seeing the grotesque figure looking at me with dark red color of blood staining against its blacken mouth and hands. There was no doubt that the blood must have been from Lisa.

It lunged at me.

My hand instinctively came down with all my might. I could feel the tip of the pen moving itself through, going down deep as it came into contact with the creature. I stabbed it right into it the monster's left eye. It fell past me into the closet as I rushed out. The creature screaming in agony, letting out painful agonizing yells. Before the thing could regain itself, I looked back up at the flames that had now made its fiery glow to the others in the closet. Hurriedly, I pulled on one of the burning coats, enveloping the creature below the flames before running away. Making my way downstairs towards the door, I looked back. No longer did I hear the scream of the creature, now I watched it frantically struggling beneath the flames, spreading the fire to the walls and along the carpet. Not daring to wait any longer, I reached the bottom of the stairs to the front door. Frozen before I could open it, I felt it. The hateful eye burrowing into the back of my head, feeling that vile creature's menacing gaze from above, staring down at me from above the stairs. Not needing to look back to see it, I just knew. Swinging the door open, I ran down the street into the cold freezing rain.

Barefoot, my body was shaking from both the fear and cold. Running right across the street, I pounded on Clarissa's door, calling out for her help.

"Help! Help! Clarissa, help me!" I remembered screaming out that night at the top of my lungs.

Begging in my mind for her to open up, for even the other neighbors to come running towards me at my calls. After a second that felt like an eternity, I gave up and ran down the street, possibly two, three houses down where I could see the lights were still on. Like Clarissa's house, I pounded on the door with all my might, again, no reply. Taking a moment to focus back towards the direction of my house, the fire was now spreading as I could see the orange glow blazing from the inside. In my burning house, a pair of eyes emerged, then a second pair, then a third; there were three of them.

A strong sense of fear rippled through my body, my heart pounded uncontrollably as I tripped, crashing down into the wet wooden steps. Weakly standing up, I took a few steps back regaining my balance as I stared towards them. Quickly turning, my legs propelling me forward down the steps, not even running down, I leapt down skipping the three steps all together. The force of the jump stung my feet as I landed, which I found both surprising and painful as I never had jump like that before. I lost track of where I was running to, all I knew was that I was running the opposite way from my house, and that was more than enough for me. How long was I running, I didn't know, all the while taking a glance back now and again, only to see those glinting eyes. I kept running; even when my legs were exhausted I kept running. When I turned around, there were now five of them. Three pair of white eyes glinted now and again, and a set of blue and yellow mixed in with them. Why did the number increase? I thought as I fell to the ground from exhaustion, scrapping both my palms against the rained soaked cement. Pushing myself back up, beginning my endless escape again, but I was tired, I couldn't last much longer. So far, every look that I took behind me propelled me forward against my limit, to strive for a continuation of my life so that I wouldn't be captured and done in like Lisa or that woman down to street. My feet was now numb, I was sure of it, I couldn't feel anything below my ankles. My hands and knees were scrapped, my lungs near the point of bursting. I couldn't run anymore, I knew this, I was moments away from collapsing, they would come, and I would disappear.

I stopped running, exhaustion had won over. Looking around, I spotted a narrow passage, something like an alleyway. I ran in, looking for somewhere to hide, but it was empty. There wasn't a single place to hide, no trash cans, no garbage bags, no boards or crevices, nothing. What was worst, I stared at three towered walls, it was a dead end. As I looked down the street, a growling howl was heard, muffled by the rain. They were much closer now, I couldn't turn back anymore. Defeated, my body limped to the end of the alley as I fell against the hard brick wall. My arms and hands were up against my face as I wept. Truthfully, I believed I was crying much earlier after running out of the house, when I started pounding against the second house, that was when I had begun to cry. It didn't matter anymore. I had thought that it was the end for me. The rain wasn't as bad now, it was still pouring down harshly, but now the wind had stopped its blowing howling screams.

Feeling their presence, I move my head away from my knees to look up. The six of them were at the end, including the one that I had stabbed the pen in its eye. They saw me and I them. Approached me, two scaling the wall to my left, two other on the right, while another two slowly approached me down the middle, which included one eye. My arms went limp against my sides, my legs sprawled apart, thinking that I would die now, I was ready for them to take me, but I was wrong. I could hear a muffled yell getting closer, growing louder. "Evan," they called out to me, the muffled scream drawing nearer. The six creatures stopped in their tracks. One eye stopped in its tracks, placing his head to the ground as did its companion besides him. Moments later, its companion next to one eye gave a long leap, clinging firmly to the wall. The other four fled out of sight with the exception of the one eye. Standing on all fours looking hatefully at me, I could tell. Even if I couldn't see its face clearly from that distance, I could see its hate in its eye, the wanting to rip me to shreds with its own two hands. The other four had already disappeared with the exception for one. The creature who took the long leap away from the one eye, now watched its friend. It exchanged words that weren't human in anyway, they were more of grunts and growls, exactly how a monster would make I thought. After a second of communication, one eye pounded the pavement with both fist repeatedly. Charging angrily at me now, his companion leapt at him with such speed, it was nearly a blur. The companion was bigger than one eye with about twice the muscular build, obviously he wasn't a match. With a powerful throw, he sent one eye up and over above the roof. Then scaling the walls, he followed, disappearing.

The call of my name was loud, much clearer now as my mother stood at the end of the alley, facing away down the street. My mother called out my name once more before turning towards my direction, now noticing me. Wanting to call out to her, no sound came out. There was only the movement of my lips. Was it exhaustion, perhaps the events of the day made me too frighten to utter any words? There was no need for me to make any sound, she saw me, after turning her head; she had seen me. Soaking wet now, blonde hair drenched, her purple dress clung to her skin. She was barefoot as I looked at her in her black coat that looked even blacker under the current weather. I could see her hands moving to her face as if she kept wiping the water from her face. I wasn't sure then if she was crying or not, she was too far and the rain made a good camouflage for tears, in fact, I wasn't sure if I was crying then either.

My mother ran towards me, relief grew in me with her every step, with each splash her bare feet would make as they made their impact against the wet ground. A little more than half way, the top of manhole behind her slid open. A large black hand rose out as dark as the night sky, its long finger much longer than any normal human's hand clung to the cement. My mother stopped running now, even though she was so close to me, she stopped to turn around to look. It came out slowly, different from the others that I had seen. This one was a much larger. Even when it hadn't fully emerged, it was already the same height as my mother. Its right hand wasn't a hand at all. Instead it was a long black blade shaped hand, directly attached to its body.

Completely emerged, the monster towered over my mother. Its physical body like the others was shaped very much like a human, with a bludgeon gut that would've seemed to been impossible to have fit through the manhole. Staring down at my mother with deep red colored eyes, they radiated a magnificent lava red glow. Giving a heinous smile extending ear to ear like the others before it, the smile of the devil I thought. Its abnormal teeth were sharp and neatly aligned unlike the others, but unevenly long. Some short stubs while others were so long that, some point of its teeth burrowed deep down into its own lips. My mother continued to stand there, frozen in silence in front of that devil spawn.

With a large quick swipe, the creature used its blade like arm and swung it at my mother. Before I knew it, she stood there at that very spot, still standing, no longer with a head. Too intent on looking at the monster, I didn't see where my precious mother's head was, instead, all I saw was my mother falling to her knees, her headless body toppling forward. A little later, I saw her decapitated head falling down front of me. I remembered the look of her eyes as I looked into them before hitting the ground. Her beautiful face rolled looking away. Parts of her hair still long, other areas now partially cut, enough still to covered her entire head.

I slowly looked back up at the monstrosity, through the gap under the creature's armpits I noticed a police officer standing at the other end, looking at us with his flashlight. His grip loosened as the light fell to the ground, out of his hand. The monster quickly looked back. Without a moment's notice, it retreated back into the manhole. Before disappearing for good, it gave a hard look at me, no longer showing its grotesque teeth. Its head finally disappearing, then its giant left hand emerged, grabbed my mother's arm, dragging her limp body down along with it. After doing so, it's long arm stretch out, reaching the cover of the manhole, moving it back into place.

Sitting alone in the rain, whatever that was left of my mother now laid a few feet from me. The officer at the other end still looking dumbfounded didn't move from where he was. The second that ghastly demon disappeared, another two officers arrived. The whistles they blew sounded for the others as they started to shout and call out for everyone to come, letting them know that I was found. Not running to me immediately, they seemed a bit more concerned with their fellow officer who stood there unmoved.

"Hey, you okay, what happened?" I remembered one of the police officer yell.

"What the hell are you doing just standing there?" The other officer yelled, but still he didn't respond, standing there dumbstruck.

Too tired now, I didn't know what to think. All I did was look at my mother, her beautiful blond golden head drenched under the pouring rain. There was so much rain that the blood quickly mixed with the water. Difficult to see, there was a slight bit of red flowing from her neck as the officer shined their lights towards me. My hand went out to touch her, my wanting to see her face once more. She was only two or three feet away from me. No longer being able to walk, I pulled my body over to her, dragging me body closer. Reaching out with my arm, I felt her wet hair. Dragging myself closer, nearly picking up her head, a police officer swiftly grabbed me forcefully.

"Don't worry okay kid, its okay now, help is here."

Looking up at the man in uniform, he was an unshaven short man, his hair was messy from the rain; he pulled out his radio and called for others. Looking at me, I turned back toward my mother. Again, my fingers wiggled themselves, trying to grasp her, this only made his grip grow tighter, hurting me.

"My mom, I want to see her," I said. My voice was cracking, weak, and pitiful.

"It's not a face you want see son," his expression was more sympathetic this time. He took me in his arms and carried me out, holding my head in his chest with great strength, as if he was making sure that I wouldn't be able to look back, to see the look on my mother's face. That was the last time I saw my mother, as a head, drenched, lying on the pavement with her hair in disarray.

I never was able to see her expression. Even at the funeral, her casket was left closed, making me wanting to see he one last time, even if it was the look of horror. Was it as bad as the officer made it out to be? Was it of shocking horror, of dread, to see such the possibility that such a monstrosity existed?

Taken to the police station, I was situated in a large office. In my wet cloths all alone, I sat half frozen, my feet in a tub of warm water, a large coat wrapped around me as I drank the hot coffee that I could barely hold. My hands, they no longer hurt nor could I feel anything from them, there was simply a tingling numbing sensation that course through my palm and fingers. It was the same for everything below my knees. Given a quick treatment as the station earlier, my wounds were wrapped sloppily by one of the secretaries who didn't seem like she knew what she was doing. A quick and temporary fix as the ambulance was having trouble getting to our location. Most of my body seemed intact and okay, except for my feet. Apparently I stepped into shards of broken glass while running away without realizing it. The one who treated me carefully remove what pieces of glass she could, gently wrapping my feet, then placing them in warm water. Not caring, I was simply too exhausted, no longer feel anything, not even the warmth that emitted from the cup I held. My feet at the moment were just something I didn't care about.

A slightly chubby short hair brunette woman came into the room carrying a towel and some dry cloths, even a pair of shoes that looked brand new.

"I have a son your age," she said standing by the door, "I hope it fits," smiling at me as she left them on the table.

I didn't feel like changing, I couldn't even if I wanted to. As I sat there I was drenched, and she had taken the effort to bring them to me. So not wanting to turn down her kindness, I asked her for some help. As I tried, my voice didn't come out, doing nothing but move my mouth. No sound, my lips quivered as I did, only to be depressed in the end. My sorrow for myself welled inside. Seeing my reaction, she must have gotten the message as she helped me dry up and change, leaving the shoes and socks off after realizing the conditions my feet were in, rolling up my pant legs so my feet could soak in the warm water some more. Once finished she patted me on the head, gave me a kiss and a hug, and left.

My father's voice sounded outside. Peering through the blinds, I saw him. He was soaked as he frantically yelled at two officers. Calmly watching my father as is face turning from relief, then moments later, shock, then utter agony. He stumbled, supporting himself against the wall as one of the officers helped support him. Continuing to watch him, his expressions of grief, I couldn't watch him cry. Feeling a spontaneous painful heat rising up in my chest, I looked away before he did.

Soon after, a man opened the door gently. Telling me that I needed to go with him, I didn't respond, so he picked me up and brought me outside to where my father was waiting for me. It was lively outside that tiny office. Some officers stared at me with pity; others were busy at their desk on the phone or the computer typing away. A commotion near the help desk broke out.

"Where is she," a man yelled. Bald headed in his late twenties, he wore a white tank top, drenched from the rain. There were tattoos visible all over his body.

I was able to see my father as well. His hands covered his face as he sat down. He was weeping. The officers around him didn't know what to do as the two of them stood there looking sympathetic.

"Sir we know this is hard, but we need to ask you a few questions," one of officers asked of my father, only to receive the sounds of this weeps.

"Leave him alone for now," said the man carrying me.

"But sir, we were told."

"Can't you follow directions, does it look like I'm asking, get the hell out of my sight!" The man carrying me yelled, interrupting the officer. Complying, the two of them quickly left.

"As you can see, your son is safe. He witnessed a terrible ordeal, but he came out of it alive, that's the good thing." Placing me down on the bench next to my father, the man stayed, standing. He waited for a second or two for my father to respond, like with the other two officers, he didn't get a reply.

Listening to his crying sounds as he tried to muffle them in his large hands, it brought tears to my eyes as well.

"I want to see her now!" the tattooed man was still there, this time he was more aggressive as he banged his fists down against the counter. Other officers around the area surrounded him, instructing him that he needed to calm down or be restrained. Lunging himself onto one of them, he was able to get one powerful punch at one of the officers before everyone was on top, pinning him to the floor.

Catching the attention of my father, he looked up at the commotion. Wiping away his tears, "Evan," I looked in the direction of his voice. He turned towards me, bent down before me, his large hands on my shoulders, touching my face, "I'm glad you're okay," trying to look enthused, his expression was more disoriented. He was a mess, red eyes, pale, he wasn't looking to good.

"Sir, we need to ask the two of you a few questions."

"Ask us questions?" My son's arms and legs are wrapped in bandages. Shouldn't you be taking him to see a proper doctor?" Saying this in calm manner, he slowly started to become angry.

"I'm sorry, but there seemed to have been some trouble on the road due to the weather, I was told that they're trying to resolve the issue to get the paramedics here as soon as possible. As of right now, in the mean time since we're here, there are some things that I would like to clarify with you and you're son."

"Fine, lets' make this quick and get this over with."

"If you can follow me," instructing my father as the officer picked me up in his arms once more. "It's not exactly the best room for this kind of situation, but it gives us privacy and it's pretty much the only thing we got. "It's right over here," leading us down the hallways.

The man led us to an interrogation room. Having only seeing it from the television box in my home, a part of me felt like a criminal. The small white painted room was much brighter than I originally imagined. All four walls were white, dirty with some noticeable dried blood stains here and there. Looking at the large mirror, it made me wonder if others were looking through, perhaps my father was since he didn't come in with me. The table was squared, beaten with scratch marks from over the years. Placing me on the table, the detective came back with a better more comfortable chair made of brown leather, which he then sat me in.

"Well, I haven't introduced myself, I'm detective Matthew Harvey, but you can call me Mr. Harvey," he said on one knee.

He must have gotten tired as he quickly stood up grunting difficultly as he pulled another chair around to sit directly in front of me. His chair was made out of hard metal without padding. It screeched and scratched the floor as he pulled it along. It was understandable for him to need a seat. He was showing gray in his hair, looking around the age of sixty-five.

"Listen kid," he paused, "Evan, we know that some," again he paused, his facial features was telling me that he was thinking of right words to say to a child my age, trying to be both considerate and careful with his words. "Difficult things had just happened to you," he continued. Once more he didn't say anything for a moment, this started to bother me. "We know you don't want to remember about what just happened, but we, the, 'good guys' need to know what went on so we can help you, so we can capture those bad terrible men."

I wanted to clench my pants, the pants that the nice woman had given me earlier. I couldn't since the feeling from my hands hadn't yet return. Instead, I diverted my eyes downwards. Feeling the tears rolling down my cheeks, doing my best to hold them in, but they came and came in an endless stream.

"It's okay, you don't need to force yourself," placing a hand on my own, I suppose he figured it wasn't enough, so the detective got up, hugging me in his big burly arms.

Wanting to speak, my voice wouldn't come out. Trying once more, still nothing, finally a third time, "I saw it." My voice was high pitched, cracking, making me sound weak like the tearing child I was. Surprise, Mr. Harvey stood straight, moving backwards as he sat down again. I didn't look at his face.

"One of them was in the house," I began to speak. "One of them was outside my window, so I ran to Lisa's room because I was scared, but the one inside was waiting." The liquids still poured down my face as my voice became steadier. "It clung above the door, and when Lisa came out, it jump down and ate her." Looking up at the officer, he was expressionless. Continuing my story, "I ran into the closet and found a pen and dad's lighter. It was dark, so I used the lighter and I saw the monster on the other side. One of the jackets was on fire and the door opened, and I saw he monster, then

I ran outside." At that moment I wanted to explain it clearer, how I stabbed the creature in the eye with the pen, how I threw the flaming coat on it. Even how before it jumped down onto Lisa, I wanted to describe the evil stare that *thing* had made, looking at me in such a menacing way before attacking Lisa. Those words never came, not being able to come up with the words at that time due to lack of vocabulary, and being put in such a flustered questioning position, I omitted those parts, explaining what I could.

"There were six, one with blue eye, two with yellow, and three with white." Seeing if my words had any impact on Mr. Harvey, he sat forward looking quite serious, intently looking at me, analyzing me for any and all details.

"Tell me what happened next," he said.

"I was running, and then I was really tired so I tried to hide."

"Like hide-and-seek," the detective interrupted me.

I shook my head. "I hid in the corner," which I really meant was the dead end alleyway, but it seemed like the detective had understood what I had meant. "I ran into the space and the six saw me. Some climbed the walls, and then I heard my mom calling me. The six monsters stopped and they ran away. Then mom saw me, and she ran to me, after that, a really, really, really big monster can out from the hole in the ground with really red eyes, and he, he took mommy." Crying harder, I tried to wipe my tears on my bandaged hands. Mr. Harvey left the room to come back moments later with a box of tissue, assisting me to wipe my face with one. This lasted for quite some time before another officer came in.

"The paramedics just arrived, they're waiting outside at the front desk for the kid," the new officer said.

"Okay, let them know I'll take him over in five," said the detective. Mr. Harvey turned his attention back at me as the officer closed the door. "That's okay Evan, that's enough; you don't need to say anymore. Did you get a look at these, 'monsters,' Evan? Did you see what these five individuals and the one that took your mom appearance?" He must have been pressed on time now and wanted to get straight to the point.

My hands shook with fear as the demonic faces smiled in my head. I nodded, "the six were small like me, and the other one was really big. One arm was really long and pointy, and he had a really big smile and teeth, also, he was naked."

"Evan, one of my men said that he saw him too, but I just want to be sure. Was the man who took your mom as tall as me?" Standing up as a measurement, I shook my head. He was roughly six foot as he then raised his hand above his head, an extra foot or so. "Was he this tall," he asked, and again I shook my head no. Once again, he raised his hand all the way up as much as he could, "how about now," he asked with skepticism.

Shaking my head once more, "no, he was bigger," I said in a low voice.

"Okay, okay, one more question Evan," taking a seat again. "What color was he, was he as dark like my pants, or was he lighter like your pants." He was wearing black dress pants and I had a dark brown. I slowly pointed to his and he shook his head. "Okay, wait here."

Making a gesture to the mirror, moments later, two officers came in with my dad. "Well, it's was pretty vague, but I guess it matches the description Henry told us," the detective said.

Henry, who was Henry? I looked around, finally seeing the officer standing behind my dad. When I looked at him, he immediately averted his gaze. It was him, the officer who saw the demon that took my mother. It was the officer who had stood at the other end of the alley, frozen as he had watched the horrid giant take my mother's body away.

"We're have a description of one of the perpetrators, we're for a large black male, without clothing, extremely dangerous, carrying a large blade like object, possible seven foot or taller," Mr. Harvey said, giving the description of the suspect to his men. "He might be working with six others, a mix of nationalities." They had it wrong; they mistook the colors that I was describing. They weren't anything human.

"No!" I shouted. "It was a monster," I said as I got off my chair, screaming out to the detective as I fell to the floor. "Ask him," yelling out, pleading as I point to the officer behind my dad, the only witness I had. He knew it, he knew it wasn't human, it wasn't anything anybody knew or seen before, nothing from this world. My father came to my side to pick me up as I struggled in his arms.

Henry stood there nervously as everyone stared at him, waiting for his response. Sweat started to build up on his face, his eyes continued to shift from me to the others. "It was a large African male, standing about seven feet, maybe taller," he said stuttering, "I didn't get a look at his face or at the others."

"He's lying!" I shouted again, "it was a monster, Mr. Harvey, it was a monster!" Shouting again, I tried leaping out of my father's arms which I successfully did. My numb legs once again failed me as I fell to the floor again. The detective quickly tried helping me up, but I fought against him in a craze, "no, he's lying; it was a monster, a monster!"

A useless struggle, my message never reached out to them. After my outcry, the paramedics examined me, patching me up as best as they could before taking me to the hospital for additional checkups and to take out the remaining glass from my feet. Once verifying that my health condition was good, my father had taken us to Clarissa's house. We were going to stay there for a while until we found new housing since we could no longer go back to our burned down home. It was easier I supposed, she was right across from us, a close friend of my parents and had plenty of room in her home to accommodate the two of us. Temporary, but it made me nervous having to stay across my burnt home.

Not being able to sleep, my chest and stomach ached as I thought of Lisa and my mother, as well as being stricken with fear. Paranoia developed in me as I took caution to every sound, staying awake all night sometimes, even after morning sun. That was how it was in the beginning, suffering from insomnia. When sleep did take over, it was for only an hour or two before silently waking from a nightmare. The first time, I had stayed up for three whole days before I eventually collapsed in Clarissa's kitchen floor. This caused Clarissa to panic when she got home from work, driving me straight to the hospital where I awoken, only to be driven back to Clarissa's that very night.

A knock on the door, "Evan, it's me," it was Clarissa. "I made some lunch, do you feel like eating?" A moment of silence before the doorknob turn as I quickly faced away, pretending to sleep. I didn't feel like eating, only wanting to be left alone. The door opened as I heard her entering, trying to be as quietly as possible as she placed the plate on the nightstand next to me before she left.

Once I heard the door close shut, I looked back to see the sandwich that she left for me. It was nicely put together; she had even cut off the crust. Getting out of bed, I moved toward the window. Outside was so still clouded, but it was bright. I knew I was wasting away as I was, even at that young of an age, I knew that there wasn't much point in lying in bed all day. In fact, it bored me, as it only gave me time to remember things that I didn't want to. My stomach grumbled, so I decided to take the food and eat down below. As I opened the door to my bedroom, the doorbell rang, making me stop in place.

"Hi gorgeous, I brought a casserole and some cookies," a familiar female voice, but I couldn't quite remember who it belonged to.

"You're too kind, I just made some lunch, how about joining me?"

"I'm not too hungry, but I could use some coffee."

"You're just in time then, I just brewed a fresh batch." I could imagine Clarissa giving a big welcoming smile as she said this.

Great, I wasn't in the mood to meet others, to meet their sympathetic stares. I would have to wait for the woman to leave if I wanted to go down now. So I exited the room and sat upstairs with the plate instead, keeping out of their view.

"So, how is everyone doing?" The woman whispered, though the large house only made it easy to hear them, still I strained my ears to listen in.

"Well," Clarissa paused, "Chris is out right now looking for a new place, getting things in order you know? He told me he found a really good place just recently and is getting the papers done. As for Evan, well, he's young, and frankly I'm not too sure. I just feel so bad for him. I remember how he first came here, looked just so awful. When he came here, he was so depressed. His body was so battered and bruised, that he couldn't even stand up. His body healed up really good, he can move around and about, but you can see that he's still pretty stricken from the whole event. Right now he's upstairs sleeping. He's awfully pale, and I don't think he's getting enough rest, he has these heavy circles under his eyes and it's making me really worried for his health."

"I see, yeah, it is probably hard on him, losing his mother and sister I mean. I was actually hoping to see Evan, but maybe another time."

"Katie, what's wrong."

So her name was Katie. Remembering her now, she was one of the neighbors living down the street as well as close friend of my dear mother. Not as close as Clarissa and my mother was, but still a good friend. Katie was always one of the few women Clarissa and my mother would call up for their random ladies night.

"Actually, I came because I wanted to apologize to him, I kind of feel responsible for Alina's death."

"Oh sweetie, come here, what did you do, you didn't do anything wrong, you weren't anywhere near the place when the tragedy happened."

"If I didn't tell her, maybe she wouldn't have had to die."

"What are you saying, didn't tell her what?"

"During that night, I had thought I heard a loud banging on my door, hearing someone calling for help. So I went out to the front to check it out, but there wasn't anyone there. That's when I saw the fire from their house and ran outside in a panic. I took another look around and saw someone running right around the corner."

Her words made me choke on the food as I tried to muffle my cough as best I could. Placing the food down, I gripped the edge of the stairs to listen harder. My fist clenched the railing tightly as I waited for her to continue.

"Of course I ran back inside and called the police station. As I did, I ran back out only to see Chris and Alina just getting back. I still remember seeing her getting out of her car, screaming, wanting to rush into the house as Chris held her back. Poor Alina was in a panic, she was hysterical. When I approached them both, Chris pushed Alina toward me and told me to hold her as he ran back into the house. Watching her so shaken an in a panic, and I recalled the banging on the door from earlier, and of some person running around the corner. I mean, I guessed that it might have been either Lisa or Evan, or maybe both." She gave a long pause as I could hear her taking a moment. My tears started to well up in my eyes as I listened.

"I told her it would be okay, that I thought I saw someone running around the corner a while ago, that it might have just been Evan and Lisa, maybe, perhaps, the both of them had gotten out okay. I mean it looked like it was a kid running, but I wasn't sure.

When Alina heard me say that, she burst out of my arms towards that direction. I'm not sure. I think about a minute later, two patrol cars came by pulling up, so I frantically told them about Chris and Alina. Three of the four officers noticed Chris in the house, so they ran inside together, dragging him out kicking and screaming, while another ran after Alina. He was so emotional, Chris, I still remember how hard he was fighting against those officers. He shouted at them as they dragged him out, even punching two of them, knocking one of them to the floor before he was forced down."

"It's alright, come here, it isn't your fault Katie, you didn't do anything wrong, you hear me."

"I kept telling myself that, but if I had gotten to the door a bit earlier, then maybe I could have helped Evan, maybe if I didn't tell Alina that I saw Evan, she wouldn't have run after him, and," she didn't finish.

"Katie, think of it this way, if it wasn't for you, than Evan might not be here instead. If you hadn't told Alina that you had saw Evan running around that corner, that she might not have run after him and he would have died instead. I know Alina; she would've chosen Evan over herself any day."

So that was how my mother and the others had found me. Before I figured it was just a miracle, dumb random luck, or perhaps that it was my mother's poor luck to have been able to find me, even after I had ran so far. Because of this woman, because of Katie, I was saved moments from being consumed, but instead, my dear, dear mother had died in my place. I wasn't sure whether to be grateful towards this woman or if I should've hated her. I knew I hated myself though. Not doing anything, I continued to listen to woman blaming herself as Clarissa tried her best to sooth her sadness.

CHAPTER

8

Waking up, I felt my forehead, now a bit dampened with my sweat. That was quite a dream of the past, I thought, one that I hadn't had in a long time. I wondered why I had remembered it now, must've been of what I told Alice and Lily the other day, about what I was afraid of. Getting out of bed, I opened then curtains and stood there for a few seconds, embracing the warm yellow rays of the sunlight again, wishing for the glorious blaze in the sky to never set.

Standing in front of the mirror, I closed my eyes, remembering instantaneously the unpleasant memories again. Remembering how my father slowly became more and more depressed and distant. Those days were he tried forcing a laugh on his face, pretending to have a good time when I knew he was wearily getting tired of his daily existence. He became less and less cheerful towards me, until one day it seemed to me that he simply just stopped trying to care, stopped trying all together. No more, "how was your day," wanting to hang out only us two men, male bonding between father and son ceased. The happiness stopped as well as his love, soon only to grow so apart that we now barely talk to one another.

Always wondering whether it was because I reminded him of how things use to be, I somehow figured that he blamed me, after all, I did, so why wouldn't he. From what happened, I was the one that started the fire, burning down our house. I remembered how he told Clarissa in his grief one night, how he couldn't even recognize Lisa's body, it was burnt beyond recognition. Just hearing that Lisa's body was still there surprised me, I had figured that whatever those creatures were, they would've taken her body. It might have been that I had distracted their attention. Too occupied with capturing me, they gave up on Lisa's body all together. Well, who know what the real reason was, I didn't know how those *things* operated.

Then there was my mother, his wife. If I hadn't run off, perhaps she wouldn't have run after me, only to be left with nothing more than just a decapitated head. My father had fallen head over heels for my mother, that's how I had remembered him telling us, that he would never love another woman as much as her. He would still smile with Clarissa, his new wife, but it wasn't the same, not like how he would have smiled at my mother, and this made me sad to see every time.

I could see images of my father drinking every now and again, never to the extent where he would lose all reason. He drank calmly, very slowly, stopping altogether when he felt like it was too much. The days after had passed by, one after another. Still going to school, however, twice a week after the incident, I had appointments with a therapist, never missing a day until I was fifteen. Even when I was away, we still had our sessions over the phone or now with the latest technology, live video sessions. It wasn't until I confronted both Clarissa and my father that I felt that going to therapy wasn't going to help me anymore. That what I had learned from the last few sessions weren't helping me. I wanted to try and find a solution for my own problems myself.

Yes, growing up afterwards was indeed difficult. In the beginning, everyday was such a struggle, that even at such a young age, I had often thought of suicide. I knew of various ways to kill myself, even at such a young age, gaining the knowledge from various television shows. There were times I thought I could just hang myself, or consume rat poison. Now that I think about it, I never should have watched all of those bad television shows at such a young age, they really were a bad influence on young minds. Perhaps it was just me and all of the problems that I had.

It didn't come to a surprise to me when I came to school and both Alice and Lily would only give me a wave or a smile as I passed them in the halls and in the classrooms. I supposed that it was to be expected. Usually, people would be afraid of spiders or clowns, I was a grown teenage senior still fearful of the dark night outside.

As the day ended, I casually walked to my bike, no longer needing to rush to avoid Alice as I figured she would now avoid me. She didn't. Alice approached me from the front entrance of the school. "Evan, can I talk to you," she asked, stopping me right as I exited the front of the building. "If you don't have any plans tonight, so let's do something."

My eyes widened, shuffling with the words in my head. "Uh," was the only thing that came out.

She chuckled, "wow, I don't really see you so speechless too often. Listen, I know you don't have anything to do tonight, so lets' do something." She continued to talk as we move to the side to make room so that the other students could come and go from the building. "I mean, I know you're not comfortable going out at night, but think about it as a step towards getting better."

"Listen, I appreciate the offer, but why at night? I'm sure," she intervened before could utter another word. As she did, I felt uncomfortable and angry, not at her, but at myself. Having said those words out loud made feel me ashamed; a bit disgusted at myself for trying to weasel out.

"Oh why not," she began, but I stopped her.

"Alice, you're right, maybe it's about time I stopped acting like a kid."

She smiled at me and nodded, "okay then, I'll pick you up at eight?"

"You bet," I replied as she headed to her car. I was relieved, and at the same time, happy that she hadn't shun me, to not think that I was overly strange or pathetic enough to, 'hang,' with. She was a good person, and perhaps I didn't give her enough credit.

Night fell as Alice rung the door bell. She was a little early, and I was nervous. Opening the door, she stood outside wearing some jean pants, long sleeve sweater, scarf, and a heavy looking jacket, she still seemed cold. Outside was freezing.

"If you're cold, you're welcome to come in for a bit."

"A little bit cold, but I'm more or less fine. The car has a heater, so hurry up and lets' go, no postponing," she headed to the car as I followed along.

Jumping into the vehicle, it was still cozy warm. This time I was much more relaxed than the last time I had gone out at night. A bit tensed still, however, my could feel that my anxiety wasn't as great as before.

"So, were exactly are we going," inquiring after some time had passed.

"Actually, I thought that we could just hang for a bit at the Cafe Lux where Lily's working, so free coffee and snacks."

"Thank god, I figured we were going to do something drastic like hiking in the middle of the night."

"Hiking in the middle of the night? What do we look like, some mountaineers to you? I know you don't like coming out after sunset, so I'm not evil enough to throw you into the ocean when you can barely swim. I'm capable of taking things slow you know. Well, maybe I am just a teensy bit evil. I have to confess, me and Jason just broke up, so I'm kind of using you two kill some of my free time."

"I'm sorry to hear about Jason, I thought everything was good between the two of you."

"No need to be sorry, I was the one who broke up with him. As you experienced firsthand, he can be a really big jerk at times, I suppose I eventually had enough. Being with him for a while, I realized that I wanted someone who really knew me, knew how to respect me as a woman, someone that was both gentle and kind. As she said this, her voice sounded shy, a bit awkward as she stroked her hair gently back. We didn't talk much after that, only making little comments here and there along the way.

Cafe Lux was the same as I had remembered, emptier this time around with Lily in the back leaning on the counter, skimming through a magazine, looking bored without much care. As the both of us headed to the counter, Lily took notice of us. As she did, she made her way back behind the counter and started working.

"Hey, you trying to ignore us," Alice said.

"I'm not, give me a moment would you, and keep your voice down. It's not really crowded right now, but there's not enough background noise where you need to shout like a mad woman, you'll bother the other customers," retorting back, still fiddling away behind the counter. Moments later, she turned and placed two coffee mugs in front of us with a giant muffin. Lily then stood up with both hands folded, leaning over the counter. "Good to see you out and about," directing the comment towards me with a smirk.

"Thanks, by the way, what's this, we haven't ordered anything?" I asked a bit puzzled as I looked at items.

"You're kind of slow," Alice said. "It's ours, on the house."

"Yes, that's right. It's for the two of you. I'm sorry, you're right though, did you want something else?" Lily said stumbling with her words.

Quickly, I took a sip of the coffee burning my mouth as I did, "its perfect, thanks."

"You'll get used her going off randomly on her own, but honestly, you really don't have much customer service skills."

"You say this, but this is your usual, and I kind of figured Evan might actually like this kind of coffee as well. Besides, unlike him, you've been here almost every other day, so you of all people shouldn't be complaining. If you two don't like the coffee, too bad, don't complain when I'm being nice. I'm sure you'll like the muffin though, most people usually do."

Both Alice and I seated ourselves as Lily helped the customer that arrived behind us. The two of us talked for a little while, this time I was being more attentive, responding and contributing to the conversation more often than I usually would have. Perhaps it was me, but Alice seemed a bit happier than she normally was, as was I. Being in this place, out at night, it felt good to be with others, to enjoy another's company, just having a good time without much worry. This really helped take my mind off of things.

It had been roughly half an hour since the two of us came in, each on our second cup of coffee. "Wait here a minute," Alice said as she walked back to Lily. A minute later she came back, "let's head out."

"Okay, sure, but where are we going?"

"Well, are you hungry, because I am, I could use a bite to eat? I mean the muffin was good, I'd admit, but it didn't really fill me up."

"Now that you mention it, I am a bit," I replied as I could feel my near empty stomach grumble the more I thought about it.

"Good, Lily had a feeling you wouldn't have eaten anything before you left."

"Oh, is she coming with us," I said as we started to head outside.

"Well, the girl that's suppose switch off with her isn't here yet, so she told us to just go ahead for now and she'll meet us there later. The restaurant is about four blocks away. In case you're wondering, it's a nice Chinese place, you good with Chinese food?" Opened the door, Alice shivered from the cold air while I felt nervous again.

"Yeah, it's fine," was all I could say.

Walking, we got closer to the car as the relief welled up in me as we did. As I approached the car, Alice kept walking. She noticed my reaction and faced me, questioning what I was doing.

"Didn't I say it was only four blocks away? You were suppose to come out tonight to help relieve a bit of your anxiety remember, or is walking the short distance really too much." Coming towards me, she grabbed my hand to pull me along.

I frowned as my stomach tightened. "I guess you're right, four blocks isn't that far," mustering the nerve to say.

At the end of the first two blocks, a group of rambunctious jocks appeared around the corner, a few of them carrying bear bottles. They were from our school I realized after seeing a few of their faces. I than grumbled when I saw Jason, which I knew it meant trouble for both Alice and I. We withdrew our hands at the same time the moment we saw him, stuffing them back into our jackets immediately. I could see Alice looking at me wearily as I darted my eyes around, looking for a plausible escape. There was a one store opened close to us a few feet away, thinking that we could hide inside and wait for them to walk by, but it was much too late. The group turned towards us, one of the guys carrying the case of alcohol made eye contact with us, muttering something towards the others. Soon, they all looked in our direction. That wasn't a good response. They started muttering something with one another. After a few moments, they refocused their attention at us.

"Looks like we're in trouble," I said to Alice, she didn't respond. Instead of being worried like me, she was perfectly normal, in fact, she seemed bursting with confidence.

The two of us stood in place as we watch them approach us. The group didn't talk anymore as they made their destination for us. Jason on the other hand who was in front looked at me with disgust, as if he was ready to knock out a few of my teeth the moment he was in range. Coming closer with every step, for a moment, I had hoped maybe one of them would stop the others, for something, anything to happen to help the two of us get out of this situation.

"Hey you two," Jason shouted out, one of the guys in the back started shaking his head.

"Dude, we told you to just ignore them, come on man," another one of the jocks said.

"Good to see you Alice," Jason said, ignoring me and his friend's advice.

"Hey Jason, good to see the rest of you guys as well," replied

Alice, the others nodding their heads while a few replied nervously back.

"So, you're dating this guy now, huh?" Not even bothering to look at me, he continued to glare down at Alice.

"His name is Evan, and," Alice was interrupted.

"It's only been two days," Jason shouted suddenly, surprising everyone including me. Despite his loud intimidation, Alice was the only one who stood strong, unflinching.

I wondered how she did it, to have remained so calm, at ease with the circumstance. Perhaps it was because she knew Jason so well. Maybe she figured that nothing would actually happen. If Jason did decided to do anything, I wouldn't be able to stop him, even if the others did try to help and stop him, he was built, large masses of muscle ripped through his body. His veins were popping out with anger as he stood there.

As I watched Alice face the tantrum of her ill tempered muscle brain ex, a strong shiver ran through me as if fear was penetrating my very core. I could feel a cold hard stare, one I felt a long time ago. It was familiar, and I knew where I felt it before. I wanted to turn around, to look behind me; I didn't. Too afraid, it could have also been due to the commotion going on in front of me, distracting my attention from immediately fleeing. No, it wasn't that everyone was distracting my attention to runaway. It was because I felt safer with all of them. If those vile beings were there, watching me in the shadows, than I might just be safer if everyone was together. It was at that point, I'd rather Jason beat me half to death than have *them* kill me altogether.

"Two days Alice, its' only been two days and you're already going off with this guy! Tell me, you like this guy don't you?" Jason seemed larger as he flexed his muscles in anger. The red veins in his eyes were more visible as his anger grew. I could see them gloss over under the street light as they focused solely on me. "Answer me!" throwing his beer can to the floor as the liquid sputtered everywhere. The carbon made a fizzling noise on the cement.

Not batting an eye, Alice stood high and mighty. "We're not going out Jason. Evan and I are just two good friends hanging out, that's it. There are actually three of us, Lily is actually on her way right now, and she should actually be here soon."

Her words seemed to have had an opposite effect. Seeing his anger growing, his jaw moved as he grinded his teeth. There wasn't anything else Alice could say. Watching, everyone saw Jason so angry and drunk, we all could see that he wanted to hit Alice. Unsure if he was going to do so or not, I didn't want to see Alice to possibly get physically harmed, so I moved in front of her to protect her.

"She's right, we're not a couple, in fact I'm seeing someone right now," saying it as normally as I could, thinking that he might just calm down a bit. The same time, I kept my senses alert still, in case there was a chance that something out there had its watchful eyes on us.

"You shut the hell up!" he yelled as his fist flew towards my jaw.

Watching his arm draw back, I was at least able to raise my left arm in the nick of time before his fist fully hit my jaw. It made me fly to the side as I clung to the nearby wall for some support. His blow was heavy as if a car had just hit me. Getting up, I looked back, ready to receive more blows, but his friends were already holding him back. Alice held my face up with one hand to look to see if I was okay.

Alice turned back at the group, "I'm glad I broke up with you, this is exactly the reason why. I told you I couldn't stand your crap anymore Jason, I've just had enough of having to deal with you. If you think acting this way makes you look tough, you're wrong; it only makes you look weak and a pathetic loser. You're too overly jealous, and you cling on to me like I'm your protective blanket or something."

Her voice was loud and clear in the cold night air. Her shouting seem to have gotten through to him. At the same time, his friends looked at her stunned, as if never seeing this side of her which they might not have. As if it was the first time they heard her shout out in anger.

"It's over Jason, I'm free now, I'm going to see who I want, when I want, the same goes for you, don't come near me anymore."

"So you are going out with him," he said wearily in normal tone, his friends still holding onto him, even tighter now.

"I told you we aren't, didn't I, we're just hanging out, and like he said, he's already seeing someone."

"Bunch of bull and you know it, who's he seeing, Lily? That arrogant stuck up woman think she's too good for anyone?

"No," another voice came from the shadows out in the distance, "I only act that way because dumb idiots like you annoy the hell out of me, that occasionally includes you too Alice. As I turned around, Lily was walking into the light, coming closer, but I wasn't concern about her now. Instead, I looked behind her, to see whatever that made me feel so uncomfortable before was there. No, I didn't see anything, no shadow, no glow, no eyes staring at me as if it was coming for my life. My imagination I thought, however, I didn't feel at ease, not even in the slightest. I could still feel it; *it* was watching me, like the invisible darkness drowning out the light, inching towards my life.

"Lily, how long have you been here?" I asked.

"Just got here, these jocks over here saw me walking towards you guys a mile away. I came over as soon as I saw what was happening. You know, I'm actually really glad that you finally broke up with that clinging gorilla."

The anger filled in Jason's face again as he struggled to get his friends hands off of him. "Let go, I'm telling you guys to let me go!" They did, but they stood poised, much more ready than before to stop him.

Lily walked towards me and placed her hand under my chin, forcibly turning my head to the side, getting a good look. "You seem okay, are you okay?" she asked me. I didn't respond as I was still somewhat out of it from the strong blow earlier, even if I did block it with my arm. "Good enough I suppose," then Lily kissed me hard on the lips.

Surprised, but I knew immediately that she was acting, she must've heard us earlier, so I acted normally, enjoying her soft lips until she released me. "My arm's in a lot of pain, but I'll survive." A thought came into my head as I smiled. "Maybe if could kiss me again, I could forget about the pain entirely."

I could see Lily's looking unsure of what I was asking. She laughed then nodded. I took a glimpse at the others as they simply stood to the side, watching us, Alice especially was baffled. Lily this time moved in again, this time lifted my arm up, and kissed it. Not exactly what I was hoping from her.

"There's a crowd behind me you know, this isn't the time for dirty thoughts," Lily said to me. Turing around, facing everyone, "we're going out, Evan didn't lie when he said he was seeing someone. I'm also Alice's best friend, so it isn't unusual for her to be friendly with my boyfriend now is it?"

Jason looked at me with calm, he wasn't fooled. "You better watch your back, guy," he said as another person from his group placed his hand on his shoulder. He darted a look of disgust at the guy making him remove his hand right away.

"Hey man, lets' go back to my house, well stop by a liquor store on our way back, get some food, you can drink and eat it off."

"Yeah, sounds good, you're treating though," the others in his group joined in, trying to lighted the tension. "Come on," they said, one of them nudging him as another wrapped his arm around Jason's shoulder, trying to move him along. He followed. After few steps, he glared back at me before making his way out of sight.

Once the pack was out of view, Alice turned towards Lily and I, who were silently waiting. "Sorry about those guys, I didn't expect a scene like that."

"You don't need to say that to me, I'm pretty used to you causing me trouble," Lily said, giving a comforting smile. Alice hugged her as Lily looked bothered by it.

Releasing Lily, Alice faced me again, "again, sorry, I mean, you got hit because of me."

"Don't worry about it, I'm just glad you're safe and that the situation was resolved." The air suddenly felt stiffer, something was coming, getting closer to the three of us. I felt it, so sure of it that I was on the verge of a near panic. I had to get out of here, now. "So much for getting rid of my fear of the dark, I think this little event might've traumatized all over again. How are you going to cure me at this rate?" I said while giving Alice a joking smile, hoping to bring back her normal happy self.

"I'll try extra hard to help you then," Alice said back.

"In the mean time, I'm starved. Why don't we head out to that meal we should've been eating by now," I said, hurrying things along.

"Yeah, hey, it's my treat tonight, alright guys?" Alice wrapped her arms with Lily as we all started walking the short distance.

Once inside, the unnerving feeling went away. My body released itself of the uneasy feeling. Staring back, I saw nothing through the glass door, nothing was there. My imagination I suppose, it had to be. It was illogical for them to suddenly come out and attack me now, so suddenly after so much time had passed.

Taking our seat, I pushed the thought of evil beings coming for my life out of my mind. As I made eye contact with Lily, I starting to think about her soft lips against mine, it was hard not to show how happy I was about it.

"You can stop being so overjoyed," Lily said, noticing my glee. "That was a one-time event, the situation called for it."

Alice looked at the two of us, "so how was it?" Alice asked me.

"I'd never seen Lily kiss anyone before, actually she never even dated anyone let alone kiss, so I'm pretty surprised how experienced she looked."

"It was good, softest lips I've ever had. Why don't we move along and order our food?" I said trying to move the conversation along as the question made me uncomfortable. This only made them both giggle at my embarrassment.

"I never took you as a guy who was this shy about making out," Lily teased. "Besides, weren't you asking me just moments ago for a second kiss? A bit late to be shy now isn't it?"

"Okay, well did you like making out with me?"

"I did, it actually gets me thinking that should start making out with boys more often."

"You definitely should," Alice joined, "I was actually a bit worried that you hated all men."

"I only hate dumb men like those we just ran in to, especially the guys at our school. I can't wait until we graduate so I can meet some mentally mature people."

"That's pretty harsh, that means that Alice and I aren't people you'd like to hang out with."

"Um, why don't we just order," Lily said jokingly, giving us a decent laugh.

We didn't mention about what had happened regarding our run in with Jason that night. We simply had a good time while enjoying each other's company. After the meal, we left the restaurant. The moment I stepped outside, I felt the pressure again, not as strong as before, but it was there. As we walked back to Alice's car, Lily took off towards her own vehicle.

'What is this feeling, it really my imagination?'

Getting into Alice's car, she drove me home. Once home, it was on my mind for the rest of the night, it ruined whatever good time I did had, not even the thought of Lily's rosy lips helped.

CHAPTER

9

Since yesterday, I couldn't help but constantly be agitated. Constantly worrying, peering around the corners in the shadows, I became paranoid at everything. As I sat in my second period, I couldn't concentrate on anything the teacher was saying. There was no point to listening to her tedious lecture anyway. The material was all covered in the book. Her voice irritated my eardrums. It was louder than usual. Mrs. Burgundy was her name, she'd been teaching at the school for the past nine years. Watching her red curly hair, overly large glasses, she was a pudgy woman that dressed and looked like she was a teacher back from the 60s. I watched her large lips move in slow motion. Her red lipstick was smeared just a tiny bit. Something was wrong with me, panic was taking over. I needed to calm down, to think straight. Using the rest of first period, I spent the remaining time to calm my nerves, inhaling, exhaling.

"Evan, what happened," the guy next to me asked. Hair cleanly cut and neatly done, his name was Jeremy, a real nice guy. Being both smart and athletic, he was considerate of others while at the same time comical, making getting along with others fairly easy for him. You could say he was the male version of Alice, the good thing about him was that he didn't talk as much, in fact, unlike the others, I didn't mind having him around from time to time.

"There's nothing to worry about," I smiled as I gestured towards the front of the class where the teacher was eyeballing us now. Jeremy nodded at me, getting the message.

Class ended. Before I got out my seat, Jeremy was already standing up next to me. "So, from what I heard, you got into some trouble with Jason."

"I'm amazed, rumors travel fast," I replied back. Having the rumors spread about my run-in with Jason last night made me feel even more on edge than I already was.

I had always tried to keep out of gossips and rumors. I supposed I didn't want any unwanted attention, having my fill of it during my younger days. Being reminded of last night, I felt my arm which was now covered up with a long sleeve shirt. My arm was now a purplish bruise from Jason's monstrous punch from last night. It felt fine in itself, I could do everything like usual, the only time it did hurt was when I applied some pressure.

"So, what about it," I said, getting up as I headed for my next class. "I don't exactly know you that well, but you don't seem like the guy for gossip."

Jeremy smirked, "you know me pretty well when you don't know me at all. I guess that's one of the reasons why the girls like you."

His comment made me grin.

"So, the rumors are saying that you're going out with either Alice or Lily, but," he paused looking at me uneasily, "uh, no one really knows."

Arriving to my class, we still had a good amount of time left before the bell for the start of the class rang. "Let me guess, you're attracted to Alice?" Catching him off guard, he didn't respond, standing there, twitchy. I assumed it was due to the fact that he wasn't sure if I was dating her or not. It could have been that he didn't want to admit it in front of me if Alice and I were going out. "You really don't need to be so surprised, rumors you know, they spread pretty fast," giving him a slap on the back, though it was an obvious fact that I didn't need to hear from others to know. I knew that he had liked Alice for a while now, with how he'd always awkwardly talk with her compared to other girls at school.

"Yeah, I do," replying back weakly. "Okay, to put it bluntly, I do like Alice. I have since we've been in middle school. Now that the Hulk is out of the way, I was hoping, I guess you could say I was hoping to, 'make my move,' and wanted to know if you're in my way."

He did have a dilemma since Alice did show some interest in me I knew. "You don't need worry about me, if you want to ask someone out, just do it," reply back to him. Starting to move inside the classroom, I had wanted to end the conversation. I wasn't in the mood to discuss about his crush on Alice with him. What I wanted to do was relax, calm my nerves and figure out what to do about my fears and what I felt might be watching me last night.

"Everyone knows that Alice likes you."

He grabbed my arm, stopping me, which made me highly irritated with him at this point.

"I'm sure you're noticed it too, you're not dumb Evan, she has feelings for you and you must've known about it for a while now. I just wanted to know whether or not I should move on before prom, you know? She likes you, but if you won't go out with her, than I want to, at least want to try before we graduate." He released my arm, waiting for my response, needing the verification from my own mouth.

Alice never seemed to stop causing me problems I thought, even when she isn't even here, there was some sort of trouble that involved her. I gave him a warm comforting laugh. "Listen, yes I know how she feels about me, and I've tried keeping my distance, I really have, but she has a way of catching me off guard. The most I can do is reassure you, Alice and I will not be in going out, I just don't feel that way about her." Again, I tried to leave, but his expression showed that he still wasn't satisfied. Time was limited as he wanted to keep talking. I gave a sigh, "no, we're not going out, I'm going out with someone else right now."

"I heard about it, you mean Lily?" he asked. "I didn't believe it when I heard about it, since, her personality isn't what I would call friendly, but I'd have to admit, she is attractive."

"Yes," I continued, "I am going out with Lily, so spread that around would you."

Turning around towards class, it had seemed that he was now contempt with my response. Leaving him behind, I did wonder what he was going to do now. Would he gather the courage to ask her out? I would've guessed that the chances were not too good for him as I was in the way. Prom was coming up in a few months, so he might actually have a shot then, as I knew Alice's personality fairly well by now. Prom was something she would definitely did not want to miss. This was her adolescent teenage dream, of the importance of prom, the needing, the wanting to go no matter what.

Lunch came around quickly as I sat quietly on the bench beneath the big maple tree again. A perfect spot I thought once more as it helped relax my anxiety over last night. Away from the crowds, cool shade, lots of room. The mixture of orange and red blended, moving the leaves as a small breeze blew. My eyes caught Lily approaching around from the side, carrying a small paper brown bag. It felt good to know that she was once again comfortable around me to eat together again. Reaching into the bag, she pulled something out, tossing it to me. It was a small bag full of green plump grapes. She then seated herself next to me, pulling out a fat free Greek yogurt and a salad.

"You don't like grapes?" I inquired.

"I do, I was hoping to have half of your sandwich as an exchange."

I smile as I started eating my half of the sandwich, leaving the other half in the middle of the bench between us.

"You know, there's a rumor going around campus," she began.

"About what?" asking uneasily. Did rumors really spread that fast?

"About you and me being a couple, something about it being confirmed with your own mouth earlier this morning."

"Sorry, I did tell someone that we're going out," saying as casually as I could. "I thought it would be beneficial for the both of us."

"Hmm, that's probably true. I'm not mad by the way, however,

I'd like you to elaborate. What do you mean, 'beneficial for the both of us?' I'd like to get a clearer picture of what you're thinking."

Being relieved now as she picked up the other half of the sandwich. "Well, it's good for me since Jason might finally leave me alone now, plus now I won't be pestered with others asking to go to the prom with me. I'm kind of assuming guys won't be asking you out for prom now either."

"What make you so sure that I would even get asked to prom, people find me highly intimidating you know?"

I laughed, "that's true, you're personality is something else, but you're also attractive, and maybe other's might not have seen it, but you do have a nice side to you. Sometimes I kind of wish others would get the courage to talk to you more often, maybe then they'd realize how great you are, like I do." I could see her cheeks lighting up. Realizing what I just said after having blurted out everything that came to my mind. She was embarrassed as I thought it made her look even more attractive, acting so feminine. When she made a face like that, it gave me a warm feeling inside, forgetting all of my worries. "Why don't we?"

Stuffing the last bit of the sandwich into her mouth, swallowing, she turned in my direction staring at me. "Why don't we what; be a couple?" The way she said it, I knew she was only making a joke of it, not realizing that that was exactly what I wanted.

My body heated up quickly from the nerves. "Yes," I responded as calmly as I could, though my palms were starting to sweat.

"Okay," she responded. Leaning forward, she gave me a quick kiss on my cheek.

She made me flustered from both the kiss and her reply. What about her, "personal problem," that she told me the first time when I confessed my feelings to her? I didn't want to question her, fearing that she would remember and turn me down. So I kept myself from asking.

The day proceeded quickly as sixth period approached. I felt great, terrific even. Things were on the right track between Lily and I, we would finally be going out. Only being a few hours, and already I felt my fear of yesterday's seem like nothing more than a bad dream. Monsters, demons, creatures of the night, I laughed. It'd been too long, they wouldn't show up now. No, now was the time to seize back control of my life, and being in a relationship with Lily, I felt that it was going to help me. Already I felt the courage do anything, that anything was possible if it was with her, for her.

Walking to class, Alice spotted me, waving, calling out to me. The way she did it, it was hard not to take notice, so I stayed off to the side as she came hurriedly over.

"Thanks for waiting for me. Listen, do you think we can talk in private, like right now."

"Sure, what's the matter," being a bit tense, did she hear about the rumor, or did Lily tell her. It could've even been something else like Jason wanting to exact vengeance upon me. Whatever it was, it didn't sound good.

Alice dragged me into the auditorium which was currently empty. "Listen Evan, I heard the rumors about you and Lily, and I know it's not true."

As I began to interrupt Alice to let her know that Lily and I was now officially dating as of lunch time today, she was talking too quickly before I could. That was when I heard her say those words.

"Evan, I really like you!" she said. As she did, she didn't look in my eyes, instead she tried to look away in unease.

A seemingly long silence as I didn't respond. I stood petrified, not sure how to respond, it was just so abrupt.

"So," she said after I wasn't responding, brushing her hair behind her ear, still avoiding eye contact.

I collected the words in my head, putting them together as best I could. I wanted to say something to let her down easy while trying not to offend her. Alice was Lily's best friend after all, and even though I would say she was annoying and bothersome at times, I still did like her as a friend. She was kind hearted and full of joy all of the time, and I took a turn to liking her as a real friend at some point.

"Alice, I'm sorry." Those words uttered from my mouth created a reverberating look of sadness in her eyes, making me feel sorry for her. "The rumors are true, earlier today, I asked Lily if she would like to be a couple with me, and she said 'okay.' We're officially dating as of lunch time earlier today."

Her facial expression was of surprise as her eyes began to water over. No longer her peppy usual self, she reminded me of an image of a young child, falling to ground. As they got up from the fall, tears would well up from the pain. That was how Alice looked to me now, like precious innocent child that I wanted to hold her in my arms, to comfort her.

"Oh, I guess I was too late huh? Um, okay, well, she can be difficult at times, but you can handle it." Mustering a smile, she looked into my eyes. Her eyes were red, fighting back the tears as she began stepping away. "I'm sure you'll treat her right," an awkward wave before she left me all alone, wanting to leave my vicinity as quickly as possible.

When sixth period ended, I made my way home. Walking, I caught the two of them all the way near the front, about to exit the school building. Alice seemed somewhat depressed while Lily was oblivious to the fact. It might have been that she was acting that way intentionally though, I wasn't sure, it had always been hard to read her, which was a reason why I liked her. When I did reach home, I would give Lily call to see if everything was okay with Alice.

Exhaling tiredly once I arrived home, I laid myself on the sofa, I wondered if life as a teenager was supposed to be this complicated.

Was a real relationship suppose to have this many problems, it had only a few hours since I was in a relationship, and already I felt that there was too much drama. The soft comfortable couch made me doze off, my tiredness reaching me now after having stayed up all of last night.

I woke up with the clambering of Emelia coming home.

"Hi, did you eat yet?" Emelia throwing her coat to the side before lazing beside me. She hadn't realized that I was taking a nap.

"No, I guess I'll make something to eat, do you have anything you'd like me to make?" I asked.

"Hmm, I feel like some pizza, so how about we order some, unless you really like cooking?"

"Pizza sounds good."

We spent the night with two medium sized pizzas, tasty buffalo wings included. While we ate, we watch a sci-fi movie airing on TV. At the end, we both cleaned up and she headed upstairs to sleep. It was around ten o'clock when I decided to give Lily a call.

"Hello," she responded after picking up the phone. "I know that we're dating as of today, but will you be calling me every night too," teasing me.

"If you want me to, I will." We talked for a while as I became pleasantly surprised with how much we talked about ourselves.

"I'm glad you're enjoying yourself," I said.

"Why wouldn't I be, after all, I don't not like you?"

"So, how are you and Alice coming along?"

"Fine, she did seem more quiet then usual when the school day ended," Lily sounded unfazed, as if she didn't notice something was wrong with Alice.

"Okay, well it is getting late," I said. As we said our goodbyes, "wait, there's something else," quickly saying, but she had already hung up.

I wanted to let her know about both Alice and the truth about those hell spawns. Feeling that she now had a right to know, but perhaps it was best if I didn't mention about those demons. And, maybe Alice had not wanted to let Lily know about her confession, to not have things made into a too big of a deal. 'Okay, I won't tell her,' at least not for now. Getting off the couch, reaching the stairs, I looked up. Reminded of those beasts, my stomach turned as I felt that I had wronged Lily. If she was going to have to deal with my troubles, she might now be at risk, just like how I had putted my family at risk all those years long ago. 'If only I had just stayed back in the yard back then, if I didn't peek behind that woman's fence,' I began telling myself in my head. Their appearance flashed through my head, memory of the woman laying in her yard as the three monsters swarmed around her dead body.

Reaching my bedroom, my hand caressed over the curtains that covered the window. I didn't dare open it, at least now while it was dark outside. "I'm sorry Lily, but bear with me for now. I'll protect you if the time ever comes."

The days passed while I didn't see much of Alice. Seeing this, I noticed that Lily had become more depressed. I knew I was part of this problem. We both sat on my couch, Emelia was still not home, nor did she know that we were dating. I myself was actually quite tired. Those vile things didn't show up, nor did I have a feeling of them watching me as of late. I didn't much sleep at night, worrying that they might still be coming for my life at any given moment. I didn't show my concerns when I was with Lily, not wanting her to worry, but I knew she saw the growing dark circles below my eyes.

"I've noticed you and Alice aren't hanging out as much, is it because I'm taking too much of your time," I asked.

"I have no idea," Lily replied, still focused on the movie in front of us. "Well, I think she's ignoring me," a moment of silence. "Actually, you don't need to feel bad, but before we started dating, I knew that she had feelings for you."

Her face saddened as I brushed her hair back, gently kissing her. "I'm sorry."

She smile, "there no reason for you to apologize, you didn't do anything wrong, I'll do my best and talk with her tomorrow."

"Listen, I have something to tell you."

"What is it," she seemed worried now.

"When I had asked you out on the bench a few days ago during lunch, Alice later that day had confessed to me. I told her that I had asked you out earlier that day and that you said 'yes.'" She didn't respond. "I figured Alice wouldn't want me to say anything to you, that she'd want to play things out normally, I guess she decided to avoid you instead. Truthfully, I wasn't going to say anything, but it just seemed that you were becoming more depressed by the day by it. I know she's a special friend to you, so I figured that maybe if you knew the reason, the two of you would be able to reconcile."

She didn't respond so I took it as her not wanting to talk. I left her alone as we concentrated back on the movie. Once it ended, she still hadn't said a word. I walked her out to the door, "let's do something tomorrow night," saying, hoping that a night out with me would make her happy.

She look at me suspiciously, "you don't like going out at night remember, you're fearful of the dark."

"I'm working on it, and I've become much more comfortable, especially when I'm with you to take my mind off of it." Leaning forward to give her another kiss, she pulled back before I did.

Giving me a warm smile, "okay, be at my place by seven," she held my face with both hands, giving me a peck the cheek.

Beginning my trip to Lily's house right after work, regretting my refusal of the car Emelia had offered. I felt uneasy having to always rely on Lily to drive us out to places we wanted to go to. Lily had stopped working herself just yesterday I realized when she told me over the phone last night. Cafe Lux had announced that they would be closing shop as I recently found part time employment of my own.

To start off, this wasn't a big surprise for Lily. Lily was informed a little over two weeks ago as the owner had decided to move to California. It wasn't all bad for Lily. She wasn't in need of the money since most of her daily necessities were provided for her by her mother. Lily initially wanted to work to kill her free time, and she wanted the extra money to purchase things without relying too much on her mother, which I figured was pretty admirable of her.

I on the other hand found work which I just started today at a fairly small bookstore close by to my house. On the week days on Tuesday and Thursday, my shift started right after school from five till ten, and on the weekends from ten till six, which wasn't too bad I thought. Sure I would be working during the nighttime on the weekdays, but I felt that it was a step forward towards recovery. The feeling of discomfort persisted at night still, but it was becoming more bearable each night. On an extra plus side, I didn't have to overly rely on Emelia and the allowances she'd give out to me. Emelia was upset upon hearing my decision though, blaming her for not giving me enough allowance which I insisted it wasn't the case.

Telling her it that it was all so that I could kill some time, having so much of it, which I did. She didn't buy it. Telling me that a young boy my age should be going out on dates, enjoying movies and love with a girl in arm, while I was still young. Then she kept on insisting to raise my allowance which she finally gave up after a bit of time.

Once arriving at Lily's house, she opened the door before I could ring the bell.

"I was just about to call you, you think we can reschedule?" Lily asked.

"Oh yeah, sure, it's fine, another time then," responding as she leaned in to kiss me, rushing me to leave.

Wanting to inquire on what came up so suddenly, she seemed like she was in a serious hurry to make me leave, so I decided to do so. She would have to tell me over the phone I guessed. As I stepped back to leave, she suddenly pulled me inside the house.

"Take your bike too."

"What's going on, first you want me to leave, and then you want me to come inside?"

"I called Alice earlier and we decided that it would've been best to discuss things over in person. So she's coming over, and I just saw her turned the corner just a moment ago."

"Then I should probably leave," I said as I went for the door.

Quickly grabbing my hand, "maybe it would be a good idea if she didn't see you, that's why I pulled you in. It might lessen the tension a bit."

I nodded, "right, I'll be waiting in the garage then," hurriedly carrying my bike with me. It was my second time in her house, so I knew the way. Lily's house was as beautiful as ever, with plenty of sunlight.

The doorbell then rang. Waiting, I was curious to how the conversation would go. Cracking open the garage door, all I could hear was muffling noises. The voices grew closer, then clattering dishes; I opened the door a bit more.

"About Evan," Lily began. "I know you asked him out, and that's okay, I just don't want you to feel so uneasy to be around me because of it."

"Lily, I'm sorry, I'm not sure we can be friends anymore. That's what I wanted to say to you in person instead of over the phone." There was a moment of silence. Even I could sense how uncomfortable the atmosphere was as I listened behind the door. Its' been only a few seconds and already the conversation was crumbling.

"Is this really just because of Evan? Alice, we've been friends since elementary, even though it may seem like I'm annoyed with you, I do like hanging out with you, no, I love hanging out with you, we've been best friends for so long, to just have everything be torn down just like this."

"Then," Alice said something in a low voice which I couldn't hear.

"How can you ask that?!"

"I know it's selfish of me Lily, I know, but I still really do like him. I don't know why, but I can't stop thinking about him, and to have him go out with you of all people. You're my best friend Lily, I want to wish you the best of happiness, but I'm so jealous of you. When I think about it, I get so frustrated, so angry, envious. You should already know how you are. You're always so completely serious and moody towards everyone that I don't know what he sees in you that he would choose you over me."

"Alice, that's enough, stop talking, if it was anyone else I wouldn't care as much, in fact I wouldn't bother to even care, but for you to say these things to me, it really hurts. For you to say these kinds of words to me in this way just shows me how much you really like him."

"I don't just like him; I've fallen for him Lily. Whenever I'm with him, my heart starts beating faster. My stomach feels like butterflies are swarming around whenever I talk to him. He's smart, sophisticated, charming, and has a good heart. I suppose his qualities are why you like him as well."

"Alice, don't do this, please, I care about you so much to let things end this way."

"Lily, I want him, he's the one for me, the only one." The sound of Alice's voice was shaky. I knew she was in tears by now. "If you continue you're relationship with him, I don't think it would be possible to be friends anymore. It would just be too difficult to see the two of you together."

"Then is this it? Our friendship's over, just like this? I never expected things to end this way between us."

A long silent pause.

"I should leave now."

"Alice wait, we can work around this. I can't give Evan up, I feel, I mean my feeling towards Evan. You know by now how I feel about him if I'm not willing to let him go, even if it would cost our friendship. My feeling for him is probably just as strong as yours, if not stronger."

"Let me go for now, I need time to think, a little distance is probably the best for the both of us right now."

One of their footsteps began to move, I assumed it was Alice taking the initiative, moving towards the door first, Lily's soon followed. I could hear them approaching the entrance of the house with the final sound of the closing door.

Opening the garage door, I headed to the front of the house. What I saw made my heart ache. Lily had her back facing me. A low noise could be heard as she leaned her head against the door.

"Lily," I said, placing both my hands on her. Her shoulders stiffened as she was startled.

"I'm okay," turning around she said to me, giving me a weak smile on her face, trying to be strong in front of me.

"I heard everything, I'm sorry for eavesdropping. Lily, I'm so sorry things turned out this way, because of me, if it wasn't for me, you wouldn't have to feel like this."

My hand caress her soft cheek, wiping away the wet line on her face, only to have one fall down replacing it. A falling tear wiped away with my hand, only to be replaced with another. She couldn't hold it back, no matter how strong she tried to be. It pained her on the inside. I pulled her close to me, to embrace her, hold her, sooth her sorrow; she resisted by pushing me away.

"I said I'm okay," her tone defiant.

She wasn't okay. Grabbing her forcibly before she had the time to react, I forced her into my chest, holding her tightly. "You're not okay, you can cry when you're around me, you don't need to be strong all of the time, especially in front of me."

I caressed her hair, doing my best to ease her with my other arm. Sure enough, I felt my shirt dampen as she let her the sadness come out as she embraced me back, feeling her hands gripping the back of my shirt into tiny fist balls. She seemed so fragile. No longer was she the confident strong willed woman she always was. My heart softened seeing her this way, wanting to protect her, I wanted to be with her more than anything now, to hold her in my arms like this when she was happy and when she was sad. As her heart ached, so did mine, as I knew at that moment, that I didn't ever want to let her go. Knowing that my feelings for her was strong before, but now it was with certainty.

We cuddled on her couch as I held her close in my arms, continuing my caressing in the quiet room.

"Do you think she'll give up on you," Lily spoke again after the long silence. "I'm not sure if she will. We've been friends since forever, and I've never seen her act this way about any guy before. It's the first time she acted that way towards ME before."

"As for Alice giving up on me, I don't know. If she doesn't, I just want to let you know that, the only one I want to be with is you, and if she truly values your friendship, she would."

Moving her hair to the side, I kiss her forehead as she dozed off in my arms. After waiting for a long time, I decided that it was best to leave. It was nine and Lily's mother hadn't come home yet. I figured that it would've been best for me to leave before she did. Retrieving my bike from the garage, I placed it outside near the front. Before leaving the house entirely, I pulled the blanket over Lily before I left. She slept so quietly, so innocently, she was the one and only thing that I worried about now.

As I left the house biking my way home, I no longer felt fear.

No longer did I worry of creatures crawling in the night, no longer did I have the need to cower back, the night didn't strike horror into me as it had always done so, no, I only felt alive, more so than ever in my entire life. Embracing the night air, the clean air filled my lungs, taking heaps of it in like never before. I was exhilarated, I was living now, that I could finally, after so long, live my life how I should truly live it. I was free of them.

That night as I slept in my bed, a loud noise woke me up. There was a banging sound coming from below. I sat up in my bed, listening intently to the sound. Cautiously getting out of bed, I turned on the bedroom light.

A knock resounded against my door. "Evan; Evan it's me, there's a noise coming from downstairs."

Not being able to ignore Emelia, I opened the door slowly. Emelia was waiting with a robe wrapped around her, holding onto a baseball bat and a gun.

"What are you doing with a gun, where did you get that?" I whispered.

"It was left in the safe in my bedroom, my ex-husband left it when we divorced," she said as she handed me the bat. A good choice as I never even held a gun before.

The sound stopped for a moment as we waited. We didn't move or speak, than a louder bang on the front door below, repeatedly banging before it went back to its steady rhythm again.

"Are all the windows and doors locked?" I asked.

"The windows are always locked, and I made sure to lock the back. Evan, I'm scared," Emelia said as she clung to me. "Do you think you could go down and take a look?"

What? Emelia knew of my fear and she was asking 'me,' of all people to check things out? Unfortunately, I knew I had to. It was the right thing to do in this situation. 'It should be okay, I'm a brand new person,' thinking to myself as I sweated rapidly. Just hours before I was braving the night not too long ago, and now I was afraid again, I couldn't shake off this feeling of discomfort. How odd my emotions change depending on the situations.

"Okay," I said meekly, "get the phone and pre-dial 911," I said steadily going down the steps. This was one of my reasons why I had moved down here, this was the reason why I'd been going out the last few nights, it was so to help get rid of my fears.

My movement was slow as I made my way down, turning on every light switch I could. Reaching the bottom, I surveyed the surrounding area, checking to make sure that there wasn't anything unusual. There wasn't. I only had to look to see what was on the other side of the door now. Warily, I place my hand upon the door, holding the bat tightly with me other. Looking into the peep hole, I didn't see anyone or anything on the other side, yet the banging sounded persisted against the door. I felt the vibration it made on the door as it shook from the force on the other side.

"Who's there?" I yelled. "What do you want this late!" again I yelled. No one responded.

I began to imagine the worst. Those beasts' sizes varied, they could've been the short evil little devils that had once terrorized me down the street. Looking back at Emelia, she didn't say anything as she now held a phone in her other hand. Gesturing for me to open the door while holding the phone to her ear, at the same time she aimed the gun downward towards the door, and at me. In my head, I began to question whether she should be pointing the gun while I was standing near the door, but I quickly removed the thought. What was more important to me was what was behind the door.

Standing back with the bat held high, I unlocked the door, then quickly taking a step back, ready to swing at whatever opened it. Nothing happened. The loud sound went on, reverberating throughout the house. Finally, I placed my hand on the handle and started hyperventilating. It wasn't the time to back out. Hyperventilating or not, I swung the door open as the cold air outside rushed into the warm heated house. The house alarm went off making a loud noise, alarming us of a possible intruder which there weren't any as of yet.

There was nothing there. Cautiously moving forward, I took a peek outside to the left, to the right and even above just in case. There was no one, it was now dead quite. The cold continued to rush in as I rushed to close the door, locking it immediately. My attention went back towards Emelia to see if she was okay, she was. Peering into the other rooms to make sure everything was in order as they should; they were.

"I don't know, there wasn't anything there," I finally said.

The phone in Emelia's hand rang, frightening her as she dropped it to the floor. It was the security agency calling to see if everything was alright. She let them know that everything was okay, gave the secret password, and then proceeded into her room to turn off the alarm.

"This is creepy, it just had to happen on one of the rare days that I'm home," Emelia said making her way down, still clutching closely to both the phone and gun. "Well, what do you think that was?" she asked looking though the peep hole. "Something must have been making that noise."

"Absolutely no idea, but thankfully it stopped. There's nothing we can do about it right now, we should head back up to bed and figure out what it was tomorrow."

"I'm too afraid to sleep now," she said hold onto my arm as we went up the stairs.

"You're not the only one. I'm shaken up as well."

Trying to go back to sleep, I couldn't. I felt restless, wide awake, keeping a constant eye on my bedroom door.

A squeaky scratching sound came from the window, straightening me up instantaneously. I sat there as the noise went away. I still had the baseball bat Emelia had given me, which I had placed near my bedroom door. It seemed so far away, so out of reach. Motivating myself, I gathered the courage, jumping out of bed to take hold of the bat. Grasping it tightly up, I was ready to attack at whatever that would come crashing through my window. As I waited for the *thing* outside, nothing appeared, then a small audible whisper.

"Evan, Eeeeevan. I know you're there. I know you can heeeear me. So frighten and afraid you must be. It's been a long time, hasn't it boy? I remember you well. You're that little, BRAT, that took my, EYE! Do you remember me?"

Motionless, I knew what it was, which one it was, I remembered it so clearly. So it's finally come for me after so many years to finish me off.

"W-what do you want, its' been years already, why are you coming for me now?" I asked, my voice was weak, trembling.

"You know why. I'll be seeing you again soon, boy."

I stood there for a while, not moving a muscle. After about an hour had passed, I walked towards the window. My hand moved up to the thick curtain, shaking uncontrollably. Gradually I pulled opened the curtain. I didn't see him there. Instead there was a scratch mark on the window. Five long straight lines were scratched down the glass. I could see it clearly in my dark room, taking in the details of how that, *thing* made these marks. I visualized it pressing its hand against the glass first. The dark being dragging its hand down before arching its fingers, connecting its nails against the glass as it scratched down against the glass.

I fumbled backwards, falling to the floor, unable to comprehend what my eyes were seeing. It was real after all, all of it, *they* were real. The therapist was wrong, everyone who laughed at me was wrong, *they* existed. Being repeatedly told they weren't real, a dream, hallucination, illusions that I drastically conjured up as a child out of the tragedy of losing my family members. I've starting to slowly believe in everyone as their hypnotism persisted growing up. In the back of my mind, I had always known that they were real, but I never had any evidence to prove it. I slowly started to believe that it was my own thoughts that gave birth to them. Trying to fight my fear against them, thinking that possibly those creatures couldn't have existed. Now it was different, there was proof right before my eyes.

"No, not yet." They may or may not be real still. As I grew older, never seeing them anymore, I had always believed in them, but my fear of them had gradually started to dissipate. At this moment, after what I'm seeing, I wasn't so sure anymore. Could I be creating this in my head? They had to be real, there was clear evidence right in front of me, including what had just occurred downstairs. Aunt Emelia was there; even she had heard the banging on the door. I wholeheartedly believed once more.

Moving to the corner of the room, farthest from the window, I sat there with the bat until morning, not moving, not sleeping; simply waiting for the sunrise.

"They can't be real, no they can't be. I was finally starting to get better enough to go outside again. Why is this happening, why now? I'm sorry Lily."

CHAPTER

10

Things became different afterwards, everything suddenly became more frightful. The very next day after Lily's and Alice's friendship ended, I had gone to the nearby department store, brought some items, and quickly boarded up my window. Not even a single part was left uncovered. Still, the appearance made it highly visible to what I had done, so I brought larger curtains to hide the visibility incase Emelia happened to come in. She had never entered my room unannounced before. Still, I didn't want to give her a reason to worry if she ever did. This was the most I could do.

During the nights that I did sleep, I felt something, something evil constantly watching me, causing me endless sleepless nights. Soon, I started to feel their presence even during the day. A strong sense of malice crept out of the dark corners. The darkness cursed me, wanting me, readying to devour me. With them creating such pressure, my fears grew. It wasn't just the nights that they forced their darkness upon me, now they had become so audacious to even come during the day? I didn't of course see them as did no one else, nor were there any traces or evidence of their presence. I simply knew. I sensed them.

For days I kept my tiring body up and active, forcing myself to stay up, going without sleep for long periods of time before my body just couldn't keep up anymore. Before I did pass out, I could feel my own weary body being dragged along by nothing but shear will and fear. Calling out to nothing; wanting, craving for sleep. Before passing out, I prepared myself. I fetched my baseball bat, holding it in my hands, ready, and waiting for any unexpected surprises.

It wasn't just my own safety that I was afraid of, I was afraid for Emelia's and Lily's as well. I couldn't let them know that they might be in danger. I knew Emelia would simply make me go and seek psychological help again. As for Lily, it was hard to say how she would react. Fearing the worse, I decided to leave her in the dark. They wouldn't believe me even if I told them anyway. Worst case scenario, I would be sent back to live with my father and Clarissa, only to put them in jeopardy instead. The possibility of running away had crossed my mind, of leaving to save the others. They only wanted me after all. After careful consideration, I decided not to. I wanted to live still, to be with Lily, grow old and die as an old man. Selfish of me I knew, but was it so wrong to want to live? No, what I needed to do was keep on living, and to act normal in front of everyone, at least for the time being.

Hiding my anxiety was difficult in front of Lily. So far we had gone out on our first few dates during day while the sun was in the sky, somehow managing to come back home before sunset. Steadily, as I sensed those monsters presences becoming more frequent. I increased the number of excuses that I would tell to Lily. The most common one was due to work. Being low on staff they needed me, that I didn't have much choice. The truth was that I had abandoned my job only after a week, not even Emelia had known. I suspected Lily caught on soon after. I could tell that she become more doubtful every time I turned her down, running the same reason by her time and again. She was sharp, but I kept my act up and my story consistent, making sure my lies always somehow added up. She didn't question me strangely, simply agreeing, letting the conversation end as is.

After a few weeks had passed, I caught a glimpse of both Lily and Alice talking in the early morning near the front of the school. They didn't seem emotionally depressed or distraught; surprisingly it was the exact opposite. They were laughing gleefully as if nothing ever happened, or at least Alice was. Lily did seem to be pretty happy, happier than I've ever seen her in the past few weeks she'd ever been with me. She was showing that rare beautiful mesmerizing smile that most people wouldn't ever see.

Watching them, I wasn't sure what to do. Best to avoid them for the time being, to let their friendship further solidify, I thought. Lily caught sight of me as she started to wave me over. Uncomfortably, I briskly walked over.

"Hey Evan, its' been awhile," Alice said.

"Its' been some time, I'm glad you two are so back to talking again."

Subconsciously my hand extended out to Lily's, holding her soft delicate hand. She was startled by this as Alice seemed surprised. The two of them began to look embarrassed and shy, as if that simple gesture reminded them of why they're friendship was in jeopardy not too long ago.

"Oh, uh, looks like the two of you become pretty intimate with each other," Alice said, forcing a noticeable fake grin.

"Yes, you could say that," Lily replied back.

In that response, I let go of Lily's hand. "You know it's strangely cold this morning," shoving my hands into my pocket.

"Well the two of you should bundle up, especially when we go out this weekend."

"This weekend, what's going on this weekend?" I asked.

"Well, Lily and I were chatting it up last night after we resolved our little disagreement, and a few topics came up. One of the things that was brought up was of you and of how comfortable you've become at going out at night. I mean, I've heard you've been working a lot of night shifts the past few weeks, right? So, we came up with this idea of doing some nighttime exploration, I mean it shouldn't be a problem anymore, right?"

"I don't think it should be a problem, I mean your aunt seems like the type that would let you go, and we'll be doing this at around eleven o'clock at night, so your work won't get in the way," Lily said.

"Eleven o'clock!" I said concernedly, the time greatly intimidated me.

"It shouldn't be a problem since you've been working the night shifts. I'm kind of assuming that you're okay by now. We haven't actually planned much of anything yet, so we can still cancel if you need some more time getting, '*adjusted*.'"

The way Lily said that last word made me cringe, making me feel so weak and feeble. I had a feeling that she was testing me, knowing I'd been lying all that time to her. I knew I couldn't turn her down, however, I knew I also couldn't stand being out so late. What would I do if we got attacked? Those creatures were waiting for me, and they were waiting for an ideal moment just like this.

"Evan, you okay Evan?"

Coming back to reality, I looked down at Lily who had her hand on my arm, shaking me back to reality.

"I'm sorry, we don't have to go, why don't we do something else?"

Her worries melted most of my fears. "No I'm okay, really. I mean, give me some time to think about it."

"Listen, I sorry Evan, we really don't have do this," Alice said. "I can tell you're not comfortable doing something like this. We can tell how uncomfortable you got when we mention it. You're still not ready for this kind of leap."

"Right, the two of us figured it would've been fun. Alice and I have done something like this before, and it was pretty exciting. We just figured it was a good idea, you know, since you were feeling better about being out so late at night recently. Also, it would've been nice for all three of us to get together to do something exciting."

It was hard to argue against her reasoning. My lips quivered as I said, "okay."

"You sure about this?" Alice asked concernedly.

"I'm okay with it, I'm sure one night won't kill me."

The bell for first period rang, making me jump a bit. Saying goodbye as I started to walk away, gathering my strength to simply walk forward. I didn't look back at them; I was too lost in my thoughts of what would become of us.

Playing it casual, I didn't think about it as I calmed myself down by thinking of other things. No one mentioned it during the rest of the school day, but Lily did call afterwards to see if I was doing okay.

"You don't have to do this; listen, I know that you've been lying. I know you still haven't gotten over your fear of going out at night, and lately, it seemed that its' gotten worse. You haven't been working late at night, and I'm going to go as far and assume that you've even quit your job. Am I right?"

Hesitantly, "you're right, about everything. Come over tonight, I want to show you something," replying.

"Okay, I'll head on over right now."

I couldn't lie to her anymore. I knew I needed to tell her everything, the truth of what actually had transpired those many years ago, and of what happened recently. It would have been only a mere matter of time before she would have known about everything, letting her know now was for the best. In a way, before our relationship would escalate any further, she would now have a full understanding of my situation, choosing to stay or leave me if she wanted to. It pained me to think of her leaving me.

Waiting for her arrival, I sat in the kitchen with a glass of apple cranberry juice left untouched. I was silent, nervous; my right leg wouldn't stop shaking. What would she think of everything that I would tell her? I had never told anyone else for years and years, and the times when I did, I was left with the feeling of self-hatred and agony in the end.

She took her time coming as I waited there. When the doorbell rang, telling me of her arrival, I hesitated to go answer it. There was no use in delaying it I thought when Lily rang the bell again. Getting up slowly, moving my heavy legs towards the door, my shoulders felt heavier than they used to, it must've been the weight of my truth. As I opened the door, Lily was standing there beautifully with her long black hair in disarray.

One look at me and she quickly expressed concern for me. "Is something the matter, you don't seem too good?"

Was I showing my discomfort that much? I must have, and I was too exhausted to hide it now. "There is something wrong," I replied. "Come inside first, I need to tell you something," I said stepping aside, making a path for her. As she did, I caught a scent of something like raspberry on a spring morning. She must've taken a shower just earlier, which was probably the reason why it took her awhile to get here. "Come on, lets' head up to my room first."

"You're room? Oh, I wasn't exactly expecting you to call me over for '*that*,' I mean…"

Cutting her off. "No, I didn't ask you to come over for sex, I do like that idea, but there's something else."

She made me feel more comfortable now as I couldn't resist grinning as I saw her blush for a moment. She caught my eyes before looking away awkwardly. I had never imagined that she could be this innocent, to see her so shy, acting so timid, but it only made me crave for her even more, knowing that it was me, that I was the one to make her look and act that way. That was a rare expression for her to show, and it was a look that only I would ever see, no one else. What made it special was that I knew that she had purposely said those words to ease my discomfort. She forced herself to act that way for my sake.

As we reached my room, I led her inside, pulling the newly brought midnight blue curtains open, revealing woods that boarded up the window. Turning around, she already had made herself to my bed, sitting down gently with room for me next to her.

"Well, what is it, you're making me really worried, what's going on, why is your window like this, what do you want to tell me?"

"I'll tell you everything," I said, seating myself on the opposite side of the bed, my back to her as I did. I didn't want to look at her as I told her the truth. "There's something wrong Lily, ever since I was a young boy, I've seen things that'd instilled fear in me, so much that I've never recovered from it. It's all because of *them*. Even worse, *they* started to reappear again; they've come back for me Lily, that's the reason why I've been acting so strange lately. I'm sure you've noticed by now if not long ago, after all, I can't hide anything from you, you can see everything."

Her hands gently pressed against my back as it slowly moved to my shoulder. I felt her soft lips kiss the nape of my neck. "Then tell me, I've been waiting for you to tell me for a long time, I didn't want to push you because I wanted you to be ready to tell me. I'm here for you Evan, I always have, and my feelings towards you won't change no matter what you tell me."

Her kiss was warm; her voice was soft yet still confident and comforting. I reached out, touching her soft delicate hands, they were warm. Taking a deep breath, once more I took in the scent of raspberry spring as it started to fill the room with the intoxication of her scent.

"It was a long time ago that it first started," I began as I told her of my childhood.

I delved into everything, the love of my mother, what I had seen in the alley way with the feline, even the taste of the pastries that I consumed when my mother and I had gone to buy them before the tragic events. The hard loss of both my mother and sister which had driven my father into coldness towards me, the psychological help for years that I had seek the disbelief and mistreatment of the other kids growing up when I did reveal the details of the horror. I told her everything, not leaving a single detail unturned. My story must have lasted for hours, yet she remained silent, listening beside me, never interrupting, not even a word. She simply listened silently to my story. Moving on in the timeline, I then told her of the current events, why I had boarded up my window, and the cause of my lack of sleep as well as the reason for my lies to her. At some point we laid down on my bed as we held hands.

"That's it, that's everything. So what do you think, I can only image what kind of things that are going through your head after everything I've just told you, and I'm sure you don't really believe me." I waited for a moment for Lily to respond.

"Your story is really something. I mean it's a lot to take in, it's not really something anyone can accept so readily," she said. "Okay, lets' say what you just told me is really true, that would explain a lot about your actions up until now. Those creatures or monsters, or whatever they are, sounds something along the lines of mythical demons from the bible or something."

"I know it's hard to believe, no one ever does, but it's true, everything I told you is real."

"Okay, then show me. You told me that there was one recently that made scratch marks on your window right? Kind of like claws marks with smear lines outlining its hand? If what you said is true, than it should be there."

I hesitated, it was still dark outside. They wouldn't be outside waiting right at this very moment, would they?

"Evan, it's a good way to prove to me that what you just told me is true, isn't it? It's difficult to believe in you right off, a little proof would be nice," Lily said, interrupting my thoughts.

I knew she was right, those markings were evidence of them, and it could at least prove to her that there was some truth in what I was saying. "Okay," I finally said, "I'll show it to you."

Getting up, I opened my drawer to remove the battery powered screw driver. It felt much heavier than when I first held it. I began to unscrew the bottom portion of the window where the marks were, one screw at a time. Lily sat on my bed waiting patiently as I worked. Finally, out came the last screw. I place both hands on the sides, readying to reveal the marks to her. When I uncovered the window, there wasn't anything there. What was there was a smooth clean glass; there were no marks or smears from the creature before, simply clear glass with water stains from the rainfall that showed out into the night. I was speechless; I dropped the board as it made a loud 'thump,' as it landed to the floor.

"T-there," I said, the words leaving my trembling lips, my unsteady hand pointing towards the window.

"What's there, I don't see anything," said Lily. She stood up and gripping my shoulder, "Evan, there's nothing there."

Her hand startled me. "No, it's there, it has to be, I saw it, I heard its voice, I made sure it was real."

It was the bottom half wasn't it? Doubt now filled my head. The top portion of the window as sill boarded over. Grabbing the curtains, I viciously pulled them off to the floor, and then I quickly drilled off the remaining screws, uncovering the top half of the window as well. Once I finished, I threw the large board to the side. Once again, there was nothing. I tripped backwards in disbelief, nearly falling over; I caught myself on my desk. My hands were shaking as I started breathing rapidly. My body broke into a cold sweat; I could feel the blood leaving my face as my body weakened, as if something sucked the vitality out of me, leaving me as weak as new born infant. My body was heavy, oh so heavy, no longer could I move from the invisible weight that held me down as I dropped to my knees.

"Evan, Evan, listen to me, everything is okay." Lily called out to me as her voice resounded in my head. I very slowly regained some self-aware consciousness of myself.

"It was there, Lily, I'm not lying, I'm telling you the truth, they're real, you have to believe me, I need you to believe me."

"Okay Evan, just calm down first, okay, everything's alright, remember to stay calm and take deep breaths," she said to me caressing my hair. She stood up, grabbing one of the boards and the electronic screw driver with the intent of covering up the window once more.

"Wait, don't cover it," I yelled. Standing up, I lost my

balance nearly falling over again, only to grasp onto the desk nearby. I sat down on my bed.

Lily dropped the materials, came over and held my head in her chest, caressing me, calming my trembling nerves. I wasn't even able to think of anything else at that moment, not being able to do any of the exercises my therapist had once told me to do in moments like these. Too shocked to even think, the only thing, the only one that was able to calm me down now was Lily and her touch, and her calm collected breathing. Calmed down, I touched her arms to let her know that I was okay. She released me as she gazed into my eyes, holding my face with one of her hands.

"I'm sorry; I lost it for a moment. I just thought it was there, I was so certain. Lily, I can't tell what's real anymore, I don' know what's going on with me."

"Don't say anymore Evan, why don't we go downstairs for now, out of this room, let's try to calm you down first and then we can talk about this reasonably."

The word 'reasonably' struck hard at me. "They're real," I shouted standing up again, "it was there, I know it, I don't know what happened, but I'm not imagining it."

"Evan, there's nothing there," Lily yelled back at me. She went to the window, pointing to it, to show me that there were no markings. "You don't need to be afraid of anything because those creatures that you told me don't really exist."

"Don't tell me that I don't need to be afraid of anything!" I fiercely grabbed her arm, not being able to compose myself, I threw her down on my bed, pinning her with my strength. "You don't know anything of what I went through, what *they* made my life into. Cowering in fear for these past years because of them. I know they exist!" Even so, my eyes began to cloud over. Drops of tears fell down on her perfect beautiful face.

She lied beneath me, expressionless. She remained calm, even when I grasped her and threw her down, she remained undisturbed. Not showing any fear, pain, or distraught, she laid there and waited, listening to my tantrum.

"How can you lay there like this, how can you do it," loosening my grip.

"It should be obvious by now. Evan, I'm like this because I know that you wouldn't really hurt me."

My grip was loose enough now that she pulled out one of her hands to touch my face, wiping a tear away.

"I probably know, because, well, I love you." Her face reddened from saying those words. I kept my eyes connected with hers before she eventually diverted them away.

"You really know when to land that on me," laughing. "Your timing couldn't have been better." Getting off of her, I took a seat at the end of the bed.

"What did you expect me to say, I was being so calm because my heart is cold as ice?"

"Actually yes, that does kind of describe you."

"That's not exactly what I'm hoping to hear from you as a response, especially after just opening out my heart to you, but whatever. At least you're acting a bit more like yourself now."

"I know I really lost it. I was just so sure that they existed, that they were real, everything, every detail was, seemed so vivid. When I saw the marks," I paused, "when I thought I saw those marks on the window, I started believing in them again. I guess I really am crazy. Losing my sister and mother really did a number on me, I believe it now, those creatures aren't real, nothing's real."

"What are you talking about, aren't you forgetting something? You have me don't you, I'm at least real, and I'm here with you."

"Why would you stay with me, I'm a guy that see things aren't real, I've lied to myself all my life, hid away in my comfort zone, running away from reality because I've been too afraid. I don't even know what really happened all those years anymore. My therapist has been right all along, losing both my family members cause me to start mentally hallucinating. Maybe they were right, I could be schizophrenic. Lily, I might be this way for the rest of my life, and you're saying you still want to be with me?"

She pulled me towards her and kissed me, then pulled away.

"That's why I'm with you. I don't think I can exactly change the way I feel about you so easily. Sure you got problems, but I do too, and my problem is that I still want to be with a paranoid psycho like you."

Looking into her eyes, her being here with me, I no longer felt fear or anxiety. No longer did I tremble in a panic. I loved her; I loved her so much, that I wanted to let her know how I felt. Reaching out for her, I kissed her passionately, more so than ever before. My hand moved to her legs as I sense her body stiffening as I did. She soon relaxed as I continued. We laid down on the bed as I began to kiss down her neck.

"What the heck happened to the window?" A loud voice came from the door way.

I stopped what I was doing, immediately the two of us looked towards the doorway where Emelia was standing. Reacting right away, I got off of Lily, standing up as she did the same.

"Oh, about the window, some stuff happened so I boarded it up, everything's okay now, so I took it down, and I'll do something about the drilled holes."

"Hi Dr. Lawrence, it's good to see you again," said Lily, flustered.

"Oh, uh, right, sorry, I didn't mean to interrupt the two of you, but the window just surprised me is all. I probably should've been more surprised of Evan on top of you, but for some reason the window just caught my attention more."

"I'm sorry, I know I'm living under your roof and all, so I shouldn't be doing this kind of thing with Lily in your house," I said.

"No, no, it's perfectly alright, I'm actually really glad you got yourself such a beautiful eye-candy. You kids can continue of course, do you kids need some condoms?"

"What, no!" I said. I could see Lily laughing next to me.

"That's alright Dr. Lawrence, nothing was going to happen anyway, and I was going to stop him before anything really happened. It's pretty late; I should probably head on home."

"Oh, are you sure you want to leave, it's so late, why not just stay. I'm sure Evan would like that, you could keep him company," Emelia said nudging her.

"Aunt Emelia!" I shouted out of embarrassment.

"Okay, I understand."

The three of us walked down the stairs to see Lily out, Emelia stood close by, watching, which made the atmosphere awkward.

"Listen, I'll let Alice know that we'll be canceling our plans to go out exploring," Lily said.

"Wait, don't do that, I'll go, I want to go. It's about time I stop being so afraid, and a giant leap is sometimes better than a small step."

"Are you sure?"

"I'm positive."

"If that's what you want, than okay. If you feel that you're ready, than I won't stop you, but if you feel like you can't do it, than I don't want you to force yourself."

"Alright," I said, leaning forward to kiss her goodbye. I could tell Emelia was watching the two of us behind me, so I stopped midway. I could tell that even Lily found it too uncomfortably to kiss goodbye. Instead, Lily gave me a hug and left.

"Somebody's a lover boy," Emelia said, making slow feint punches which made her look ridiculous.

"You're so embarrassing."

"It's my job as you're guardian. You two sure are cute together," reaching over to pinch my cheek. "This is all the teasing I'll do for now, I need to shower and get some food. Six hours of surgery can really exhaust an old lady like me," Emelia said rushing up the stairs.

Following after Emelia, I made my way inside my own bedroom. My room was a mess. "There's nothing to be afraid of," I told myself as I looked outside through my window. I placed my hand along the smooth cold glass. "I've been making them up all this time. This time, I won't be afraid anymore. No, I won't, no matter what, this time around will be different. I will get better."

Looking at the curtain on the floor, I rolled it up, placing it neatly on my desk. Turning my attention at the window, it seemed a bit unsettling to me, seeing it so open and bare, at the same time, proud to see it like so, as if I had grown. I took some cloths and headed for a shower.

We watched the boy that night, surprised to see him bringing down the protective cover which allowed the darkness to see inside. Something must have happened to make him do so; it must have been the girl's doing. We had thought the boy to be too afraid, to have lost his spine. It matters not. We are ready for the taking. The boy will soon cease to exist.

"It'ssss only a matter of time before we devour you."

CHAPTER

11

When I see my window at night, I sometimes shudder, as if I'm being watched through the darkness. Always wanting to cover it up, I simply stared at the perfectly flawless window pane, to be reminded of what I think that could've existed out there was nothing more than my own thoughts tricking myself. Reminding myself that they weren't real. My fears were decreasing, I didn't feel as afraid anymore, but I couldn't help but to look into the dark corners from time to time. The logic of their non-existence had greatly propelled me forward, to recover myself of my fears. Of course, it was without question that a part of me still believed in those demons, but no longer did I tremble every time I was outside.

The days slowly went by, filled with much more joy and

fulfillment with each night that I stayed out. As Lily and I became closer, we started to go out nearly every night, increasing my comfort level each day. There were times that Alice came too. It was strange having Alice around at first, trying to act how we used to, as if nothing ever happened. As we continued our nights out with the three of us, Alice made it apparent that no matter how hard she tried, she still had lingering feelings for me. Showing visible slight actions such as avoiding eye contact, shifting her gaze away when our eyes did meet, or being embarrassed or self-consciousness when she said or acted a certain way in front of me, something she never done so before. Lily noticed Alice's unusual moments too, probably even before me, having known her so long. There were times when Lily would just seem depressed when Alice wasn't looking, feeling burdened somewhat after watching Alice acting in such ways. Caring for Alice very much, they had known each other for so long, she didn't want their friendship to end, or at least not again. Seeing Lily's moments of sadness made me want to say or do something during those times; I never did, I couldn't, not knowing what I could do, it pained me to see her like so each time.

We were together eating dinner one night, the three of us together, Lily, Alice, and I. It was a quaint Chinese restaurant with very traditional decorations. No, not the same one as we first went to, this one was different. The lights were dimmed. A casual mood was set with the low mellow Chinese song playing in the background. I had always preferred nice little places like this more than the fancy high end restaurants. Sure, service weren't always the best at places like these, in fact they could be downright deplorable at some places, if there were any at all, but at least you could act and look how you wanted. Places like this would be filled with other normal regular people, simply wanting to have an enjoyable casual meal, to hang out with others. For people who simply just wanted to eat and be left alone without the waiter coming back to you every ten minutes, making sure we were having the 'best time of your life,' experience. Somewhere where people could be alone and eat and relax.

"You know we never did go out and explore like we had planned," said Alice, biting into a piece of steamed dumpling. It was filled with juices which came unexpectedly gushing out, catching her by surprise. She gave a satisfying happy look eating it, making both Lily and I craving for one.

"That's true, it has been about two weeks, and you do seem pretty okay with going out at night during the past few. Do you think you'll be okay with it if we did go exploring?" Lily had asked me as she went for one of Alice's dumplings.

I had an inkling that Lily had talked it over with Alice to postpone the outing, at least for a little while. Having known Alice long enough, I knew she was the type to always be on top of things. She would have never let a planned event or scheduled meeting to just quietly be forgotten without a proper excuse.

"My dumpling!"

"You can spare one," said Lily after snatching one of the tasty morsels, devouring the piece whole.

"Well if you can spare one, you can spare two," I said stealing another from Alice's plate. Alice gave me a menacing playful look, where in turn she stole a piece of my salt and spicy pork chops. "Why don't we do it this weekend, it's like you said, I've gotten pretty comfortable with going out a night, so I think I'll be fine now."

It was true in the fact that I've greatly recovered from my fear. It was as if that night's uncovering revealed the truth to me, a revelation to my own self. At first I was still nervous as I always were, but as I spent time walking around with Lily and Alice, I realized there was nothing in the dark, nothing ever came popping out. The cold menacing stare lingered in the air every time, but I soon learned to shrug the feeling off in due time. Lily was especially helpful with my recovery. Spending time with her simply made me feel more alive, my attention was drawn to her instead, distracting me from everything else. It was because of her that a part of me wanted to hurry up and adapt to the night, wanting not burden her with my delusions. I wanted to be able to go out with Lily without her having to worry about me.

"If you're that sure, than lets' do it," Lily said, looking at me with a bit of skepticism.

On the other hand, Alice looked quite delighted with the outcome. She must have been waiting for this outing to happen for a while.

"You seem really happy about this," I said to Alice.

"I am, and I already have the perfect location in mind. I've been thinking about it for a while now. It's an old abandoned building on the outskirts of town. No one goes there since it's pretty far out, and it's restricted area due to safety concerns."

"Safety concerns? Like what?" I asked.

"The building is poorly developed. The design was poorly done, and really cheap materials were used in the constructing of the building, causing it to literally start falling apart after a few short years. Outside it looks like normal regular building, but it's really collapsing from the inside. If I remember correctly, it was abandoned about twenty years ago completely after the ceiling had collapsed during a heavy rainy day. The incident ended up killing one and injuring multiple others."

"Have you been there, you seem to know a lot about it," I asked, surprised at her knowledge.

"I've been living here for a long time, plus I like researching these kinds of things, they're interesting, and no, I haven't gone to it. I can't really go to places like these alone now can I, because you know, I'm delicate girl," she said a bit awkwardly.

Lily laughed. "You're far from delicate."

"At least I act more feminine that you," Alice retorted.

We spent the majority of that night eating the good food, having a good time, while planning for the weekend. The two ladies created a list of what we would need. Gloves, boots, backpack with emergency supplies, multiple other necessities. Discussing the event made me excited to do something like this. I never quite imagined myself going out on a minor exploration. There was a feeling in my gut telling me not to go. Once I began to head on home, a feeling of worry filled me inside, my stomach felt twisted, my muscles tensed as I thought of the our mini adventure to come. 'What was I feeling afraid of now?' asking myself this. I knew, it was a backlash of own paranoia, I was afraid still, which was why I told myself that this was the right step, this was the direction that I needed to go towards.

Asking Emelia if she had any of the items on the list already, she seemed excited to see me going out on this little exploration. I would've figured her to be concerned, but she welcomed the thought of me venturing out. She had most of the gear that we originally needed. The few other things left that I needed, I went out and brought.

When Friday came, I geared up and was ready to head out. Alice arrived with Lily to pick me up, both also geared up, ready to explore into the unknown. It was just the three of us as we headed to the abandoned building. As we continued driving, the surroundings became more and more deserted. A worried feeling swept over me. I kept it hidden from the other two. I didn't want to let the two of them worry over me, not wanting to seem weak.

"This is pretty far out, why did they build the building somewhere that's so deserted," Lily suddenly asked.

"Well, it's some sort of research institution. You're not the only one that thought it was weird, so I read up on it. It was originally used to experiment with a lot of toxic chemicals that was harmful to the public under normal circumstances. They had actually had a research institution in town, but they had to relocate after public outcry regarding safety concerns. I don't really know all of the details, but the company had insisted on staying within the area, so they spent some money to build it out here, away from the public. Far enough from the population but close enough to still drive." After a moment of silence, "don't look at me like that," Alice referred to Lily. "I was a bit bored at home and had some time to kill. Plus, it's always good to do your research before going somewhere you've never been to. Knowledge is the key to survival in the world."

After driving for about an hour and a half, we went off road through thick foliage, we then pulled up to a large metal gate. Getting out of the car, I took a good look at the building which looked ominous. Alice was right about the place, it was really run down. It was a large and vast facility which might have at some point employed and filled the rooms with hundreds, even possibly up to a thousand employees. The building had deteriorated quite badly. On the far left and near the right, you could see that the structure had partially collapsed. The plants in the surrounding area had over grown in some parts, while in others areas, they had all but died out.

An uneven mix of over grown life and desolated death made it looked rather uneven, adding to an unusual mysteriousness under the night sky. If there was one beautiful aspect about the place, it was due to the stars that shown showering the sky above us. The scenery was beautiful yet gloomy.

"The gate's locked," I yelled back as the two caught up.

"Well, that's why we have tools like this," said Lily holding onto a large bolt cutter. "It was pricey, but the reviews said that it can cut even industrial high-strength steel bolt-cutter proof chains."

"You really brought something this high quality for this run downed site?" asked Alice in disbelief. "I mean look, the gate and chains are rusted over."

"Well, I like quality," Lily said back, a bit flustered trying to find a good argument, as if what she said was the best one she could come up with.

"I should've known, you're pampered, you're mom always did give you the best of the best," Alice said teasing her.

"Whatever," Lily replied, handing me the cutters.

It was heavier that I thought, but it did the job it was intended to do, cutting the lock off from the gate. Looking at it, it did seem kind of a waste to buy such a high quality cutter. A part of me kind of liked it; it made me want to test how good it was at cutting. Handing the cutter back to Lily, she placed it back into her backpack as I unraveled the heavy chains. Pushing open the left side of the gate, it detached itself from the hinges, clanging to the floor, making a loud sound that echoed throughout the area. It startled all of us.

"I did say the materials used to build the place were cheap, but who knew it was this bad."

"Are we going to be okay?" I asked. "I mean I don't want to stroll on in and have the roof collapsing on us."

"That's the risk of exploring, there's a bit of danger involved, that's part of the excitement and mystery. Since the gate was still locked, it looks like we're the first few people in the past twenty years. Are you afraid?" Lily asked me with a stern face. It was her usual intimidating confidence, but this time it bothered me. It wasn't how she said it, but what she said, asking if I was afraid or not.

"I'll be alright, I was just making sure it would be safe enough, I don't want you to get hurt is all." Leaning forward, I kissed her forehead. She didn't give much of a reaction, instead she quietly walked ahead, Alice and I following behind.

"Hold on," Alice called back, pulling out a camera.

Entering through the front, the glass doors was still intact, but chained up as well. After breaking in, we saw the place was completely dark inside, giving me a shudder. For a second, there was a small panic that ran through me. I could picture those creatures emerging ghastly from the complete and utter darkness. I recomposed myself once Alice turned on her flashlight. The light pierced through the darkness forming shadows. Lily turned on her flashlight as well, as I reached into my bag for mine. Moving inside, the doors creaked closed behind us. We took a minute to looking around, staying within the vicinity. The front lobby was a large spacious open area, multiple tables and chairs were spread about. The ceiling was starting to crumble a bit. You could see countless cracks as if the whole ceiling could come down at any moment. The air smelled dusty, and it was quiet. Much too quiet, so quiet that there wasn't a single sound but those that the three of us made, it was unsettling for me.

"Come on, I found the stairs, lets' head to the roof," yelled Alice. Her voice echoed throughout the building. The building made her voice clearer and more audible than it should have.

When I heard her, it suddenly became hard to breath. It wasn't the dust, I was hyperventilating. It was because I was afraid, I could see my hand trembling as I held the flashlight in front of me. If they were here, they were sure to have heard Alice's yell. Lily was looking back at me in the distance with her flashlight pointing to the ground in front of me. Looking at the shine of the blinding light helped bring me back to my senses.

"Remember, they don't exist, it was just you imagining everything," I softly told myself, unsure if the others had heard me or not due to how clear the building made of our voices. Forcing my lungs to fill itself with the dusty air, calming myself, I walked ahead towards the stairs.

We progress up the stairs slowly. There was nothing but the sound of our footsteps as we carefully climbed. Reaching the third floor, we saw that the roof had collapsed, blocking our path. There was no way to go around.

"It's blocked, looks like we have to continue from the second floor," saying into the camera that Alice pointed at me.

We back tracked down the stairs to the second floor. Lily pushed open the door which to our surprise, was unlock.

"They didn't lock the door. Well, I suppose it doesn't matter now that no one's coming here anymore," Lily said.

"Who would besides us," Alice replied. "The place is uninhabitable, and they probably realized that the building didn't have any resale value anymore, seeing how it's falling apart and all. Even if someone did decide to buy this place, it would cost a fortune to reconstruct it. It would probably cost them less to just bulldoze and rebuild from scratch."

"You know, I'm surprise neither of you are afraid," I said.

"Does it seem that way? I know I'm afraid, but more than that, it's exciting for me," Alice replied as we continued down a corridor.

Reaching a door to the right, Lily tried opening it, but it was locked. "Now I'm surprised."

"Do you think we could break it down?" Alice asked.

"Do we really need to? I thought we were going to the roof?" I replied.

Lily smirked, "what's the point of exploring an abandoned building if we don't explore?"

"Alright, lets' see what I can do," positioning myself in front of the door.

"You can do it Evan, we're counting on you, if you can't do it, you're not a real man," cried Alice.

'Not a man huh?' thinking to myself. With a deep breath, I lifted my leg and gave a heavy hard kick to the door, successfully breaking it down. The kick might have been a bit too hard, never doing such a thing before, the impact sent a somewhat paralyzing sensation up my leg. "I really hope I don't have to do this all the time," saying as I rubbed my leg.

Walking inside, we saw lines of test tubes all along the tables. In the cabinets were various chemicals in brown bottles. Along the counters were microscopes and jars of insects that were now dead inside. Looks like Alice was telling the truth about them being some sort of a research institution and hazardous chemicals. The insects were used in their experimental testing. It made me curious as to what company it was. What work did they do exactly?

We moved along to the next room which was also locked.

This time, instead of having to kick it down, Lily pulled out a large hammer. "Let me try something," saying this as she rose the hammer up. Swinging down, she connected smoothly with the knob as it fell to the floor. "Good thing it's cheap," saying as she fiddled with the door a bit before it officially opened. It was a much better alternative than kicking the doors down each time.

As we toured each room, we passed multiple offices, rooms with the same lining of glass tubes and materials as before. A kitchen, bathrooms, and finally a conference room near the far end. As we stood in the conference room, we looked out the large window right out to the front.

Staring out, I thought I saw something move in the shadows near the tree. Not knowing what to do, I simply stood there, looking at the location, not diverting my eyes away. Waiting for some movement to ensure myself that I wasn't seeing something.

"Evan, come on," Lily called for me as she and Alice exited the room.

I had no choice but to turn around. Not telling either of the two about what I just saw, I kept it to myself, assuming it was another delusion that I possibly had created for myself. Even if it was a hallucination, I continued on more cautiously than before.

After walking for a while, we made a few turns while skipping a few rooms, not having the time or patience to look through all of them. When we did finally reached another exit and a flight of stairs, we heading on up until we hit the fourth floor. Unfortunately, the top of this flight didn't have access to the roof as we had wanted.

"Looks like we can't go any further than the fourth," Alice said. "Kind of makes me sad, I was really hoping to go up there, I brought a few things too."

"There might still be a way up," responded Lily. "Why don't we look around a bit more before giving up?"

In agreement, we headed through the fourth floor door which was very much similar to the second. Moving through the doors, this particular level was a bit more technologically advance. The equipment used was outdated of course, but still much better and more expensive than what we had previously saw. In a few rooms, we found what seemed to have been labs that were testing various chemicals on a variety of plants. Multiple plants were listed from a varying type of exotic flowers to normal corn and tomato plants with lamps hanging above them. I could have imagined the room being filled with lamps running constantly, the room filled with the smell of chemicals. Breathing in the air, it wasn't the dusty smell we've been inhaling all this time. It wasn't irritating or particularly bad, but it did make me uncomfortable not knowing what it was that I was breathing into my body.

"I guess they must've been some sort of chemical producing company for plants. Possibly discovering the formula for the next generation of all kill pesticide," Alice joked.

Moving along, I thought of what Alice said about the company possibly being a pesticide company, which did make some sense putting together all of the information we had gather so far. We soon realized that that might not have been the case. There were a few rooms near the end that seemed to have been broken into before us, looking out of place. All of the rooms up until now had mainly been locked, with the exception of the few ahead. These doors were broken down. I took a good look at the door. There were scratch marks on them. They looked very similar to me, as if I had seen them from somewhere. Not liking the looks of things, I didn't want to continue further. Swallowed hard, I began picturing of the happy moments of the past few days, how free I felt. The days I spent with Lily, walking in the parks at night. How far I've come, how mature I've become, how happy I finally was.

"This is really weird, who broke these doors?" Lily asked, but no one gave an answer.

"Well, it saves us the effort," Alice said as she moved towards one of the rooms. "But really, it creep the hell out of me."

'Then why don't we just head on back,' thinking to myself, only keep quiet and follow along from behind.

"Oh my god," Alice exclaimed. "What the hell happened here?"

Both Lily and I rushed over to take a look. There were lines of animal cages all forced open. Streaks of blood covered the walls and floor.

Alice went in to take a closer look. "What happened, these cages looks like they were forced open? I guess that means this wasn't just any pesticide plant."

She was right, the doors of all the cages were forced open, and something wanted whatever animals that were caged up. From the looks of it, they kept a variety of animals here judging by the different sizes of the cages.

"The other room is like this one," Lily said as she came back. "There's actually more rooms like this further down. The doors were broken down, rooms full of cages inside of them with blood all over the place. What do you two think happened?"

"Wild animal maybe? Maybe a bear so something smelled them and broke in," Alice responded, trying to come up with the best logical answer.

It did make some sense. None of the exit doors were locked, and an animal might have come in somewhere other than the front entrance. There wasn't any complaints from Lily with Alice's answer either. I wanted to believe it wasn't *them*, but the more I tried, the more I was reminded of those monsters. I felt faint as I left the room.

Seeing this, Lily came after me. "Hey Alice, why don't we keep moving, lets' hurry up and get away from this," she called back as she caught up with me. "You okay, should we start heading back?" she said, looking at me concerned.

"I'm okay, really. We can keep looking around if you two want to." In reality, I wanted to leave the place as quickly as possible, to never set foot on this property ever again.

"Alice," Lily called to her again, "do you want to keep going or is this enough?"

"After seeing this, I do kind feel like heading back now, but how about we at least head down to the end of the hall, it looks like there's an exit, this one might has stairs with a roof access. If it doesn't, then we'll head home."

Agreeing, we moved towards the stairs, passing the other rooms. Like Lily had said, they were all the same. Streaks of blood, cages forced open, doors broken down. We reached the stairs which did have a roof access.

"Looks like we're in luck, kind of wished there wasn't one though, I kind of want to get out of here," said Lily.

"Oh, this is surprising, you usually don't show that you're scared, always the brave Lily," Alice mocked her.

"I'm still human, even I get scared now and again. Letting you know ahead of time, if something does show up, I'm going to leave you behind to get eaten," retorting as she headed up first.

"What a cruel hearted woman, it breaks my heart when you say things like that," Alice saying in a comical fashion.

Reaching the top of the stairs, Lily pushed the door wide open. Being so old and rusted, the heavy door stayed open. Still, Alice pulled out a door stopper from her bag wedging it in just in case. They were so well prepared, and it somewhat surprised me. As I reached the top, I went outside into the open with the others and was awestruck. The view from above was magnificent. Looking at the stars was a completely different experience than from below. Up here, the trees didn't obstruct your view. There weren't other objects within view that deterred your vision. As you looked up, there was nothing but the midnight sky, illuminated by the light of the moon and stars. The roof was large with lots of open space. Carefully, I made my way to the edge and saw the view from above, overlooking the front. We were above the trees now. The view below still looked gloomy and strange, so I pulled my eyes away to focus on the sky once more. Moving to the back, I caught a glimpse of exactly how large the place was. There were multiple buildings constructed behind this one. It really was as large as I had imagined. No wonder they cheap out on the construction, the cost for such a large space would've been a fortune.

"I wanted us to get up here because I have something." Alice said as she knelt down on one knee, opening up her backpack. In it, she pulled out a multiple smaller black bags, then slowly she unzipped them revealing telescope parts which she quickly put together.

"A telescope. You know, we could have done this on the ground too," I said.

"We know," interrupted Lily, "but we've always liked the rooftops when looking up, it's a different feeling than looking up from the ground with the trees and other buildings obstruct your view." Saying this, she started taking out her own portable telescope as well. "Come on, did you bring the stuff?"

Knowing what she meant, I started rummaging in my own backpack, taking out a large picnic blanket, laying it out. It ended up as a small midnight stargazing picnic on the roof. Forgetting all of my worries as we enjoyed our time, blocking out the bloody smears that we saw just right below us, the overall atmosphere at that moment was nice. The thought of being on top of an abandoned building out in the middle of nowhere still unnerved me. Alice and Lily didn't seem to mind; at least they acted as if they didn't care. Were they just used to this?

The three of us spent a good amount of time on the roof; most of it was spent teaching me about the constellations. It was hard to pick it up in the beginning, but soon I started to connect them. A small laugh came out of me.

"What's so funny?" Alice inquired.

"Nothing, never pegged the two of you to be the geeky types," replying.

"It's not geeky," Alice proclaimed, "besides, experiencing new things once in a while can be beautiful thing, and we're still women, we like to look up, to watch the glimmer of the night sky." Saying it in an embarrassing fashion, she went back to looking into the telescope, and I realized that perhaps this was another of the reasons why so many guys at our school had taken a liking to her.

"I'm glad I came," lying next to Lily. "I never thought I could do something like this again. When I was a kid, I camped out with my family a few times, never out in a desolated creepy place like this, but it reminds me of what I've missed out for so many years. Being on a roof under the stars like this seems like dream to me. A part of me is still afraid, even more so being out in the middle of nowhere like, but I'm happy."

"Glad to hear," Lily reached for my hand.

Alice came down to lie on the other side beside of me as we lay, for a silent moment we simply enjoyed stargazing quietly, taking in the scene.

"You're right you know, being out in the middle of nowhere like this can freak you out," Alice said after a long pause, making all of us chuckle.

"I know right, especially after the bloody scene below, mentioning it kind of gives me the shivers now. I don't exactly want to make our way back down there." Lily grasped my hand a bit tighter.

"Yeah, thinking of it really bothers me now, kind of ruins the good atmosphere we just build up." Alice got up and walked off to the edge of the roof, looking over towards the front of the building. "Hey!" she yelled, "get over here."

Hurriedly, the two of us moved next to her, wondering what her sudden outburst was about.

"What is it, what's going on?" I asked her.

"I think I just saw something move down there," she replied.

"Don't see anything, where was it, what did it look like," Lily asked tensely.

"I don't know, it was in the corner of my eye and it was really fast, but I know I saw something move."

Standing there silently, my left leg shaking rhythmically, my hands trembling, feeling my body temperature rise slightly as my forehead began to produce small particles of sweat. Waiting, standing, shaking, we watched for any signs of movement from below on the unmoving bottom floor. There was no wind to move the surroundings below, so we would've notice if anything to be moving.

"There's nothing," Lily whispered. "Are you pulling a prank on us?"

"What?" surprised, "you should already know I'm not like that, I would never do something like that when I know how sensitive Evan is. Just because you're dating him right now doesn't mean you have to be so protective," Alice whispered back.

"Why do you have to say it like that, you kind of make it sound like I stole him from you, I thought you were okay with the two of us dating now."

"How can I be okay when I see the two of you together, I'm really happy for you, but" Alice stopped herself, biting her lip.

Still standing there, I listened to their whispering argument as they tried to keep their voice down. Not stopping them, my attention was directed downwards, my eyes shifting all over the place, taking in everything, every detail. The height of the trees, the size of the water puddles, even how the mosses grew long the wall to the far left. From how the dead leaves piled up against the gate, to the size and shape that each shadow made. I listened past the two's argument for possible movements, a shifting of leaves, sound of movements of any kind, even the sounds of insects or frogs. Like before when we first came, there was no noise, not even the croaking of a frog. Noticing the dead silence was unsettling when we first arrived, however, now it seemed more apparent to me. So quiet, so disturbing. No movement, no sound, not even a shifting of a single leaf. How unsettling.

"Alice," Lily began, but as she did, a loud creak came from below.

Creak

It stopped short for a slight moment. It was short yet loud, and then a longer one followed.

Creeeeeeeeeeeeak ~

We stood silently listening to the sound beneath us, and then once more a long creak as we knew we heard the door closing behind whatever it was that had entered the building, from what seemed like the front entrance.

"The hell was that," Lily asked.

"Don't know but I don't like it," Alice replied

From the distance, we heard the sound of a car pulling up. The headlights were seen far off in the distance as it pulled up to the entrance next to our car. Becoming more noticeable once the headlights were turned off, it was a large truck. As someone got out, we noticed that it was Jason; Alice's used to be boyfriend. Alice ducked, pulling the two of us down to do the same.

"Alice," Jason yelled out, "you're here right? I know you are, and you're dating that guy aren't you!" he yelled out into the open night.

Alice and Lily peeked up to take a look, I too did the same.

Jason walked strangely to the front over the fallen gated entrance. "I'm sorry Alice, I love you, I love you so much, but for you to leave me for some scrawny guy like him," he yell, fumbling, walking to the building strangely. He had come drunk, and was holding onto something. It was a glass bottle in his right hand as he took a swig from it.

"My god, I never seen a guy break down like that in real life, I mean, we've broken up for a while now and he's still that attached?"

"There you are, my Alice," stumbling, watching the three of us as we quickly withdrew our heads from sight. "So I see Lily is with you, and I saw him too, he eventually came along with you did he? You know, it really hurts me to see you with him, I know you love him, no matter what you or everyone else says. I know you after being with you so long. I know how you look when you stare at him, you love him," stretching the sound of the 'o' in love, "and I HATE his god damn guts!"

Shortly after, the sound of the door below opened again, making the same creaking noise as before. The three of us looked over to see no one. Jason was now inside the building as well, with whatever that had come inside before him.

"No, this isn't good," I said. My head felt light, and everything started to spin.

"Evan, calm down, look at me," Lily came over, shaking me as I faced her. "They don't exist Evan, we came to that conclusion remember? Try to take deep breaths to relax."

Staring at her, my hazy mind began to recollect into sensible thoughts. Doing what Lily had instructed the breathing help.

"Alice, why the hell is he here?" Lily whispered angrily next to me.

"I told a few people that we would be doing some exploring, but I never told them where. I guess he connected everything from when we were dating, I did tell him a few times that I wanted to see this place," saying in a panic. "I'm sorry; I didn't think that he would come here." She sounded frightened. I could see her peaking from the side, looking at me concernedly. She was sorry for me, wanting to apologize to me in some other way than her words, but she didn't know how.

Touching Lily's arm to let her know that I had calmed down, she released me. Reaching over, I grabbed Alice's shoulder as she looked into my eyes. "Alice, I'm okay, you don't have to be sorry about anything, a few moments ago I told you how glad I was for coming out here, remember? Nothing happened yet, so right now we just need to focus on getting out of here."

My words had an unexpected effect as she her lips began to quiver and her eyes watered over. "Okay, lets' get out of here."

"Glad the two of you are getting your act together, but we have a big problem. Besides from the drunken angry muscle head coming for us, something else is here and we have no idea what or who it is. For all we know, it could be anything from a psychopath to a wild wolf."

"Okay, hold on, I have a stun gun and some mace," Alice said, pulling out the items, "this is all I got."

"Great, you keep the stun gun, I'll take the mace. I have a military knife, you take it," Lily said, pulling out the knife from behind her, handing it to me still sheathed.

I looked at the two of them dumbfounded, unsure of how to respond. I wasn't expecting the trip to so dangerous, so I came unprepared unlike these two in front of me. They knew well ahead of the possible dangers that might occur, and they were more than prepared.

"What did you think; we would just wander into a place like this expecting everything to be okay? You have to be ready for anything," Lily said smiling at me.

Calmly, Lily took charge of everything, the opposite from Alice and me. Standing stiff with knife in hand, the blade was about six inches in length, heavy, and looked sharp enough to easily cut through flesh and bone. I saw the moon reflecting from the blade as I gazed at it, realizing that this was really happening. Alice was next to me shaking, worried, she was similar to me, nervous and afraid.

"Hello," Lily said next to me. She was on the phone calling

for help. "Yes, this is Lilith Rothschild, I'm calling from an abandoned building in the outskirts west of town and we need help, it's an emergency, please, get someone out here as soon as possible." She paused as she waited for the voice on the other end. "I don't know the address, but it's an abandoned lab or chemical facility, whatever it is, it's about seventy miles from town, or about an hour, an hour and a half's drive. We have a crazed psychopath that entered the building trying to kill us, and something else. I'm not sure what it is, but I think a wild animal came inside too." Again, she waited for a response on the other end. "I'm with two other classmates, Alice Rivera and Evan Gray." Waiting, Lily seemed irritated as she listened to the other end. "Somewhere safe to hide? Okay. Hello, hello? Damn, lost reception now of all times. At least someone's coming, lets' do what they said and find a safe place we can try hiding until they come, I'll keep trying to contact them as we do."

Nodding our heads, Alice and I agreed with her. As we quickly packed up everything, we started to move towards the door. A loud noise could be heard close by as we froze in place.

"Alice, Alice! I know you're up there, I'm here," Jason yelled from below the stairs. His voice rang loud and clear.

It was too late for us to hide, there was nowhere to escape. The roof was nothing but vast open space, so hiding was not an option. Jason had come much too quickly in the five, seven or so minutes after entering. He must have sprinted straight here after seeing us.

Loud running footsteps sounded as Jason ran up to the roof. Once he reached the top, he yelled out Alice's name. "Alice!" he roared. "You, what the hell are you doing here," directing the question towards me, panting from his sprint up, holding onto a small keychain light which was still on.

"Damn, he's already here," shouted Lily.

"Get away from her, I'm so god damn tired of see your face near her all the time," Jason yelled at me. His anger grew ten folds the moment he saw me, his face redden, veins protruded from his arms and temple. "I'm going to kill your scrawny ass," walking briskly and angrily towards me.

"Jason, stop!" Alice yelled, standing in front of both me and Lily.

He didn't. Instead, he quickly motioned his arm for a backhand with the full intent of striking her. Seeing what Jason was about to do, Lily, almost inhumanly pushed Alice out of the way. As Alice fell to the side, she dropped the stun gun which Lily caught in midair, then jamming it into Jason's ribcage electrifying him. It seemed painful as he stood shaking, paralyzed where he stood before Lily withdrew the gun. He collapsed to knees and fell to the side.

"Alice, you okay," running to her side to help her up.

"God damn it," Jason was forcing himself to stand.

"Shit, I can't believe he's already getting back up, we need to get out of here, now!" yelled Lily as she ran for the door.

Alice and I quickly followed after her down the dark stairs. Lily already had her flashlight out as we quickly followed the light. Unfortunately, Alice and I left everything up on the roof, we were lucky that Lily was at least keeping it together enough to remember taking hers. Past the bloody rooms, we didn't look back. We trusted Lily's direction, blindingly following her. Reaching the next flight of stairs, we ran down them, bursting through the door as we were once again were on the second floor. After a few steps, Lily stopped.

"Why did you stop," I asked her.

"Quiet, I think there's something up ahead," saying as she directed the light in front of her. Her light caught a glimpse of the legs of something running away. It looked dark, black colored, hairless. It moved quicker than thought possible for any normal animal as it disappeared almost instantaneously. Seeing this, no one motioned. Lily then pointed to the far end of the hall, catching the glimpse of a body moving around the corner. Whatever it was, it was standing on two hind legs before disappearing.

"The hell is that? Is that the thing that came inside before Jason," Alice whispered quietly.

Lily turned off the light, which made us panic. Did she have something in mind to warrant turning off the flashlight? We continued to look down the long silent hall, frozen. Glowing lights darted from one end to the other, then another. It was hard to see after turning the light off, but I could see something. It was faint as my eyes adjusted to the dark, but we saw it. It was a faint glow in the dark, a pair of two similar glints, like the eyes of a hyena in the night, looking mockingly at its prey. Another pair appeared shortly after.

"What are they," Alice whispered.

Before anyone answered, the three pairs of glowing eyes quickly moved closer, we could see them bobbing up and down as they rapidly approach.

"Evan!" A loud yell called out to me, almost like roar. "Where the hell are you, I'm going to pound that smug face of yours, you and that little bitch," referring to Lily who stunned him.

The three creatures stopped shortly before us, roughly forty feet away, retreating immediately after they heard Jason's roar. Once they were gone from sight, Lily turned on the flashlight. Hurriedly, she grabbed Alice's arm, opened the nearest door, and forcibly shoved her inside. Getting the message, I followed. Alice was already glancing around trying to find a place to hide as Lily silently closed the door behind us. It was a poor choice of a location as there wasn't any place to hide. There were no furniture, no closets, nothing to hide behind. There were just a bunch of metal tables, but even they had a see through bottoms and were drilled into the wall. There were also small cabinets hanging about which held nothing inside for us to use in defense. We could hear the loud running of Jason as he ran down the steps like a mad bull. Lily turned off her light. It wasn't completely dark, there was a slight glowing light, illuminating through the window from behind us. Gathering near the window, we waited. Noises were heard filling the building, reverberating audibly as they reached our ears.

"Alice! Lily! Where are you three?!" Jason yelled, kicking a door, one after another, looking through each room on the second floor. The force from his kick sent the doors flying open with force. "Where the hell are you all?!"

"Why don't we just run for it," Alice asked.

"We could, but we might risk running into those *things* again. I don't know what the hell they are, and I don't want to know," Lily replied, taking out her phone again. "No use, there's no signal." Putting her phone away, she looked over the stun gun she held, making sure it was working okay.

Seeing her, watching her, it made me feel small, unworthy to be with her. How could she be so strong in the face of such danger while Alice and I cowered in fear, shaken, disoriented with confusion and of what would become. It was only after seeing her that I realized I was still holding the knife she had given me. My grip on it was tight, holding onto it firmly. It was strange how still I held it so still while my other arm quivered in fear.

Jason was getting closer as we heard the doors crashing open from the impact from his muscular leg. We did nothing but wait for him. Not taking long, he reached us eventually. The door flung open, breaking off its hinges, with him standing behind it. He placed both hands above the doorway with satisfaction, almost as if intentionally blocking our escape.

"There you are, you know, I'm going to enjoy beating you and you're electric whore."

"Listen, you need to calm down, you're drunk, why don't we go somewhere and talk this out," Alice pleaded.

"Shut up! You don't tell me what to do!" shouting over her reason. "You got a nice piece there," he said looking at my knife. "You know how to use it, because I don't think you do?" Motioning his right arm down behind him, he pulled out a small pocket knife, dropping his miniature flashlight, the light went out. "It's not anything like yours, but I'm sure it can get the job done."

Pulling his other arm down, we knew he was going to come after us as we readied ourselves. Taking a foot inside the doorway, he was thrown out of sight. All of us saw it. Three pairs of shining glints darted straight across at him, pushing him out of view.

"Aargh."

Hearing the sounds of struggles close by, it lasted for two seconds, maybe three, before silence followed. Then, they appeared once more, at the doorway. We heard them growl at us. Not being able to see them completely, they stood in the shadow of the hallway. We were still able to see some slight details of them. Their eye color;

two pairs of white, one blue, one standing up roughly three foot tall, hunched over, the other two on all fours. As one of them slowly moved towards us, it made a disgusting menacing laugh. Placing a hand into the door, the weak light from the moon was just enough to show the details of its long grotesque fingers. Dark like black ink, even though there was hardly any light, the light faintly reflecting off its hand. We stood frozen, not a twitch, not a blink, not a breath as they motioned ever closer. Like Jason, it disappeared from our sights, along with its companions.

It was something much like them, but larger, tackling them out of view. The sounds of growls and roars were heard, vicious noise of fighting and struggle. We caught quick glimpses of them as their bodies darted back and forth from the view of the open doorway. The fighting stopped. We didn't hear anything for some time.

"We need to get out of here," Alice whispered to us.

"No, we don't know if they're still out there," I said, my hand gripping a hold of her arm. I was holding onto her too tightly, I knew it as I saw my hand gripping her arm. I was holding onto her with all my strength, probably hurting her I thought. My hold on her didn't loosen.

She didn't seem like she was in pain, instead she looked at me, touching my hand. "It's alright Evan, let me just check it out, to see if they're gone. It would be better if we made a run for it instead of waiting for them to comeback."

"No," Lily interrupted. "We're going to wait here. I already called for help; someone will come for us eventually."

"Lily, we're out in the middle of nowhere, it would take time for them to come to us, even then, they would still need to find us in this large facility, it might be too late by then."

"I-I'll go with you," saying with a slight stutter. Loosening my grip on Alice's arm, I released her. "Don't wait, they'll be back for us, I know it," trembling.

Alice reached for Lily's flashlight, but she held onto it with an iron grip. "Alright, at least let me take a look instead," Lily said.

"No! I can't let you do that," my hands reached out to her, gripping her by her shoulders.

"I have to, I'm the one that's thinking the most calmly out of all of us, and you should be careful when holding a dangerous weapon," gazing at my knife which was dangerously close to her ribs. She gently placed the flashlight on the floor and forced my hands off her shoulders. Her strength confounded me. I thought I held her tightly, but she was still able to push my grip off, with ease almost. "You two wait here, I'll take a quick peek, if the coast is clear, then we'll leave this place."

Taking a peek around the corner, she glanced to the left, then the right. Turning on the flashlight once more, she shined it down the hallway taking her time to examine patiently, making sure nothing was there. I walked over to her as she turned around.

"Okay, it's clear, lets' go."

We stood at the door way, but Alice didn't come.

"I can't move," she said.

Not noticing until now, she wasn't like Lily who collected and altogether, Alice's whole body was trembling. She was just being brave a moment earlier. She was still just a delicate frightened girl after all.

Walking back, "Alice we need to go," I said as I held her hand, helping her up.

Turning around, we walked over towards Lily. As we did, two small figures darted over, grabbing onto Lily, pulling her away and out of sight.

"Lily?" I dropped my knife, as it made a clanging noise. "No, not you too." I ran to the door and look down the hall in the direction she was taken. "Lily!" I called out from the top of my lungs.

Taking a step in the direction she was taken, then another. I picked up the light Lily had dropped. Not knowing when, but my body was running down the hall towards the direction they'd taken her. I didn't want to see them, I was afraid to face them again, but I ran to her, for her.

"Evan, Evan wait," Alice called out behind me.

I didn't look back, I aimlessly ran around, searching the building for her, feeling my cloths drench in a cold sweat from the fear of what would become of her. Calling out Lily's name every once in a while, making my way from one floor to another. It seemed like I spent a long time looking for her, when I knew it must've only been a few minutes or so. Aimlessly I ran, I wasn't sure if I was in the same building or not, or if I was in one of the interconnected buildings. I was in a panic as I continued my search, running without direction. Reaching the third floor, I continued to run before the floor gave way below me.

I laid dazed having fallen through the third and second floor, landing now on first. I could tell, seeing how open the space was. Even as my head was spinning from the fall, I was at the front entrance of the building were the three of us had initially entered. I wondered than if all I was doing was just running around in circles.

Hearing the sound of a door opening, I looked in the direction of where it came from.

"Oh my god, Evan!" it was Alice's voice. I could see her coming towards me.

As she did, I saw a glow behind her. I knew which one it was. How could I forget that look, that white glowing eye as it caught sight of me? It's one eye, large and round, glowing in the dark, a perfect sphere. Its eye became menacing with rage as it ran for Alice.

"Alice, behind you," I said softly, not being able to shout out to her. My voice didn't project. "No, please no."

It caught her. Taking Alice like it took my sister. The creature jumped onto Alice's back, pulling onto her hair, whipping her fiercely to the floor. Hearing her loud scream, I couldn't do anything, just like so long ago.

"Somebody help!" she screamed out loud. It was too late. The tiny demon made quick work of her.

The small figure looked at me as it stood upright, on top of Alice's body, triumphant. *"Finally, we found you. A long time we waited, but we found our way back,"* it said.

Uttering its last words, another larger figure came down from above. It was the much larger one. It's large hand grabbed hold the small one by its hind leg. Picking the smaller one up, slammed it to the floor with such force, the cemented ground below shattered apart. Letting out a loud roar, it attacked the smaller one, clawing, thrashing away at the body, ripping it to shreds. The carnage continued before me as my eyes closed shut, passing out.

CHAPTER

12

Waking up, I laid blinded inside of a brightly lit room. There was sound of a repetitive beep, a slight pain in my arm and leg, the safety of a hospital and its bed. I looked around groggily. Emelia was sitting reading a book when she noticed me waking up.

"Evan, thank goodness you're away," moving over towards me. "I'm so glad you're alright, I'm so glad you're alright." Tears streamed down her face. "Everything's going to be fine, alright, you're safe now. You're mom and dad is flying in as we speak, they should be arriving in a few hours. You hurt yourself pretty badly when you fell, but the doctor, a good friend of mine, said that you should be making a full recovery, and even able to leave in a few days. Of course I'm going to make you stay a little bit longer, just so you can heal a bit more properly. I wanted to look on you personally, but I couldn't, they said I was too emotional. I made some arrangements however, so you'll be directly under my care starting tomorrow."

Taking a look down, it was difficult as a painful shock reverberated throughout me. I knew I was hurt in a few places, but didn't know where. "Where," I started to choke, "where's Alice and Lily," managing to say, doing my best to hold back my coughs. It was difficult to talk as my chest was in pain. I had the feeling that they were dead by now, but I needed to confirm it, to hear it.

Emelia was hesitant. "Lily; well Lily is alive and safe at least. She's a bit beaten up, but she'll be making a full recovery like you."

Hearing that filled me with relief, I was so happy to hear that she was alive. I was overjoyed knowing that I would be able to talk and be with her again. I wanted to see her right then and there, to make sure that she was alive with my own eyes. Knowing I wasn't able to, not in the condition I was in, I laid there simply glad. "Alice, what about Alice," I asked, hoping for similar good news, wishing that what I had seen was just a dream, a hallucination.

"You're hurt, not badly, a few scrapes, a few stitches, lots of bruises, you're extremely luckily you didn't break anything," Emelia responded, trying to avoid my question.

"Who cares about me, I'm at least still alive. Aunty, is Alice alright?"

"Yes, well," she paused, not being able to look into my eyes, and I knew what that meant. "She didn't make it sweet heart. Right now you need to rest. I'll tell you what happened since you have the right to know." Stroking my head, wiping my sweat, doing what she could to settle me down.

"Roughly two hours had passed before help arrived. Their excuse was that the place was in such a deserted area, it was difficult to find the road leading to building, which is why it took them so long. Going through the front entrance, they found you lying in a pile of rubble. You had fallen through a few floors above. You were the first person they saw actually. In the same room not too far away, they told me they found Alice's body. Something had taken a large bite from her throat, which is how she died. Searching the entire building, certain parts were not accessible due to the poor integrity of the building, but they were able to located Lily in another building all the way in the back. She was found bloodied on the third floor, but alive and breathing. She was covered in blood which they tested and confirmed that it was her own, coming from her own wounds. She suffered large cuts on her back, stomach, and both legs. They'll leave scars, but she'll be okay. As for Jason, they're still searching for him. They haven't find a single trace of him as of yet, but they're not giving up. They're trying to find ways to look into other parts of the buildings that they haven't accessed yet. I was told that they might have to call off the search since the building had deteriorated to such an extreme extent, its' become a safety concern to continue search any further."

An investigator came around to take my statement. I told him everything that occurred. When I asked him about the building, certain parts it didn't seem to add up. The details were off, things that I told him didn't appear as they should have found. Having taken Lily's statement before me, apparently her version of the story happened exactly as I told them, but the investigators never found the bloody rooms with cages. Correction, they did find the rooms with animal cages, which were forcibly open, but there was no blood. They also didn't find any traces of the beast, animal, demons, or whatever it was that they thought Lily and I had seen. I was so sure that some traces must have been left on the first floor. How the monster tore through the smaller one so viciously, some traces must've been left. They didn't find anything, no blood except mines and Alice's. There was a large dent on the floor nearby Alice that they admitted was unusual, this was what I thought of where the larger monster had slammed the smaller one to the floor, but that was it. Other than that, there were no traces of them. It was as if they never existed. However, I knew that they were real. The officer had admitted Lily telling the exact same story as I did. There was even similar detailed description of the beasts and of the blood covered rooms.

My feelings were mixed. What was best now was to simply recuperate as much as I could so I could see how Lily again. My father and Clarissa didn't believe me of course, overhearing them talking of how the event was making me relapse back to how I was before.

"My poor boy is starting to see things again, I can't believe this is happening, just when I thought that he was finally recovering," remembering what Clarissa had said as I overheard her.

There was no point in telling anyone about it. Everything would be just like when I was child. 'Lies and delusions,' people would think, that was how they always thought. My father and Clarissa stayed with me in the same room for the first two days before deciding to stay in a hotel. Clarissa absolutely refused to stay with Emelia, blaming her for the current events.

Clarissa was sitting comfortably in the seat next to me when Emelia came in.

"Oh, it's you again," Clarissa bemoaned.

"Of course I'm here again, I work at this hospital and I'm currently the doctor in charge of him," Emelia exasperated, throwing her arms up in the air. "Anyway Evan, I'm dropping by to let you know that Lily was discharged just now. She wanted to come see you, but her mom insisted that they head home. I guess she blames you for what happened."

"Blame him, it was obviously that it's that little vixen's fault," Clarissa yelled, standing up.

"Settle down would you, this is a hospital, and do you mind not acting like a crazy lunatic all the time."

"Well what do you expect from me?"

"Do I have to call security on you again, I did it once and you know I'll do it again."

Clarissa grumblingly sat back down quietly.

"In any case, you're recovering well. You should be able to be discharged soon too. You'll have to continue to wear the casts, but at least you can leave the hospital," Emelia said.

"I already talked it over with your dad earlier. Once you can leave, you'll be taking the next flight home with us."

"When was this, he's almost done with the school year, it would make more sense to let him stay and graduate," Emelia interrupted.

"And what, let something like this happened to my little boy again; under your care might I add?"

"Little boy? How old do you think he is?"

"So what, he's going to continue living with you? Just look what happened to him while you were supposed to be supervising him."

Emelia was baffled. I could see her hurt by those last few words that Clarissa had yelled at her. A part of her felt responsible for the condition that I was now in.

"I'm staying," interrupting their argument.

"Evan, don't say such nonsense, you can recover with me and your dad. Besides, we missed you so much at home, if you don't comeback with me, I'll only pace back and forth everyday worrying over you."

"Thanks, but I'm about to graduate soon." I could see her wanting to say something, but I interrupted her before she could. "Mom, please, I want to stay," I said as I reached for her hand.

"Oh fine, I'll discuss it over with your father, he's on his way with some food, so we'll talk about it then. Just to let you know, I'm not too happy about this."

When my father did arrive, he was the same as always. He did everything that was asked of him, and everything a father was supposed to do. He visited me, talked with me, brought me random things to occupy my time, not because he was asked to, but out of his own concern. Still, he barely smiled while I was around, and something told me that he wasn't too happy to be here. Eventually Clarissa brought up the topic of allowing me to stay a few days before I was being discharged, and he refused at first. When I heard him refuse in front of me, demanding for me to come home, I was taken aback, it even surprised Clarissa hearing him so adamantly arguing to take me home. Even more so was that he was genuinely angry of the idea of having me continue to stay with Emelia. It had been a long time since I'd seen him so angry, so concerned for me in that way, that he seemed like my father to me once more. It took two days with both Clarissa and Emelia collaborating to finally make him agree.

I left the hospital a day early before my recommended discharge date to attend Alice's funeral. It was a depressing solemn scene. Lots of people came, gathering around. Classmates I never talked to, her parents grieving off to the side. Her mother stood weeping in black, her father trying his best to comfort her while keeping it together himself. He did not try to hide his grief as he comforted his wife. They cried for their beloved daughter. The father wiped his tears with his hands to keep up his strong appearance; they persisted.

Overhearing some talk right before the procession. Jason parents would not be attending Alice's funeral. Even more, they had already decided to hold Jason's funeral the day after, adamant to have the two funerals on separate days, even though they had not found his body yet. The search crew had stopped searching after only a few days when three of the men in the search party were injured when one of the walls crumbled, causing the roof to collapse above them. No one was seriously hurt, only minor injuries, but that was when everyone but his parents decided that it was time to call off the search. I had decided not to go to his funeral. Knowing how much Jason had disliked me, it was for the best that I didn't. I would only cause problems if his close friends saw me and pointed me out. I wished he was still alive, even if he was about to kill me that night, he was also a victim of those things. I hadn't wanted him to die the way he did, with his body most likely never going to be recovered.

Looking throughout the crowd, I spotted Lily and her mother close to Alice's parents. She too was crying for her dear departed friend. I was relieved to see that she was okay. Lily wasn't in casts like me, but she still had a bruised eye which seemed to be close to healed. So glad I was, but I didn't have time to feel any joy as now was a time to mourn, as I wished Alice a peaceful afterlife. Once all was over, people started to leave, Alice's parents thanking those who came one at a time, for coming to see their daughter off. It was really her dad that did most of the thanking and talking as his wife buried her face in a handkerchief. Lily made her way to their car, walking with a slight limp, her mother giving some support as they walked away.

"We should go home," my father said.

Wanting to talk and apologize to Alice's family, and to run after Lily, I didn't do either as I nodded in agreement to my father. We drove back to Emelia's house where both my father and Clarissa decided to stay before leaving the following day, against Clarissa's wishes. Being away from work for so long, the two had to return. That night before, my father came knocking on the door.

"Come in," I replied.

"This is a surprise, your window isn't covered," my father said, moving over to hang up the curtains up for me.

"Thanks, I don't think I would've been able to sleep without it covered, at least not anymore." Having the window open as such made me tense again, as if something would appear.

"So this, 'Lily,' are you staying because you want to be with her?"

He caught me off guard with the sudden inquiry. "If I said 'yes,' would you force me to leave with you?"

"No, I would still let you stay, even more so, I would want you to stay because of it," finishing up with the curtain, he checked it over once more before sitting down on the chair nearby.

"Why would you want me to stay?" I asked, finding his answer highly unusual.

"Let me ask you first. It sounds like you've fallen for this girl, have you?"

"Yes, I have, I would even go as far as calling it love."

"I would have assumed so, after all, you wouldn't have gone out in the middle of the night to explore some building out in the middle of nowhere if it wasn't due to a woman. It may not seem like it, but I have been watching over you. Even though the therapist told me that you've made leaps in your recovery, I know better. How you break in a nervous sweat just from the setting sun. How you shun others, distancing yourself as to not get hurt like you have been many times already. Even how glad you were leaving me, getting way from Clarissa and me."

"I'm your father Evan. I've watched you as a parent, watching you grow into who you are today. I know exactly how afraid you were, so for her, this Lily, to get you this far, it must mean that she's quite the woman."

Not sure what to say, I didn't say anything, I merely listened to him.

"It's late, I'll let you rest," my father stood up to leave.

"Wait, you didn't answer the question."

"You should be more concerned about recovering," moving for the door.

"Then before you go, I've always been wondering. Do you blame me for what happened all those years ago?"

My father stopped with his hand on the doorknob. I supposed I caught him off guard with that question. Frankly, I didn't think I had it in me to ever ask him that question.

"You've really changed," he replied. "You've grown since you come here. Before, you would never have asked that kind of question to me." Turning around, he made his way back to the chair. "I don't blame you, at least not anymore."

My chests tighten after hearing that he once did, knowing for a long time he blamed me, or at least partially. Not saying anything, waiting for him to continue, or was he waiting for me to say something?

"I still don't know what exactly happened that night, and I'll let you know now that I still don't believe your story. After all, it's rather absurd to think that demons and monsters exist, that your sister and mother died in such a way. When it first happened, I was still grieving, having lost them both, I shattered under the grief I was in, and so I started to resent you. The more you told me your ridiculous tales, the more a part of me hated you. It didn't last long, my anger and displeasure of you that is. It lasted probably for a few weeks before I came to my own senses. You lost them too, and as a child of your age back then, you wouldn't have been able to remember things clearly. Besides, I couldn't hate you, your my boy, you were all I had left and I loved you so much. I still do love you son, even with how cold I might act. That's why I wanted you to come home with us, I didn't want you to stay and risk the thought losing you either."

"You might now want to ask as to why I've become so cold and desolate towards you if I'd loved you so much. It's not because I blame you. It's because I remember them when I'm around you son. I don't mean to burden you, but when I see you, I can't help but remember those times we spent together as a family, the four of us. I loved you, your mother, and sister so very much, that those days were the happiest days I could remember. With you near me, I'm reminded of those happy days, and it pains me to think that we can't enjoy them anymore. So I've slowly squeeze my emotions out, making up who you see right now."

"Don't say anything son," my father said as he caught a glimpse of my mouth moving as I was about to speak. "Since I'm explaining things to you, the reason why I'm allowing you to stay is due to your feelings for this girl. It's because I know. I know what it means; after all, I loved your mother very much. I love Clarissa, but there's no woman out there that made me feel the way your mother could have. She was something special. She was a woman that could fill me with joy just by hearing her voice. Even a hundred miles away, under stacks of paperwork, being stressed and overworked, or even during a heated argument, I was always happy to be with her. To know that even if that crazy woman made me want to kill her sometimes, listening to her voice, to be with her, I knew I was still happy, that it was with her that I was arguing with. So seeing you change so much, being able to face your fear to this extent, I'm certain that you love this girl very much, probably as much as I've loved your mother. I'm sure I can leave you in her hands as well. If she's able to be with you after seeing how you are, assuming she knows of your fear and what happened back then, than it must mean she loves you just as much. Don't let her go Evan."

Watching him leave, I called out to him, "dad," not knowing why I called out to him, I just did. "Nothing," I said, before he closed the door. Never in all those years had we ever really talked like this. I wasn't sure how to think, how to feel, how to act when we would see each other again.

There were a lot of things I needed to think over, so much had happened in such a short time. So many things went around in my head like a whirlpool. Events would swirl around for a while before vanishing, not knowing where. Not being able to sleep, there was no way I could after listening to my father. I started to recollect the past few days, starting with the window. They existed, I knew that for sure, or did they? There were no marks on the window, it was verified already, which had led me to believe I had hallucinated demons and monsters all my life. Then there was that strange knocking on the door that very night as well, but there was no actual evidence that it was cause by *them*. Then what of the attack I had experience just a while ago at the abandoned building. Perhaps I hallucinated that as well? I couldn't have. I thought long and hard of this possibility. Was what had happened in that place something that I'd conjured up, like the marks on the window? It might have been possible that I had put the delusions together when I passed out, twisting reality. But Lily had confirmed it as well; at least that's what the police officer who questioned us both had said. What was I thinking, as I lay in bed, battered and bruise still, with Alice dead and Jason missing, what was there to question?

Starting to worry for my own mental wellbeing, anxiety slowly built up from my conflicting thoughts. There was one way to confirm it, I knew one other person who could confirm everything, that was Lily. She was present and still alive. Thankfully, she would be able to give confirmation that *they* were real or not. As late as it was, having been thinking for so long, it was now two in the morning. I couldn't wait. I needed to know from her as my thoughts persisted to roil over the past events. Picking up my phone, I dialed her number. The craving to sedate these unanswered questions was a must for me.

The phone rang a few times. No one picked up. Not leaving a message, I left it at that. A second later, Lily was calling me back. "Hello, Lily?" I answered.

"It's me."

"Sorry, you're probably resting up."

"No, I was awake. I didn't answer earlier because I wasn't sure what to say to you once I heard your voice. I've been pretty emotional, everyone has, and I don't even know what to tell people anymore, about what happened, what I saw. After what I saw, after what attacked us." Her voice told me that she was becoming emotional. "I've stayed quiet, no one would believe me if I told them. I mean, they didn't find anything, not a single trace of evidence of those creatures."

"So you did see them."

"I saw them, you were right all along, they do exist. Seeing them with my own eyes and having them attack everyone, I now know they're real. I believe you now, you weren't lying or hallucinating, but what are they?"

She confirmed it, their existence which no one else ever could before. A sigh of relief swept throughout my body, finally after so many years, I was able to confirm of their existence with someone else. A cold chill came after, having confirmed that they *did* exist.

"I'm not too sure myself," I replied, which was true. This was really the second time they ever attacked me, and it wasn't as if there were readily available records of them. "They could be demons, monsters, aliens, I don't know, all I know is that I'm glad they didn't take you away from me too. If you had disappeared on me, if they took you away from me."

"They didn't take me, I'm alive, and I'm here. I'll be going back to school starting next week, will you be there?"

"I'll be there. I've wanted to see you."

When the day did finally come around for me to go back to school, I had healed a good extent. There were no signs of bruises or cuts anymore, and my casts were just taken off the day before, though there were a lot of stares and whispers when I returned. This wasn't unusual, after all, Jason and Alice were both well known throughout the school. During class, no one approached me. Jeremy who sat next to me sat fidgeting. It was obvious that he wanted to come up to me, inquire about what happened. He told me he liked Alice after all, and to know that I was there when she was killed. He never did come up to me and asked.

I began to wonder if the others wanted to question me, they must have. What would I say, perhaps I would say that something attacked us looking like a wild animal, but we couldn't see what it was since it was too dark? What were Lily telling people? Were people even asking her, she was much closer to Alice than I was?

Not being able to catch Lily that morning, I waited for her during lunch at our usual spot. As I waited for her, a group of jocks came up to me. They were Jason's buddies, remembering a few of them from an earlier confrontation. A few of them seemed calmed enough, others not looking too happy to have their friend missing, which was understandable.

"Evan, right?" one of the calmer individual of the group asked me.

I nodded, "that's me."

"We heard the story about what happened that night, but we wanted to hear it from you. We got word that it was reported in a statement that Jason attacked you out of anger. We're not questioning if he did or didn't, we pretty much figure that he did, but what happened after that?"

His statement surprised me. I didn't know how or where he obtained that information from. "He, Jason, arrived drunk that night. Having chased the three of us, he eventually cornered us in a small room, Lily, Alice and I," calmly saying as my stomach tightened as I recapped the summary of events for them. "He took a step at us with a pocket knife that he carried. That's when it happened, an animal or something attacked him, pulling him out of view, and that's when we lost sight of him. I don't know what happened to him after that."

"That's not exactly what we heard," the same guy responded.

"You're a goddamn liar!" another guy yelled as he grabbed me, pulling me up forcible by the collar. He was one of the more agitated individuals. I had noticed him from the back, jittering, wanting to grab me from the start. "We know about it. We heard all about how you said in your statement that you were attacked by these little creatures or darkened monsters. What makes you think we can really believe the hell you're saying?" The others were restraining him, forcing him to release me as he couldn't fight against their collaborating efforts.

"It was dark, and that's what they looked like to me. I'm not lying, thinking back, it had to be some kind of animal," I proclaimed. "No person can take out Jason, even if it was three against one."

"Listen, snap out of it, do you want to play in the next game, huh?" one of the others started to slap him a few times.

"Who the hell gives a damn about the next game when he's missing," he argued back.

"What the hell is going on here?" a teacher called out to us. He was a large man with glasses, tie, and a balding middle aged man, some teacher that I never had before. "Hey kid, you okay," he asked me running up.

"I'm okay, we were just talking. A bit rough, but were good," responding with a smile. Looking towards the other guy who first initiated contact with me, he got the message.

"Right, we were just messing around, guy to guys, seeing if he was okay you know."

"Nothing wrong here," another interrupted, hanging his arm around his buddy's shoulder, "just got a bit emotional hearing about Jason and what happened to him is all. Everything's alright now, no need to worry sir."

"I get it, I do, but we don't condone violence at this school, I'll let what I saw go this time, but for now, get the hell out of here," the teacher said.

'Okay, okay, we're leaving,' a few of them replied back, while the others simply turned around, walking away.

More people throughout the day began gathering the courage to confront me, asking me about what had happened. What kind of, "animal" did I think it was; how bad were my injuries? It was difficult explaining the details, forced to recapture the moment of the event, having to remember it repeatedly throughout the day. They were friends and classmates; they wanted to know, though it seemed that most of them somehow knew the full details of that night anyhow.

When school ended, the day had made me tired, craving to

escape everyone's questions and stares. Lily was at school I knew, having seen her in class. I decided to wait for a better time to discuss things over with her, figuring it would be best to meet elsewhere and talk instead of at school. I texted Lily, letting her know in advance that I would be wait for her at her place. I left immediately for her house.

Once arrive, I rung the doorbell. No one was home, Lily hadn't come back yet. Soon after she arrived, pulling up to the drive way.

"Come inside," Lily said as I followed behind.

She turned towards me, giving me a rushed kiss. "I'm sorry, I'm just so happy to see you okay."

I touched her neck where she had a slight green bruise, something I hadn't notice before. It was still healing slowly, soon to disappear completely. "I'm glad you're okay, does it still hurt anywhere? I saw you limping at the funeral."

"I'm alright, when I got dragged away, a got a really bad cut on my leg. The hospital stitched it up. It hurts still, but not as much. I was told that after a bit more time, it should fully heal and I wouldn't feel the pain anymore. I'm sure that it's going to leave a scar, but at least I'm alive."

Moving to the living room, "Lily, I need to hear it again, that I wasn't seeing things. You saw them too, right? I just can't believe in myself anymore."

"They're real, I saw them," she touch my hand, holding on to me. "When I first saw it, I didn't believe it at first, but I was able to get a good look at it as it was dragging me away. Whatever that thing was, it looked at me with these savage starved eyes. It gives me shivers remembering those eyes."

"I can't believe it, someone besides me after all this time believes me. I've been hiding, telling myself I was delusional, but they do exist. I finally have some confirmation. Not only do you believe me but you've seen them too." Sitting there, my body seemed drained of energy. My heart slowed, I could feel the blood leaving my face.

"I'm here, everything will be okay, we're together, we're alive, and we're going to get through this together."

"No, you don't understand you saw them; they'll come after you too! They wanted only me, but now they might be coming after you because you've seen them."

She kissed me, "no one's going to take me, well get through this together, and we're going to keep on living. It was just that one time since we were out in the middle of nowhere. If we stay together near other people, they won't come after us."

"You can't be so sure. I don't know how they act or think, or what they're capable of. Look at what happened. They found no evidence at the scene. They didn't find any bloody animal caged rooms, no signs of Jason, no traces of anything that had even the slightest hinted that they existed. They're not human or any kind of life form that exists from here. Those *things* can do things we can't even imagine."

It dawned on me then that they had some unique skill or ability to be able to cover their tracks. They were able to make all traces of their existence disappeared if they wanted to. That was what they must have done with the marks on my window, which was why there was nothing there anymore, no hint nor traces of them ever being anywhere. There hasn't been any record of them, or none that I could find since they always covered their tracks.

"You can't be too sure about that. They did leave you alone after all those years, didn't they? If we think reasonably, if they had really wanted to, they could have come after you a long time ago, there's no reason for them to have waited so long."

She made some sense, why did they wait so long before coming after me. Was it because I started venturing out more brashly, more often into the night? Did one of them spot me as I did so? It might just be a possibility.

"Okay, you might be right, it might just be a coincidence, but I have a feeling that it wasn't, almost as if they planned to come for me sooner or later, as if they've been watching me patiently as of late. I'm sure of it since I recognized one of them that night. There was one with just one eye, I had seen it before."

"Why don't you stay here tonight, it might help you relax being with someone else."

"Why aren't you more worried? You seem so all together, even after what you just saw."

"Outside I seem like it, but I'm grieving and terrified on the inside. There's no doubt that I'm afraid, but I guess looking over the facts, I'm assuming that they won't be attacking us, or at least I hope so. It seems to me that it would be unrealistic for them to attack us in an area that's more densely populated."

"So, would you like to stay over?"

"I'll stay, its' been awhile since I've been this close to you," stroking her face with back of my fingers, pushing her long black hair back.

She leaned forward to kiss me, and then rested her head against me. We laid there for a while, waiting patiently, simply feeling the warmth of each other's body. Thunder sounded in the distance, loud and strong did it roar. It was getting late as Lily had fallen asleep in my arms. I unluckily couldn't do the same. Awake, I kept thinking and wondering about their existence, what were they, where did they come from, what was their habits, how did they choose their victims? Lighting flashed through the window, the rain could be heard coming down a bit harder than it was before. The loud rumbling of thunder came crying out so all could hear its powerful might.

The door to the front was heard opening, "Lily, I'm back, I got something you might like. We're having Italian tonight; I got it at that one place you like so much." The woman yelled as she rushed inside, shaking off her umbrella. Making her way inside, she caught sight of us two.

"Evan, what are you doing here?" The woman said, not looking too happy. It was Lily's mother Helen. Her coat was held with one arm, mostly dry still, with a few drops that had managed to cling to it. The food just recently brought in her other hand. She stood furious to see me in her house.

"Mom, I invited him over," now awake, fully alert. "We wanted to talk about what had happened."

"I'll tell you what happened, he threw you in danger, that's what he did," throwing her coat on the couch while placing the food on the table, she came over and stood towering above us, looking down upon me.

"I told you, it's the other way around," Lily hesitated, trying to come up with the words. "Alice and I were the ones who pushed him into going with us. We were the one who really wanted to go, he just tagged along."

"I need to talk to you," Helen said to Lily, using force to pull her along. Calmly as she usually is, she followed to the other side of the room. They moved slightly behind the wall, still insight. Lily's back was facing towards me as Helen glanced over at me, measuring the distance between us to judge whether there was enough between us, though it was as if she didn't care, perhaps she wanted to me see them discuss things over.

"Sorry for intruding Miss. Rothschild, I'll be leaving now."

"Wait a minute Evan, give us a moment," Helen called out to me, making me sit back down to wait.

"What do you think you're doing by staying with him," whispering angrily.

"You know I can't leave him, it should be obvious how I feel towards him. If it was anyone else, I wouldn't give a damn, but not him."

"Lily, I want you to get rid of him, doing it now will make it a lot easier."

"What!"

"Careful with your words," Helen said, taking another glance at me which made me divert my eyes.

"You can't mean that, what makes him so bad, he didn't do anything."

"That boy's the reason why you're in this shape," yelling while holding Lily by her shoulders. Quickly she let her go, calming herself down to a whisper. "If it wasn't due to him tagging along, I know that you would've been able to handle the situation on your own. He's the reason why Jason showed up in the first place and is still missing, why Alice is gone, and why they found you so beaten and bloodied. Everything connects to that boy."

"I'm sorry mom. I'm not going to do it. We can't do that to him, I'm going to be there for him, with him by his side."

"Your relationship can't last, it won't," Helen stood by, letting her daughter go. The air around her was different, seemingly more menacing. "He's not like you and I, he has problems, the only thing an immature young man like him can do is runaway and hide."

"He's getting better. One day he won't be afraid anymore."

Helen snorted, "'getting better.' Even so, I can't trust him even if you do. I don't know if one day his problems might act up again putting you in danger."

"Who do you think you're talking about, it's me? I'm more than capable enough to protect myself. You of all people should know this."

"I love you, but I can't trust him. I guess I'll have to get rid of him myself if I have to." Helen motioned herself towards me, but Lily extended her hand out, quickly grasping her mother tightly.

"I'm sorry about this Evan, but could you please leave for now?" Lily asked, her back still turned.

Seeing how things played out, there was no convincing her mother. Most likely she will forever hold some animosity towards me from now on. I left the house, driving through the pouring rain under the darkened sky. It was strange. I was much calmer driving through the night than I should have been. Could it have been that I built a stronger resistance to fear of them as of late? Possible due to the fact that I know that they're real, and there's someone else who've seen them is with me now. There was more to it. It was the thought of losing Lily. After hearing the two discuss, I didn't want to lose her, not to anyone or any monster. I would have to be stronger for her, for both of us.

Coming home, I walked through the door. My shoulders were stiff, perhaps from lying on Lily's couch with her for so long. As I made my way to the kitchen, the thunder roared. A scream was drowned beneath it. I heard it. I wasn't fooled. It was obviously a scream of fear. Though the sounding thunder might have helped to cover it up, it was inside the house, close enough to tell the difference while others might not have.

Rushing to the stairs, "Emelia," I called out fearfully, "are you okay," again I yelled, taking two steps at a time as I climbed up the stairway. 'Please dear god no,' thinking to myself, it can't be, they couldn't have been back so soon, and not to my aunt Emelia.

Reach her room, I called out once more, "Aunty?!" I pushed opened her bedroom door which was already slightly open. The shower could be heard running. She must have just gotten home, I thought, she usually jumps into the shower after getting back.

"Emelia, I thought I heard you scream, is everything okay?"

making my way inside, slowly, cautiously, I held my breath. Her bath room door was cracked open. Walking over to it, "Aunty, it's me, Evan," no response as I touched the door. Pushing it open ever so cautiously, the steam filled the large luxury bathroom.

Emelia was there. She laid in on the floor, faced down, the curtains wrapped around her head. Bathing in her own blood, two large gash wounds were visible on her bare back. The dark red blood flowing out stained the floor, created a small pool.

"No," I fell to my knees, "this can't be." I looked up at Emelia once more before someone grasped me vigorously from behind, throwing me fiercely back against the wall. Reaching the wall with such force, I landed with a thud. I was able to catch a glimpse of the tall blackened dark figure. It was quick as it moved with its inhuman speed. It was gone from sight as I heard the window. I looked around the room. The window was now open. Seconds later, the lights turned off throughout the whole house.

I pushed myself up, moving my hands against the wall to find my way. My eyes hadn't yet adjusted to the now pitched dark house. Feeling that I reached the stairs, a heavy kick from behind sent me tumbling down the stairs. Gazing up, I stared at the violet eyes, glowing in the darkness. They were similar. I knew I'd seen them back at the abandoned building where everyone was recently attacked. Walking down the stairs, the lighting continued to flash, more often now as the storm was closer by. Outlines of the creature could be seen. Taller than your average person, possibly seven feet with long wavy hair down it's sides. I couldn't catch much else, what with the quick bits of light that randomly flashed through the windows.

Standing before me, it vanished. Hearing struggles in the dark, grunting off in the distance, I couldn't tell much of what was happening. Then, two sets of eyes, rolling around as they fought each other. One violent, the other a dark green, the same green that I saw next to Alice's body that night as it beaten and ripped the one eye to shreds. The fighting ensued in the living room. Mix in the sounds of thunder, wood and glass broke as the two darting across the room with immense speed.

"Enough!" a yell cried out. It was the roar of a menacing evil. "I won't hurt the boy, why don't we have some lights and talk things over for now," it said. Two seconds later, electricity began coursing through the house once more, lighting everything up.

"Hello Evan," said Helen, who stood where the violet eyed demon once stood. Still wearing her cloths from earlier, she smiled gleefully at me. It didn't look normal. There were traces of wickedness lingering around the corners.

On the other side of the room was Lily where the other one once too stood, replaced with the supposed to be love of my life.

"You must be really surprised," Helen said, "in fact, I am too. I didn't think Lily would actually come out to save you," saying as she calmly yet effortlessly pulled the couch over inhumanly with one hand, facing me. "I suppose she really has fallen heads over heels for you," crossing her legs, resting her hands on her knees. Looking like a normal person, but her demeanor was ominous. She exuded a wicked air about her as the lights flickered when she smiled. "Why don't you have a seat too sweet heart," patting the area on the couch next to her as she stare at me, though I knew she was directing the question towards Lily.

Lily didn't move, she stood there weeping, her face away from me.

"Suit yourself. Evan, I have to kill you, I need to kill you. I don't want to, you're a sweet, sweet boy, but I just have to. However, it seems like my daughter is making this a rather difficult thing to do. So I might not kill immediately, at least for now."

"You won't?" I asked.

"Silence!" she roared, the sound of the devil came reverberating out. For a moment, black veins coursed over her left side of her face, one eye clouded over violet, returning back to normal once she had settled down. "Sit silently and let me explain."

"I can't let you live anymore because you know about us, our 'kind,' if you will. What are we? Well, there are various different races, types, and classes, but humans have labeled us as either monsters or demons all together. Most often, it would be 'demon,' which many of us rather prefer being called as. You see, we have to go after you since it puts the integrity of our existence in jeopardy.

We really would like to stay hidden in the shadows. Lily and I don't devour people like the others of our kind do, but we still do cover each other's tracks when knowledge of our existence is in crisis. After all, it would be hard to mingle in with the population trying to live a normal life in this world if others were constantly trying to hunt us."

"Lily, I'd rather not have you stand there crying. Why don't you help your boyfriend up and have a seat?"

Lily didn't motion.

"Alright, I'll help him up then."

"Wait, I'll get him." Lily moved to me, her eyes red as she wiped them away. She extended a hand out to help me up.

Looking at her now normal hand, I didn't reach out. Instead, weakly, I got up myself, a bit dizzy from the hard fall still.

"A bit hateful isn't he," Helen said, pulling another chair over, reserving the couch for the two of us. "Perhaps he no longer sees you as his girlfriend, maybe not even a human."

Passing Helen to reach the couch gave me chills as we sat down.

"So yes, your knowledge of us is a threat. Emelia of course is an unfortunate victim, but we have to make things look like an accident after all. Having her dead too would make things more believable. You know, originally I was thinking of burning the house down. I was going to put cloths on her, clean the bathroom, and light the house on fire. I was going to make it look as if she was running out of the house, only to fall from the second floor, wounding her back and breaking her neck in the process. You of course would have been trying to save her and fell down as well."

Doing this kind of cover up isn't easy you know. You have to fine tune the details, set the fire just right to be able to last in this downpour. At the same time, create a cause for the flame in the first place. Some investigators really look at the specifics, it can be quite irritating."

She sat there waiting, expecting something. "Well, why don't I take a question or two for the time being? Do either of you have anything to ask or add?"

"W-what really happened that night, a while back with Alice, Lily and I?" I took the courage to ask.

Helen sighed. "That's what you want to know? It's complicated, but okay." Adjusting her position, she crossed her legs over once more. Leaning to the side, she placed her hand against her beautiful face, supporting her head. "I told you there were various types of our kind, the ones who ruined your childhood years ago were able to finally return from the other side. Don't ask about the other side or how they returned, but I'm going with the assumption that the first time someone from the other side opened the portal for them, then closed it off. After so long, they were able to find another way to open the portal again, and so they began searching for you after coming back. I know since I felt it open and close, having the same ability as well. They're sloppy. They should have killed you long ago and finished things before heading back home. What can we do, that's what you get from lesser demons."

"Finally coming back to this world, I suppose for some reason one of them had some sort of grudge against you. After locating you, they chose a moment best to finish you off, which just so happened to be at the abandoned building the three of you went to. They most likely were in the middle of planning a scenario, something like killing you and burning down the house like I was going to, but you three were in such a desolated place, it was probably too ideal of a place and too hard to resist. So they acted then and there. On the building roof when Lily was calling the police, it was actually me on the other end, she knew they were there after you, and the best way to cover the tracks were for me to intervene. That way she wouldn't have the need to show her real self."

I looked at Lily who was staring down silently at the floor, guilty.

"It wasn't easy," Helen continued, "I created a warp, kind of like a portal that connects my world to this one. Than another where it opened near your location that night. I had to run full speed searching for the building you know, it was tiring to do. I was the one who took cared of the ones on the second floor when you three were trapped in that room. I was supposed to give a signal letting

Lily know it was safe once I finished sweeping the locations nearby. Unfortunately, it was me against three, even though I'm much stronger than those weaklings, three against one proved difficult, so it was taking me a while. While I was occupied finishing those three off, all of you just had to wander around. Lily was then attacked, luckily she transformed and pulled it out of view from you two, but she was ambushed by a few others and was also preoccupied. By the time I myself was done, I had found Lily on the first floor mutilating one of them with Alice dead nearby, while you were lying unconscious in a heap of rubble. It would have been unwise to finish you then, to have my daughter be the only one to come out alive that night might have raised some questions and concerns. Plus my daughter insisted I leave you alive. Agreeing then, but now I've changed my mind. You're a liability that I can't leave alone."

"I'm pretty angry you know. I've never had a need to raise my hand at my daughter before. Do you know how she received those wounds? I inflicted them on her. To make things seem a bit more believable, I had to hurt her enough to make it look like she too was attacked, of course only after she had called the police."

Confounded, my eyes widened, looking at her with disbelief. This woman, this cruel cold hearted demon had gone above and beyond to cover all the loose ends.

"That's right," Helen said calmly after seeing my face, "my little girl wouldn't be so easily hurt from a bunch of lower demons, even if they are stronger than the average human. She practically came out unscathed after killing them off. I had to beat her till she became unconscious, and then cut her body up myself. Afterwards, I cleaned up all traces and evidence, which included the room with blood and cages. Another sloppy job, I'm assuming it was done by another of my kind who gorged themselves on the animals left behind. If you're wondering about Jason, I had to get rid of all traces of him. They made such a mess of his body, so much, that it was no longer possible to salvage his remains. There were also particular markings on his body that were inflicted so that I could no longer able to be pulled off as, 'an attack by wild animals.'"

"It's getting late, so why don't I conclude things up? If Lily still insists, I'll let you live Evan, you and Emelia. You see, in most cases this wouldn't happen, but her father was a human just like you. I fell in love with him, and as a family we stayed together. He never knew of what I was. It was unfortunate when he found out. As Lily grew older, she one day turned at the age of four, playing alone in her room with us. This horrified him when he saw this. At that point I had to tell him everything, about whom and what I was." She sat there, depress as she told the story of her past.

"Doing his best to keep it together, he struggled with the truth. Then one day, he came to Lily's room with a knife; he was going to kill her in her sleep. Sensing something wrong that day, I stayed awake and watch him enter the kitchen to slowly pull that knife out. When he entered Lily's room, I watched him raised that knife, swinging it down, wanting to rid of his daughter's existence. I waited until the last second before the knife reached her, hoping that he would stop. I felt his strength in his arm when I grabbed his hand. He was really going to do it. I had no choice. It was either Lily and I, or him. I didn't care much about my own life, I would've gladly given it to him, but Lily, my precious girl whom I've given birth to. She had to live. So, not being left with much of a choice, I finished him off."

Helen's face saddened as she remembered the past. I almost felt sorry for her.

"So I'll let you live, seeing how much my daughter loves you. You two remind me of my husband and me. I guess the memory of old times is making me soft. Emelia should still be alive. I tore up her back to stop her from struggling too much as I wrapped the curtain around her, making her pass out. So yes, she should be alive unless she bled to death already. Now, here's the bargain. Lily, do you still love him enough to let him live?"

"Yes, I do."

"Then Evan, I'll allow you and your Aunt to live, if you can keep your mouth shut about us. Your aunt should be okay. I was stealthy enough that she didn't see me, and I'll create a setting for you to convince her just enough. The other's won't be after you, I finished all of them off at the abandoned building, so for at least right now. You should be safe from my kind, unless more of them come over and start searching around, but unless you've done anything wrong, no one from the other side should be hunting you anymore. I'll have to kill you and everyone close to you if you ever so happen to tell another. If that's fine, if you can still live a normal life after all of this, than you I'll leave peacefully. What do you say?"

Sitting there, there wasn't much of an option, it was either I agree or die. "I agree," I replied meekly, my answer wasn't able to vocalize like I wanted it to.

"Lily, take him to the kitchen, I'd rather not have him see me fix the room. I have to 'change' to use my abilities, and that form isn't exactly pretty."

Taking me by the hand, Lily led me to the kitchen. I could hear small shifting noises in the other room as her mother started to repair what was damaged in the room. We stood silently across from each other.

"I'm sorry. This wasn't how I wanted things to happen."

"Why, why did you have to be one of them, of all people, you? I loved you so much, even now, to think that you were one of them all this time."

"There wasn't a choice for me, I didn't chose to be like this, to be a demon, it's not easy living a lie no one knows, not even Alice knew. I've hidden this secret from everyone."

"Lily, I can't be with a something like you," I said, clenching my fist. I was more difficult to say than I thought. Why? Why was it so difficult? She was one of those damnations. Breaking things between us should've been easier.

"Evan, don't say that, please. I may be like this, but think of all the times we spent together."

"Enough, don't say anything else, it won't be any use. I'm afraid of you, terrified of you Lily. Just having you in this room frightens me. Your kind took away my life back then, and was about to again just now. I still love you, but I know just what you're capable of now, and I'm not just afraid of you, I'm filled with *hatred* towards you."

"Okay," hearing her voice cracking, she was on the very of crying.

As I saw her so close, it made me ache inside as I knew that I was the cause.

"I still love you Evan, I hope we could be together still. I might have this ugly side of me, but I want to let you know, my feelings won't change. You may say you have hatred for me, but I know you Evan. I know you still love me, somewhere inside. You still have those feelings inside of you for me. I won't force you, but there's a building that's being constructed. If you still want to be with me, than gather the courage to meet me there this Friday night. If you don't show up, then I'll take it that you don't love me enough to be with me, and I'll leave you alone from then after."

The door opened behind me, "it's done," Helen said entering. "Come into the room," she said as we both followed her command.

The room was in perfect condition once again, as if no grueling fight between two demons ever happened. There were exceptions, Emelia was lying on the floor faced down, fully clothed. The back of her shirt was ripped accordingly to reveal the gash wound which had ceased oozing out blood. It was still ghastly to look at. Lying on top of a broken wooden table, she was placed below the stairs. Above, the wooden railing had, 'conveniently' broke. There were traces of her blood on the wood railing as well, most likely to show that it was how she ended up with the wounds.

"Humph, I don't like this one bit. This isn't how I saw things playing out. The way things are set up leaves room for question, but I did my best. I even did my best to gather up some of her blood from the bathroom to have it as if she was bleeding down here all this time. If only I didn't make that second marking on her back, then it would've been easier to make this more convincing."

"Mom, please, that's enough," Lily intervened.

"Oh, my apologies, you're right. Evan," she began to instruct me of what to tell Emelia when she woke up. After she did, she calmly walked over to the phone, picked it up, and came back handing it to me after dialing 911. "Make it believable," she said before letting go.

After calling the police as instructed, I did my best acting.

Once done, the two of them left through the back door out into the rain. Kneeling next to Emelia, I waited until the ambulance came.

CHAPTER

13

I waited a long time for a response to Emelia's condition. When I got word, I was told that she had lost a great amount of blood requiring a blood transfusion which they had ready. Apart from that, she was going make it, but needed plenty of rest. A great sigh of relief rushed through me when I heard the news. Emelia had survived, she was alive and I would be able to hear her cheerful voice once more. Being allowed to wait by her side, watching her now pale face as the new blood was still working its cure. Her body had yet recovered enough to show her natural healthy glow. Wishing to do more, to be able to help her in some way, there wasn't anything I could do but stay by her side until she woke up. To wake up knowing that I was there, that she wasn't going to wake up not knowing where she was, how she got here, to see no one by her side. I wasn't going to do that to her, after so much she'd done for me. Was this how she felt when I was lying in her position not too long ago?

Not sleeping, I stayed up for the next few hours until she woke up. She looked confused, eyes darting around to the surroundings that were all too familiar to her, considering her field of work and that this was her hospital where she worked.

"Evan," she called out to me in a slight bit of panic as she tried to reach for me with her hand. She was so weak, she couldn't lift her arm, struggling, only being able to move her fingers as they grasped and clawed towards my direction.

"I'm here, I'm so glad you're okay," grabbing her hand, kissing it with gratefulness to see her now conscious.

"The shower," she said shifting her eyes, "I was attacked."

Helen was afraid that Emelia would remember, as was I. "You were?" I tried sounding confused. "Was that how you fell down from the second floor, did someone break in and threw you off?" The start of the lie made my mind feel as if my entire being was becoming twisted, knowing full well how her injury was caused. "When I came home, I found you lying in on top of a broken table. The police investigated the house inside and out, they told me there wasn't any sign of forced entry, and you seemed to have gotten the wounds on your back from the fall."

"No," she sounded confused, "I was naked, taking a shower, the curtains wrapped around me, they, someone cut me, then I passed out."

"Emelia," when I found you, you were wearing cloths. Maybe you were attacked after you got out of the shower, if someone did break-in, I need to call someone so they can investigate a bit more thoroughly."

She nodded in response, too say anymore. That would take care of that, at least for now. Her statement would be taken, looked into, only to find that there was nothing out of the ordinary since she had never actually saw anyone. There was also the fact that she was saying how she was naked in the shower, but was found lying on the first floor fully clothed, it would be hard to add the facts up. The most likely caused scenario as mentioned by Helen was that Emelia was leaning over and the hand railing broke. Having fallen over, it resulted in a slight memory loss and confusion of the events. There were two slight problems that created a cause of concern if anyone took the liberty to investigate in detail. There were certain unusual facts.

First, there would be cause to see that the railing was actually quite sturdy. It would not have broken with Emelia's given weight, even if she rushed at it, it most likely would have still been able to hold together even then, that was how well it was built. This gave rise to a possibility that someone might have thrown her off, someone fairly strong. Second, considering how Emelia fell and with how the broken pieces were found at the scene, she should have really sustained at most one large scar on her back, instead there were two, and they were relatively parallel to each other. Helen was gambling for no one to look at the details, even if so, no one would be able to do much of anything anyway. At most, I would be the most likely suspect of causing harm to Emelia, mainly due recent events and records of my, "questionable" past mental stability. If that was the case, it would only cause me grief, not Helen or Lily, a risk worth taking if the Emelia and I wanted to live.

When morning came, I headed to school like always. There was no use waiting there, merely watching Emelia sleep all day, there wasn't much else I could to do for her, all I could do was continue to do my best. Plus, I had missed so many days of school as is. Perhaps I would stop by and pick up a few items for her, a few books and some puzzles would do her some good to ease the boredom as she recovered. She was going to be in the hospital for some time.

Having gone to school, I began to become increasingly nervous to see Lily. Seeing her walk by in the hallway, giving me a small wave, she made me petrified where I stood. She herself now instilled fear in me, fear of what she was, what she and her mother could do to me. As I sat acting normally in class, I couldn't help but gaze at her. Doing my best to seem as if nothing had happen, I started to wonder how she could be so casual, so aloof as if nothing occurred last night. Of course she could act that way, she was obviously good at acting, hiding her true colors, having done so all this time. Her whole life, she had been hiding her true existence of what she really was. I then thought back to what she said. So this was what she meant when she said she had "personal problems" and rejected me. She was one of them.

Sitting there, thinking over and over, my fears grew as well as my hatred. Hatred welled up inside of me like the pressure in a volcano, building up for an eruption. Gradually did it start to build, its growth grew the more I thought, the longer I reminded myself upon Emelia in her weakened state. Never in my life did I hate *their* kind as much as I did now. Before it there was only lingering feelings of hate, most of that was usually directed at myself for my own incompetence, which then turned into a paranoid fear. This was different, now they harmed Emelia who was now lying helplessly, wounded. The woman whom I loved so much with all my heart was nothing but one of *them*, one of those demons whom tormented me all my life. So great was my growing hatred that I began wishing for the death of all their kind; even wishing for Lily's death.

Avoiding all areas where I might have a run in with her, the school day soon ended. Deciding that there wasn't much else to do, I headed back to see Emelia. Clarissa and my father should have arrived by now, which they did, seeing the three sitting in the room as they chatted away.

"Evan, I missed you so much, its' been forever," Clarissa said giving me a big hug.

"You were here visiting me not too long ago."

"Yes, but it feels like forever, but enough about that, what's going on lately, first you, now Emelia? How could a doctor like you end up being a patient in her own hospital?" directing the question now at Emelia.

"Evan, get her out of here," Emelia replied. Of course everyone knew she was half joking.

The mood was relatively joyful, even my father seemed to have had a decent time, most likely thanks to Clarissa's joyful personality lightening the mood. Both of them had come bringing with them a large fruit basket, a get well bear, and some light novels. I too had brought some books on the way to the hospital. Not knowing what types she preferred, I chose a few dark fantasies, psychological, and a science fiction, the ones that were currently popular and being most read by the general public. After staying for a few hours, my father and Clarissa decided to head back to the hotel where they would be staying for today until they flew back. It was just the two of us alone now, in the lonely room white room. I turned off the light as she complained that it was too bright, hurting her old eyes. She had the room all to herself, there were no one in the other bed next to hers.

"You know, I could have sworn I was in the shower when I got hurt," Emelia said, bring up the one topic I had hoped she could've left alone.

"I know, you told me. I've already told the police, we can let them look things over again. Did they come to take a statement, and did you get a result from the rape kit?" I asked since I called them earlier before heading to school on her behalf.

"They did, they'll be coming over tomorrow to look things over again after you get home, so be sure to be there. As for the results, it was good, I'm happy to let you know that I wasn't raped or anything."

"Good. Okay, well I'll head home right after school, then I'll come back to visit after."

"Oh, you don't have to. I'll just be lying here as I am now."

"I know I don't have to, but," Emelia interrupted me before I could finish.

"Dear, I know you care for my wellbeing, I get it, but you need to take care of yourself, get caught up on your school work, go on a date with Lily, she must be jealous of you spending so much time with me."

Hearing Lily's name made me cringe. Despite that, I forced a nice smile, making myself give a small laugh towards Emelia's teasing. Not being sure if she saw through me, I quickly agreed. "Alright, I won't come visit you tomorrow, but the day after when I do come, you have to be twice as healthy then you are now."

Emelia nodded weakly. That night, I decided to stay with her to keep her company, even though she told me that I didn't have to. As we talked, there were moments when I wanted to tell her what really happened. Each time, I turned the thought down, what good would it really do, the truth was too difficult to believe let alone prove, plus, it included the danger of Helen coming back for us if I didn't follow her specific instructions.

When the next day came, I saw both my father and Clarissa off in the early morning from the hospital, making one last visit goodbye. After school, I came home waiting, not knowing when the law enforcements would come to reconfirm the safety of the house, to inspect to see if there was any lingering evidence. The broken table and pool of blood was cleaned, I had to do it myself. I couldn't simply leave it there. This left only the railing on the second floor, the only thing left to look into.

Once the officer did come, he did his job and examined all the doors and windows for the possibility that someone might've broken into the house. Once confirm that there wasn't anything evident enough of a break-in, he asked me if there was anything missing. I told him simply that I wasn't sure. In response, he asked me to check each room just to be certain, that he would wait as I check the house. Not having much choice, I did just that. Calmly and patiently we walked into each room checking for anything missing, broken, out of place. Having never actually looked through each room in detail before, I wasn't sure what Emelia would consider valuable or not. It didn't matter of course, I knew nothing was missing as I went through each one pretending to check. After confirming that nothing was out of place, he checked the downstairs where Emelia was found, then went up to check the broken railing on the second floor. He spent a long time looking at it, making me nervous.

"You said that they think she was leaning over on the railing, and then it broke from her weight which is how she ended up falling down from up here?"

"Yes, that's what was they said. That was the most possible cause," responding calmly. "My aunt informed me that she was taking a shower before, and then was when she was attacked and fell unconscious while still in the shower, but somehow she ended up downstairs."

Walking down the stairs now, "her falling down does seem like the most probable cause, but I was taking a good look up there."

Did he see a reason for concern, possibly a hit of certain things not adding up?

"Looking at the wood, it seem like it was constructed pretty well, the railing itself was made sturdy, so it does seems a bit odd that it would break so easily. I'll make a note of it in a report, but you know, it is wood, and wood breaks, with enough force, it can snap apart. I don't see anything unusual, the report last time also stated nothing unusual or out of place. Tell your aunt that I wasn't able to find anything suspicious and that I hope she feels better."

"I will, thank you so much for coming," saying as I opened the door to see him out. Relieved to have him gone, I was tense for a moment when I though he found something suspicious looking at the railing for so long. It was good that he disregarded it so quickly, but it made me disappointed to have our law enforcement so casually looking over the facts, not even thinking that it was worth a more detailed inspection. But there were bigger crimes going on out there, people were being robbed, murdered, kidnapped, they wouldn't have been able to do much even if they did spend the man hours investigating Emelia's case.

Most of the sky was dark as the sun began to set beyond the horizon. It was late. Thinking of what to make for dinner, my taste buds craved meatloaf, so I began pulling out the ingredients. In the process, I noticed the calendar nearby, tomorrow would be Friday. Remembering what Lily had said about meeting somewhere close by to talk, I wasn't sure if it was wise to go. Initially, the thought of going would have been out of the question. There was no way that I was going out during nighttime. Looking outside through the window into the night, to see how I now felt of the darkness. Neither fear nor unease immediately took hold of me as it once would. There wasn't a shudder, nor did I break out in a cold sweat as I might have imagined. After all that was done, perhaps I was simply too tired to be that afraid as I used to be, or just used to it. Putting down the ingredients in my hand, I moved towards the door, deciding whether or not I should open it and go outside.

Unlocking the door, I stepped outside. Peering into the dark backyard, there wasn't anything there but the sound of the night. Sounds of crickets cricketing under the slightly warm air, the lamp above me buzzed away. Taking a seat at the small table Emelia had placed outside, I sat there waiting for nothing, simply taking in the dull view. It was strange, the feeling of not being afraid anymore. Fear was nonexistent altogether. With so many things going on, something inside of me told me that I wouldn't be killed by those demons, that I wouldn't be hunted, at least not anytime soon. After all I've been through, I had survived time and time again, guessing that it somehow made me simply not care anymore. A part of me knew that if they wanted to, they would take my life whether I hid in my shell or embraced the open. There wasn't anything that could stop them had the chose to. Being able to do things no normal humans could do, they would forever hold the upper hand on me, on everyone.

Since the darkness no longer brought fear to me, the possibility of meeting Lily Friday night was now an option. The new question presented was did I still care enough for her to see her again. Did I still wish to hold her in my arms and kiss her lips, listen to her voice as I once did? Thinking earlier of my feelings of wanting their kind eradicated, which included her, I tried imagining Lily, picturing her face, her hair, her eyes, but the image of her was soon replaced with the vision of a demon. That was what she was, a demon, dangerous, cruel, ugly, there was no feelings that I could find for that *thing*, but hatred. So there and then, the thought of loving such a heinous fiend faded away.

Heading back inside to finish up the cooking, I pulled out a large knife to cut up some onions to add into the meatloaf. In the middle of chopping, I stopped, staring down at the large sharp blade of the knife which I now held. Raising the knife up, examining it in more detail. The grasp and weight of the knife was decent, bits of onion clung to the knife, its juices dripping down its silver metal blade. Light reflected off the perfectly crafted metal as I saw a blurred image of myself. Near the hilt was the name of the manufacturer I never heard of nor cared to remember. The blade seemed sharp enough as I had already tested it the onion, how easily it had cut. At that moment, the idea came to me of killing Lily, to finish her off, a sort of revenge on one of their own. It was tempting as my disgust of them overpowered my fear of confrontation with one of their kind. This was the best weapon that I had, and it wasn't as if I could take Emelia's gun, I knew she had locked it safely away with a secret pass code. Slamming the knife down, cutting what was left of the onion in two. So be it, I would meet up with Lily tomorrow night and end what wasn't meant to be.

After school the next day, I visited Emelia. It might just be the last time I would see her. Once tonight was over, I might no longer be alive. Helen or Lily herself might do away with me. Entering her room, she was fast asleep, so peacefully, so silently. Not wanting to wake her, I placed her favorite chocolates on the table nearby, certain that it would delight her when she awakened. Seeing her so soundly asleep eased my heart, knowing that she was safe. The color had come back to her face making her look much healthier than before.

Watching her face started to remind me of my mother. If my mother was still alive, what would think of my situation, my confrontation tonight with Lily? Would my mother disapprove of my intent to kill, even if it was a demon? Perhaps my sister would urge me on, to take revenge for the both of them. Thinking about it only made me irritated.

I took a moment to look around the room. It was now filled with gifts from people who dropped by, wishing Emelia a quick recovery. She had received lots and lots of flowers, most from her coworkers at the very hospital she was in now. Stuff animals, get well cards, bottled wine, and even aged cheese and a can of caviar. Reaching for a card, I picked it up to read.

Dear Emelia,

It's so unfortunate of what happened. Get that railing fixed ASAP so that no more accidents can happen. I really do hope wish you a quick recover, Lily and I would love to see you at the high school graduation.

Wishing you a speedy recovery,

Helen and Lily

The card nearly fell to the floor as it was about to slipped through my hands. They were here. How could they come here after all they've done to us? To act like they didn't do anything, to come and seem so friendly with what they've done to Emelia. I was in rage. Holding the card, I looked over to Emelia, making sure that she was still fast asleep. I went into the bathroom, ripped up the card, and flushed it down.

Returning to Emelia's side, I kissed her on the forehead lightly as not to wake her. "Goodbye aunty, get better real soon." It wasn't a normal departing. Not the same goodbye where I would see her later, it was my departing in which I may never see her again.

My thoughts started to turn like gears of an old clock as I tried to see what the future had in store for me. Thoughts of seeing my family grieving upon my dead body, if they were able to find it, even my father would be shedding tears uncontrollably. Clarissa would be shouting at Emelia, wondering how my death came to be. She would blame Emelia for my death I concluded, just as she blamed her for the cause of my injuries the last time. She would have been more forthcoming in blame last time if it wasn't for my father being there. How about my father, would he shout and yell at Emelia too? Maybe he would he confront Lily head on.

Leaving the hospital, I waited patiently at home. Lily had texted me the address of the location. All I had to do was show up. Time quickly passed as I waited. Staring at the clock for the approaching time when I needed to leave. As the appointed time approached, the wait soon felt longer as my anxiety increased. My heart pumped loudly of the thought of what I would do. Deep breaths followed to ease my growing uncomfortable self. It was time to head out, but I didn't want to show up early. I waited a bit more; Lily wouldn't just have to wait. When I felt ready I walked to the door, put on my jacket, then stepped into the kitchen.

Standing there, the knives stood on the counter across from me. Pulling them out one by one, I laid each one out neatly in front of me. I picked up the large chef knife, stainless steel with a sharp blade and fine point. As I held it, I remembered the army knife that Lily had handed to me when we were in trouble before. That would've been much better than the one I currently held. Made with the purpose to be used as a weapon, I thought. It was unfortunate that it was lost back in the abandoned building. Reminding myself that it was Lily whom handed me the knife, it made me want to disregard the thought of wanting to use a weapon that was given to me by that demon. Placing the knife in the inside of my jacket, I left the house, taking Emelia's car, which I've been borrowing since she'd been in the hospital.

Looking up at the sky, not even the moon showed itself as it was covered by the clouds. The weather report called for heavy rain that night. As I drove to the location, it started to drizzle. By the time I arrive at the set destination, the rain came pouring down. 'It's always raining on moments like this,' I thought. How depressing was the rain, as if its appearance was a bad omen. Getting out of the car, I pulled out the umbrella as I took a good look at the building. It was half constructed, water dripping down off the plastic and wood. I looked around for a way to get inside as the building was boarded up with wood to stop anyone from trespassing. There was one piece that was removed, obviously showing a gap for entry. It was a sign from Lily announcing that she was already here welcoming me in, waiting for me, anticipating that I would eventually come, but unknown of my current changed feelings towards her.

Entering inside under the protection of the building, out of the rain, I folded up the umbrella, leaving it near the exit. Moving deeper inside near the center of the building, taking out a flash light, looking around, there were no signs of her.

"Lily!" I shouted out as loudly as I could. Waiting for a response, nothing. "Lily, I'm here, and I know you are too!"

"I'm here," she said, spooking me as I moved my flash light all around, trying to locate her position. She stood standing next to a pillar, her palm trying to block the shine of the light. "I knew this would happen, so I prepared a little something." She moved close by, switching on a lamp. It brightly lighted the area around us. Slightly covered, it was a warm white, bright light, making the surrounds around us visible. Looking at its reach, it didn't shined bright enough to catch the attention from anyone outside.

"You're always so prepared. Did you pick up that habit as you tried to hide what you really are from all humanity?" asking spitefully.

"Yes," answering me back simply, this annoyed me. "I have

to be, I learned from my mother to hide all traces of what I really am, to prepare for the unknown, the uncertain. Like a well trained criminal, always hiding from the law, but in my case, I'm always hiding from all humans. How's your aunt Emelia?"

"In the hospital, she's recovering quickly. I was told by the doctor that she was lucky, having lost so much blood, she was still able to make it."

"Good, I wouldn't feel like I could show my face to you anymore if I had known my mother had taken her life. She's an important person to you after all."

I chuckled. "I really hate her, you know? I hate your mother for doing what she did to Emelia. It's one thing if she only came after me, but she didn't, she came after both of us, at Emelia who had nothing to do with what happened, with anything."

"I know Evan, I'm so sorry, I swear, I didn't know she would've gone after the two of you that day. If I knew, I would've stopped her sooner if I could," saying as she took a few steps closer towards me.

"Don't come near me!" I shouted. "You're just like her. You're just like all of them, a ruthless killer."

"No, no I'm not, I've never killed any humans before, there was only one time I ever killed, and it was only that one night after that lower demon had taken Alice's life, but it deserved it." Tears began to well up in her beautiful eyes, those eyes that once mesmerized me before. Not being able to resist, she started to cry. "Please Evan, it's me, I'm still the same person."

Watching her, she seems so normal, so human. I wanted to hold her again, ease her pain, to be how we used to be. 'It could be an act', I then told myself. I wasn't sure what to believe from her anymore. Acting so fragile, innocent, heartbroken now, when before she would usually be so strong willed and confident. After seeing what I've seen, she wasn't that fragile either. Hiding her true strength, even as she was right now, she was still stronger than the average human, remembering how quickly and gruesomely she had taken out the lower demon from before.

"You can stop your acting Lily, how can I even trust that look, you've become so good at your lies that I can't tell what you're thinking anymore. Thinking back, I've never known what you've thought of anything." That was when I pulled out the hidden knife into view.

She looked at it in shock, not expecting such a thing from me. "Please Evan, I'm in love with you, I love you so much." She came towards me, taking a few more steps.

"That's enough! I told you not to come near me!" I took a few steps back to replace the gained distance as a response. "You love me? You know I had loved you too? So much I thought about you every day since the moment I first met you. When I first saw you, you caught me eyes, and I just knew something was different about you than from everybody else, and now I know why. It's because your one of them, your different from everybody else because you're a freak, not even a freak, you're a demon. A demon Lily, one of those monsters that," I couldn't even finish as I clenched my jaw together.

Waiting for a response from her, she didn't move, she didn't speak, and she didn't even wipe the streaming tears that continued their fall. She stood, listening to me calmly with a pained expression. So I continued.

"You know, I wish you were really were human. Before this, I enjoyed kissing those lips, touching your face, feeling you skin, your warmth. I thought we were meant to be, that if I had to be with someone, to grow old together, I would've been happy knowing that it was with you. But it's different now, I don't think I feel that way with you anymore, no, maybe a bit of me still loves you, but it's now clouded over with such hatred for you, that I don't think I can be with you now. When I see you, I don't 'see,' you. It's you, but then I remember your eyes, of those beautiful green evil glows, and then I remember everything about your kind, and what you're capable of."

"Evan," she finally said. "Look at me, look at me like you've never done before. You know me, you've been with me, you've held me, and you know I'm not like the others; that I'm not like my mother." She motioned closer, but this time I was hesitant to shout her away. "I love you just as much, I still want to be with you," she was finally within reach. "I don't want to lose you, I can't lose you, I don't know what I would do if I don't have you. These last few days, I might not have showed it at school, but I've been breaking apart on the inside." She touched my hand that was holding the knife. Gently, carefully while still looking into my eyes. "Evan, please. Don't push me away. You and I, we're meant to be. I may be different, but we can still be together." Coming closer, she moved the knife away a bit, now only a breath away. "Evan, we can be together." Kissing me softly, she embraced me.

I didn't return her embrace as she buried her head into my chest, continuing her silent weep. She had touched me, weakened my will, my conviction of what I had originally come to do. She was in my arms now, and all I had to do was raise the knife, and bring it down upon her. Now, I couldn't even lift it, there was no strength in me as my heart was now melting for her. Why? Why did I still love her like this?

"Show me then." I hesitated before I continued. It was hard to speak from being so emotional. "Show me what you really are, I want to see your true form, only then can I know if I can really be with you. I need to see it, I have to see it; otherwise I can't. I want you to show me what you really are."

Releasing me, she backed away, gazing into my eyes as she wiped whatever tears were left on her face. "Evan, you can't, I can't show you, I've seen how I look, the true me, and I hate it. You could never love something like 'that,' I know you can't, not even my father was able to."

"If you can't show me, then this discussion is over, I can't love someone that I don't ever know. I'll go to bed wondering what's sleeping next to me, what kind of demon you are. I wouldn't know what to do or think if I woke up with some unknown dark hideous demon sleeping next to me."

"If I show you my true form, you won't love me anymore, I know it."

"Show me!" I raised my voice, interrupting her.

"Okay," she replied, turning around to give herself some distance. Leaning against the pillar, looking away from me, "are you sure about this?"

I stayed silent, not responding to her question. All was silent, only the sound of the rain could be heard, water dripping down from somewhere, making an echo inside the building. I watched Lily, waiting for her. Something was different, the air felt heavier, more menacing. Her shoulders started to look a bit odd, somewhat disjointed, then she turned, facing me, showing everything to me. Her face started to cloud over a misty black. As it enveloped her face, she started to grow much larger than what she really was; a few centimeters, than an inch. One of her eye clouded over, changing color to a beautiful dark green color, a beautiful color that I so remembered. A beautiful color that draws you in, giving you a sensation that it would take your life if you stared into them long enough. Her arms much longer than normal, they too clouded over, the black darkness enveloping her skin, crawling down to her finger tips. Joints could be seen shifting, becoming disfigured for a moment as parts of her body grew. Her head grew larger in a ghastly way. Her head was probably twice as large as before, face fully blackened like the night, the light shined against her skin, making it look like fine glossed ink. Her hair started to stick together as if static course through them, giving more volume, and unlike her skin, it seemed to absorbed the light, making it a fine black, as dark as the void. What was more horrifying was how her mouth changed, only to amplify the horror of her sight ten folds. They were like those vintage metal animal traps with teeth, waiting for a prey to come by before ensnaring them. These were a bit different though, her teeth grew much as described, but extending outward a bit more, longer, thinner, sharper, a black color like the rest of her body. They now became sharp, each and every one of them like tiny spear heads. Her mouth extended from one end to the other. It was like a shark, but more menacing, as if she was laughing, smiling wickedly unintentionally. Her body outgrew her cloths, muscles protruding, then as if they were about to rip, her black dark skin enveloped her cloths, becoming part of her skin before disappearing.

I took a step back, seeing her true form, fear gushed from the very inside of my soul seeing her this way. She stood much taller than me, slightly hunch over, about seven and a half foot tall, perhaps taller. Words didn't escape my lips, my hands shaking as she stood there calmly. After a moment, waiting for me to take in what I was seeing, she stepped forward at me.

"Stay back," I yelled, raising my knife up automatically, my body telling me that it needed to defend itself. She had an air about her, just like all the others. I remembered this feeling, it was them. It was the feeling of demons watching me, wanting me, waiting to take my life. She was indeed one of their kin.

"Evan, it's still me." Her voice was deep, more course, powerful, the voice of a demon. Even so, the way she said it, there were traces of gentleness, sadness, of Lily.

"Y-you really are a d-demon," I stuttered, trying to say.

My words pained her, hearing me say such things at her. "I am, but I didn't choose to be this way," looking at her hand. "I was born this way, but you're right, I am a demon, an ugly monster, but I would never harm anyone." Clenching her fist, closing her eyes before opening them again as she looked at me once more. "I would never harm you. Evan, you asked me to show you, and this is what I really look like."

"I didn't expect you to be like this," taking another step back, all the while my eyes never deterred from her.

"Evan," she moved closer, "I still love you, I probably always will, but I understand if you choose not to be with me anymore. Like my father, he too couldn't erase this image of me from his mind, and in the end, he nearly killed me, not being able to forget this horrifying sight of me. I suppose I had hoped that you would be different. I don't want to lose you, and I knew you loved me deeply, but I was hopeful that you would still love me even after seeing me like this."

Now directly in front of me towering over, looking down at me, her eyes changed, they now seemed troubled, agonizing with emotions. She touched my hand holding the knife; it was warm just like a normal human's.

Having her hand upon mine's, it terrified me, at the same time, a welling of disgust and hatred arouse as it reminded me of my initial intent. Seeing her made me see my mother and sister, Emelia laying the hospital, Alice's gravestone, even reminded me of Jason. So I did it, I did what I thought was necessary, to end her life, to end this demon's life, this monster whom I had once loved. I plunged my knife into her chest, pushing with my other hand making it go deeper.

"I can't be with you, not after everything your kind of have done, I can't be with something as horrifying as you."

She didn't strike at me as I had expected. I was alive and well, unharmed. Prepared for my demise from her own hands, or even her mother's; nothing, she stood there, her mother didn't come out from the darkness to finish me off either. Drops of water came down, dripping onto my hands. I looked up and I saw her tears coming down. The clear liquids dripping down her face over her sharp deadly teeth. A silent cry, eyes filled with such sadness, such self-loathing, for in that moment, it made me regret my decision. Her emerald eyes looked at me, as if they were taking me in, remembering me, a picture to last forever, one last time as if they would never be able to lay their sights upon me anymore.

No words came from either of us for a few seconds. My heart ached seeing her in such a saddened state, reminding me of my loved for her. It was the feeling of happiness that I would most likely never find with another. My emotions ate at my heart, to know that a part of me still lingered for her. Words of apology, for forgiveness, I couldn't utter any of them. She stepped back, my hands letting go of the knife. They were soaked in her blood. Like her skin, it too was like fine black ink, but thick like the texture of a normal human's blood. She leaned back against the pillar, still looking at my face, me looking back at her, at my hands with her blood. I then ran.

My legs shaken, I clumsily turned and slowly exited from another part of the building. Steadily at first, I then began sprinting. Circling around in the rain, I located the one exit, making my way into the street. Safely inside my car, I drove away from the place, driving as fast as I could, breaking the speed limit. In disarray, I didn't see anything but the now diluted blood from my hands. I opened my fist to see traces of her blood left. I had ran with my fists clenched, protecting it from the rain. Seeing the blood, the water mixing in, it made me panic. I grasped the wheel, running through all the lights. It was good that no one was on the road; probably the heavy raining night was acting as a deterrent. Once I reached my house, I hurried in, turning on the light, leaning against the wall. I looked at my hands and started to cry. I didn't know at that moment why I cried, they just came. Looking at my hands once more, there were still traces of her. Rushing into the kitchen, I scrubbed my hands clean until they were red.

Making my way into my room, soaking wet, I looked at my window. It angered me seeing the curtains hanging there, as if mocking me. I grabbed them with both hands, and strongly pulled. In the first pull, they resisted from coming off, only to further my anger. This time with all my might, I pulled again, ripping them off, throwing them to the side. Looking at the window into the night, it reminded me of my cowardice. I picked up my lamp, ripping its connection from the wall as I threw it at the window, shattering it.

The lamp was my source of light that I had discarded, so I sat in the dark, not wanting to retrieve another light source. Tears came pouring out, the cold wind from the outside blew inside, water from the rain entered, soaking the carpet. There I sat, welcoming the darkness for the first time in my life as all I wanted to do was sit in it and let it envelop me. Why was I crying, I didn't understand what these tears meant.

Was it because I was heartbroken as of what I had done to Lily? Was it due to the fact that I killed her or might have killed her? I searched deep inside my soul and I knew it was because I still loved her, I betrayed her trust in me. Imagining the sight of her had horrified me, but seeing that demon cry, realizing it now, I knew she was existed there, on the inside. It was a demon, but it was Lily, and I still loved her dearly. Now it was too late, there was no going back. I had taken a knife to her, making it clear that I could not be with her anymore. Grieving for what I had done, realizing what I've just lost. Wanting for her, already missing her, now wanting to be with her, grasping her, to make love with her, I wanted her again.

I ran out of the room, bursting through the front door, not caring to close it behind me. I drove into the rain, to speak with Lily, I had to see her. Almost there I told myself. Increasing my speed, I drove recklessly. As I made a turn, the car skidded and I hit a pole. Getting out of the car, I tumbled to the ground. Picking myself up, I wasn't badly hurt. I bit the inside of my mouth, but otherwise I felt okay, or perhaps I had too much adrenaline coursing through my body at the moment to notice anything else.

I ran. Running as fast as I could, my legs wanted to give out, I urged them to continue ahead, they moved as I commanded, stretching, propelling me forward. Once I reached the building, I stood in front. My umbrella still there, now lying in the floor, the wind must have blown it over. Walking inside, the white light was still on, visible from a distance. I moved to the light until I stood where I once did. There was no one there, Lily was not there. The only traces were of the lamp and a few drops of her black blood.

Leaving the location, I dashed to Lily's house, not stopping to rest until I did. Once reaching her house, I pounded on the door. No one answered. "Lily, Lily, it's me, I'm sorry," crying out. The words gushing out of me, calling her name, I continued my fist to the door; no one answered. It reminded me of my time as a child of when I was in the rain, pounding upon Clarissa's door, crying for help. Yes, it was the scene of me struggling for my life to get away from their kind. It was ironic, how I now was struggled to meet with one of them, to be with one of them. Falling to my knees, "Lily, forgive me, I'm sorry, I love you, and I still love you, so please forgive me." After a long time of kneeling there, I lifted myself up and dragged my pathetic self home. The rain had weakened its downpour as I walked the long distance home.

My room was a mess. I sat there the rest of the night, not sleeping. Saturday came. I didn't slept or changed my cloths. When morning came by, my phone rang. Without strength, I reached for it.

"Hello," I answered.

"Evan? It's me Emelia, I asked the doctor to let me head home to continue my recovery instead of the hospital. He told me no, that I should stay a bit longer, but I can move somewhat now, and I would feel more comfortable at home. Could you pick me up in a few hours? Also, if you could, bring a change of clean cloths."

"Alright, I'll be there, see you soon."

"What's wrong, you don't sound okay?" she asked.

"I'm alright, that's just me waking up," I lied.

"Oh yeah, it's Saturday, well okay, see you when you arrive, bye."

"Bye."

Not wanting to, I had to move from my spot. I got up, my cloths now damp, I showered, cleaning the house up before leaving, retrieving the lamp I through earlier outside, which was now in pieces. Then I biked myself to where I had gotten into an accident the night before. I got there right when it was about to be towed away. Spending a lot of time taking care of that mess, I was able to walk away with the vehicle, thankfully in a drivable condition still. Throwing me bike in the back seat, I headed straight to the hospital. When I arrived, I handed the cloths over. Emelia got dressed and was wheeled out. The hospital didn't charge her for the treatment and stay, and gave us the wheelchair as well, after all, she was a highly valued doctor there, plus she was well liked by her coworkers.

When I pulled the car up front, I helped her into the car and drove us home. She didn't ask or mention about the obvious state the car was in. Was she waiting for me to say something? I was expecting her to grill me over or at least give a comment, but nothing.

"Sorry Emelia, I kind of broke the window in my room and I got into an accident with your car," after a certain point while on our way back home.

"I can see that, and that isn't exactly what I was hoping to hear after getting out of the hospital, but okay. What happen? Is everything okay? Did something happen to you while I was gone? Did something happen to you and Lily?"

The mentioning of Lily stroke a nerve, but I bottled it in. "Yeah, I don't think we're together anymore, so I got a bit emotional and threw the lamp at the window and drove a bit recklessly, sorry," telling her the truth while omitting much of the details. I couldn't delve much else to what had occurred.

"I could care less about the window and car, what I want to know is if you're okay," she asked. I didn't dare to look at her caring eyes, fearing that I would spill everything to her. Even after wrecking her vehicle and house, she worried for me.

"I'm mostly alright, just a bit depress is all. I found that I really cared for her, maybe just a little too late."

"To find such love for someone while being so young, I envy you so. You know when I saw you two, you looked like a match made in heaven, like how my sister and your dad used to look at each other. I envied that, since I was never in love in such a way. Don't get me wrong, I used to care for my last husband, and a few other men that I'd been with, but I never did have the kind of love like theirs, possible like yours and Lily's. I can't do much since this is your life you're living, but I want to let you know that I'm here for you if you need me, I'll support you in whatever decision you make."

We drove home in silence the rest of the way. I didn't feel like discussing anymore of what happened, I suppose Emelia saw that.

CHAPTER

14

After taking care of Emelia, ensuring that she was comfortable, I took cared of the broken window and my banged up car by making various phone calls. The burdensome task of my recklessness was burdensome to clean up after.

I headed toward Lily's house, wanting to see her, hoping that she would be there so I could apologize, I would go over as many times as it took. I at least was sure she was alive. I knew because I was still breathing. If my knife had killed Lily, her mother wouldn't have let me live, that was for certain. When I did arrive, out in front were large trucks and movers, transferring furniture, their furniture.

"What's going on here, are the people living here moving, did they already leave?" I asked one of the men.

"Don't know; you've got to ask my supervisor inside, he's the one that knows the details."

As I hurried in, more than half of their stuff were already packed and hauled into the trucks. Looking around, I spotted two men on the first floor. One dressed like the many other movers, the other standing next to him was giving him instructions. He was a much older man in a suit and tie, standing out amongst everything that was going on.

"Excuse me, do you know what's going on here, where is Miss. Rothschild and her daughter?"

"And may I ask who you are and your association with the Rothschild's?" asked the man in the suit, the other took notice and left us alone to monitor his men.

"My name's Evan, I'm a close friend of the daughter of this house hold, Lilith. So what is all of this?"

"Hello Evan," reaching out to shake my hand. "I'm Helen Rothschild's lawyer, Patrick Davidson, and I'm not entirely too sure myself. I was told that she wanted to me to hire some movers to pack and move everything out of this house into storage. Now I don't usually do this kind of service, but I've been her lawyer for a long time, and she is paying me a large sum to do so. If you're wonder where they are, unfortunately I have no idea, they didn't tell me. Even if I did know, I'm not at liberty to disclose that kind of information to you."

"Than what about her work, what about Lily's school, graduation is right around the corner," I asked franticly.

"I'm sorry, Helen didn't inform me about her work, and I didn't inquire about it. As for her daughter Lilith and her upcoming graduation, I can't disclose that information to you, all I can tell you is that I'll be meeting up with the school later to discuss the situation," the man said before going to a table nearby to finish up a bunch of documents.

I was lost, was there no chance to see her ever again?

He looked back at me for a moment. Taking pity on me, probably seeing how devastated I was, "but," he said, "I can see that you're not a bad kid, so I'll let you know that she should be getting her diploma still, or at least I'll do whatever I can to get it for her. I'm sorry that they left so unexpectedly, in fact I was just as perplexed when Helen gave me a call in the middle of the night, literally demanding that I do this for her. That's all really all I can tell you, I'm sorry." He patted my shoulder as he left me standing there.

She had left me. A feeling inside of me grew. It was the knowing that I would never see her again. That night was the last night, only to have it end so poorly. Remembering her eyes, of those emerald green eyes that looked into me that night, oh how she looked at me then. She knew it was going to be her last time seeing me then, the moment I stabbed her with that knife, she would no longer appear before me.

There wasn't anything I could do, she was gone, and there wasn't any way for me to find her. Hearing the news, I became a living corpse, simply moving through the motion of daily life, listless. When people asked me what happened to Lily, I simply ignored them. Prom came and I didn't attend. As others celebrated the once in a life time event, I stayed solemnly at home, thinking of how beautiful she would've been in a dress, of the two of us dancing together.

Graduation felt much the same. Unlike the others, I accepting my diploma with a forced dead smile as my Father, Clarissa, and Emelia stood cheering for me. There were no feelings of excitement, joy, or satisfaction about the finalizing of high school life. Parties were held, I attended. Barbecues where thrown, and I pretend to have fun to please everyone else, but inside of me was only sorrow. As I looked around me, acting as if I was enjoying the monumental celebrations, I wasn't. The lights, the glitter, my fellow students surrounded me having a time of their life before venturing off to who knows what. All I wanted was to be with Lily.

When the celebrations were over, I bided my time. Most of my days, I would spend staring into the night sky. Other moments, I would wander around, taking short walks in the middle of the night, hoping that Lily might show herself to me, not giving a damn about the other demons anymore. Fright no longer overcame my senses, uncaring if they took my life as I just wanted to see her. She never did showed herself, nor was there any feeling of being watched by their kind. They were gone from my life completely now.

That was how I had lived my life for a while. Being lifeless, unemotional, I entered college like that. My reasoning to live was near a breaking point, regained only when Emelia had pointed out how worried she was, right before I left for college. Seeing how I was acting, it concerned her. She knew something was wrong for a while, hoping I would recover or come to her when I was ready to talk, but I never did. Much of the time, I spent my days inside, not doing much, and I hardly smiled anymore. Even when I did, it looked so forced, so painful, like how my father sometimes would look at me. Telling me that I had kept going as I was, I would become like how my father was right now. That was when I knew I had to snap out of the slump. I didn't want to end up like him.

Deciding to start opening up, socializing with others grew more frequent until I started to enjoy them again, the company of talking to another person. At some point, an attractive girl came up to me after class one day to ask me out, I turned her down. My heart yearned for Lily still. Knowing if I dated anyone now, it would throw me back into depression as I would only look to see Lily instead of her. I wasn't ready for the next step, so I politely turned her down. My heart agonized some nights when something reminded me of Lily, and then nightmares would remind me of what I had done inside of my dreams, seeing her blood on my hands. Not as much anymore as time passed.

It'd been six months since that time. I came along nicely, being more alive and active. The college campus in California was large and open, the sun shined down every day with constant warmth, sometimes too much making me sweat just leaving the house on some days. Having decidedly to take a walk after finishing all my classes, I stopped at a park near my apartment. The sun was just starting to set, the orange, red, and yellow, stretched out from the sun as I watched the colors spread across the endless sky. Taking a moment to take in the sight, I noticed a woman on the other side of the lake, reading a book on the bench. It looked like Lily, though it was hard to see. I felt my heart throb achingly, as if someone was gripping it with their hand. After six months, my love for her held strong. Hoping it would be her, I began to walk, then a jog, soon running full speed, hopeful that it was Lily as I ran to the other side.

The woman must've noticed me closing in, me being only a few feet away from her as she glanced over in my direction. As she did, I saw that it was definitely her, it was Lily. Still beautiful as she once was, she had changed how she did her hair. Still long and straight, she cut it shorter and styled it a bit. Looking more mature since the last I saw her. She had looked mature back then too, but now for some reason, she looked more like a real woman.

Her eyes grew wider, being surprised to see me running to her, to see who it was after all this time. She got up and started to run, but it was much too late as the moment she got up, I had reached her from behind. The soft touch of her delicate body, feeling the warmth that emitted from through her cloths, from her skin that fill me with thoughts of grief for what I had done, what I had lost.

"Wait, please don't go. Lily, I'm so sorry for what I did back, I regret it so much. I think about it and regret it every day." Breathing frantically from my run, I said the words while trying to catch my breath.

"You made it evident already. I knew the moment I saw you look at me that night, being the demon that I was, that we could never have a normal relationship." She didn't look at me, as if she would break where she stood if our eyes met for too long. Looking uncomfortable to see me, she seemed smaller, weaker than she normally would. It was the innocent side of her that she would only have ever express in front of me. I was able to see it again, and I missed it.

I let her go so we could stand facing each other.

"When you thrust that knife into me, when you said those words that night, I was torn inside. Not from the wound of the knife, but to know that you couldn't stand that sight of me. I cried over and over for days, knowing that I couldn't be you anymore, it solidified what kind of demon I really was, that I'm not human. You know, I really loved you, and you crushed it. Even if I knew you were going to reject me, I expected it, but I had some lingering hope."

"I did loved you, but when I saw you that night looking so different, my feelings were clouded over with hate and fear for all the things you kind had done to me over the years. How I was endlessly tormented of the thoughts of demons, not knowing when would be my last days alive, taking away my family, harming those close to me."

"We can't be together, I won't work," looking down at the floor about to continue, but I stopped her midway.

Grasping her, "I do love you, I still love you. I didn't realize it until after I ran away, but I realized it now, that I care for you deeply. I didn't realize how strong my feelings were for you. Lily, even after all this time I've wanted to see you again, wanting to touch you again, to let you know how sorry I am for hurting you, and that I want to be with you. Without you, I've been and empty shell. I've been wandering in the middle of the night, hoping you would show yourself to me." My hand reached out to touch her face, but she grabbed my wrist before I reached her. "Lily, there's a gap inside of me, and you're the only person that can fill it."

"That's enough, we can't be like how we used to," she said, gently looking into my eyes now. It was the same look of goodbye, the look of us departing, to never see each other again. Reminding me of what I had lost, the time we lost together. "What would you do if you woke up one night to see me like that again, in that form, what if we had kids that are like me, you've already shown me that you can't stand it," releasing me.

"Lily, don't do this, I love you and I know you do too. We can still be together. I'll love you and our kids if you want to have them."

She looked up at me, hopeful, giving me hope for the two of us. Shaking her head, "I'm sorry, just let me go, I've had enough of feeling depressed, of wanting you, missing you, crying time after time. This is goodbye, for good." She turned around, leaving me.

Was that it, an official end to us? Would we never be together even though I knew with certainty that she still felt the same way about me? No, I was losing her again, slipping through my fingers. I reached out to her, reached out my hand, stretching to catch her. I didn't want us to end. We loved each other and I knew it, knowing that these feelings would never be the same, that they could never be replace or duplicated for another. No, she was the only one. She was the one that I wanted to hold on to, and this time I would hold her tightly, never letting go. Grasping her wrist, I swung her around. She looked shocked as I placed my arm around her waist and kissed her.

"I'm not going to let you go this time, no matter what happens, we'll be together, together till the end. If you leave me, then I'll follow you to the ends of the earth, even to the other side if I have to."

Kissing her again, feeling something wet against my face, I opened my eyes only to see her in shedding tears.

"Damn, I really hate you. I never cried so much before until I met you."

"Don't worry, when you do, I'll be here to gladly comfort you," wiping her tears, kissing her again. This was it, she was mine again, and I was hers. The sensation of life filled my soul again. The bright warm sky welcoming us both, feeling her soft lips as I kissed her again, over and over, those lips I never forgot.

We sat down for a moment, watching what remained of the sun.

"My mom won't be happy to see you, she wants to tear you limb from limb just thinking of you."

"I can imagine, but I'll see her. I'll see her and I'll let her know how madly I love you, and that this time, I'm not going to run away."

FROM THE AUTHOR

Hoped you enjoyed my first book of the Dark Chronicles. This is my first ever book that I've written, so I hope it was enjoyable, it makes me self-conscious to know there are others reading my material. I know there are errors in my grammar and writing, but self-editing your own work over and over can kill a person (exaggerating of course, but still). So I did my best by myself since I'm too poor to hire an actual editor (life is hard you know!), so please forgive much of the errors.

I plan to have my second book out by January 2016 the latest, so a full year from the publishing of this one. Though due to my full time job in finance/accounting, I find it difficult to write as my job makes me work rather unexpected long hours, but I'll do my best to persevere. I've already even started the second book, which in my opinion is better than my first. So look forward to it.

A bit about my second book. So a few of the characters you'll be seeing are from this one, but it's a completely different story with a completely different main character. So don't expect something of a continuation where Evan or Lily is the main character with the whole story revolving around them, but be surprised. I'll try to do a better job this time around. Hopefully I can use the income from this book to get someone to review my second book.